The Diamond Man

The Diamond Man

by

Michael J. Molloy

Gypsy Shadow Publishing

The Diamond Man

by
Michael J. Molloy

Gypsy Shadow Publishing, LLC.
Lockhart, TX
www.gypsyshadow.com

Library of Congress Control Number: 2014943725

eBook ISBN: 978-1-61950-099-0
Print ISBN: 978-1-61950-228-4

Published in the United States of America

First eBook Edition: June, 2013
First Print Edition: July 1, 2014

Praise for The Diamond Man

With the soul of a poet and a fondness for sports, Michael J. Molloy has managed to combine the two in a surprisingly sweet novel about a sportscaster whose life changes after he performs a heroic act and falls in love.

This is one of the most charming books I've ever read, with an unusual premise; a romance written from the man's point of view.

Get yourself a copy of *The Diamond Man* and be prepared to revel in romance and sports. Something for both sexes to enjoy, with no undue emphasis on either to annoy those who prefer action to romance or vice-versa.

—Ida Vega-Landow
Lincoln Heights Literary Society

Dedication

This book is affectionately dedicated to my dear companion, Connie Colvin. Her sweet tenderness and unbridled love are captured in the character Anne Finley.

Appreciation

I wish to thank Denise Bartlett and Charlotte Holley at Gypsy Shadow Publishing for recognizing the merits of my work. I would recommend their publishing company to any aspiring writer, especially with their diverse acceptance of various genres. And to my family, fellow writers from my RWANYC group, and friends, I say thank you for your devoted support and encouragement. You make the difference.

Chapter One

Hours after the late August game and its broadcast, Diamond Jim Monahan maneuvered his Honda Civic through Richmond's waterlogged streets. The spirits of the play-by-play announcer of the Richmond Flying Squirrels had been flattened like a pancake. After all, the team had kowtowed to the hated rival Bowie Baysox, 6-5—thanks to the play where the visitors' Lamont McGill uncoiled like a cobra in the top of the ninth inning and jacked the pill until it was a blip off the radar past the left field fence. The loss eliminated the Squirrels from postseason consideration, thus rendering the team's upcoming season-ending series that weekend in Reading moot. The severe thunderstorm the forecasters had predicted was a fitting end to the evening's proceedings. Mother Nature was venting her anger as she wept profusely for the saddened city.

The rain, which began shortly before the conclusion of Jim's post-game radio show, came down in sheets. The upcoming trip to Reading was the farthest thing from Jim's mind. Making it home through the torrential downpour became a struggle for survival. As fast as the windshield wipers swept away a collection of water, another waterfall soon followed. Jim might as well have been driving blindfolded. He wanted nothing less than to curl up in his bed at his apartment.

Inching along Jennie Scher Road, Jim suddenly noticed the rear lights of another vehicle off the side of the road below street-level. His initial reaction was to press past and head for home. But something peculiar about these rear lights peaked his curiosity. Had a fellow motorist's vehicle swerved off the slick road into Gillies Creek? Compelled by his own burning desire to know, Jim opted to forego the need to sleep.

"Oh, my God. I wonder if anyone is hurt down there."

Parking his Civic in a safe spot, Jim cautiously made his way down the incline. The rain continued to pelt him unmercifully, a thousand needles stinging his face. He wasn't the least bit concerned about getting drenched. Someone was in dire need of assistance, and that was all that mattered.

He stopped in his tracks when he saw the vehicle, a late model Ford Explorer sport utility vehicle, its front wheels almost totally submerged in the rising waters of the creek. The rest of the vehicle would soon fall in. If someone were still alive in the Explorer, he'd have to act fast.

The driving rain made it difficult for him to see. Through squinted eyes, Jim noticed a figure in the driver's seat. He tapped the window with his knuckles to get the attention of the individual, but there was no response. He tried to open the driver's side door, but soon discovered it was locked. There was only one thing left to do: he had to break the window.

Time was critical; he frantically looked around for a sizable rock. He spotted one the size of a football and hoisted it. But before he struck the window, Jim yelled, "Hey in there! I'm going to smash the window! See if you can move away or at least turn your head away!"

The shadowy figure nodded and moved his head to the side.

With adrenalin pumping throughout his body, Jim heaved the heavy stone. The impact cracked the glass in the pattern of a spider's web. Jim hit again and again, before the window shattered and he could reach inside to unlock the door. The third attempt was the charm.

He extended his left arm through the narrow middle opening of the broken pane. As he did, he nicked his forearm on one of the jagged edges. *Ouch!* He winced in pain, but pressed on in search of the button. Five seconds later he fingered what he believed was the door lock. When he pressed it, a sudden click sounded. Relief enveloped him, but the task was far from over.

After delicately pulling out his arm to avoid another cut, Jim opened the door from the outside. Just then he heard an eerie noise from the SUV, signaling it was another step closer to being totally submerged. The clock was ticking.

Jim focused on the object of the task: an elderly man, incoherent save for a few moans. The man slowly moved his head side to side. His wailing grew louder, almost ear-splitting.

"Hey, mister!" Jim yelled. "C'mon! You've got to get out of here! This truck's about to fall into the creek!"

"I can't move," the man groaned. "I think I broke my leg."

"You can't stay here! I've got to get you out!"

"No! No! Leave me alone! I'll be all right."

"Like hell you will!"

Jim quickly released the man's seatbelt. The baseball announcer was about to position his arms around the back and behind the knees of the man when he heard another creak. The vehicle was yet another inch closer to slipping into the waterway.

Water rapidly filled the floor of the vehicle. There was no room for error. Jim instructed the old man to grab him around the neck. Jim fought to lift the man out. After he succeeded in doing so, he struggled up the embankment with the man in his arms. He managed to go only six steps before he heard a very loud sound behind him. He turned his head and saw the Ford Explorer sinking completely into the creek. Seconds later, only the top of the vehicle stood above the water. Diamond Jim Monahan had saved the old man's life—but there was no time for celebration. Jim continued to transport the old man until both of them managed to reach street-level.

The announcer safely guided the injured man into the backseat of his Civic. Seconds were precious. Despite the teeming rain, he used his cell phone to contact 911 and request an ambulance. When he was finished on the phone, he noticed the old man reaching for him with his right hand. Jim clasped it as a handshake, as if he were greeting an old friend. Still writhing in pain, the old man looked at Jim through tired but grateful eyes.

"Thank you," the man quietly told Jim.

Jim smiled softly in reply. He shut the door so that the man would be out of the torrential downpour, got into the driver's seat and closed the door behind him to shelter him-

3

self from the rain. His clothes were soaked, but Jim wanted only to relax all of his taut muscles and be swallowed up by the bucket seat. The wait was now on for the emergency vehicle's arrival.

Chapter Two

Almost a full half-hour had passed before both the emergency medical service unit and the Richmond city police arrived at the scene. The paramedics successfully transported the elderly man and Jim to Capital Medical Center on West Grace Street. Jim checked into the emergency room, at the behest of the paramedics, to see if he was okay. He also stuck around to learn firsthand the progress of the old man.

The elderly man was immediately taken into an examining room. Jim, on the other hand, had to bide his time. But waiting didn't faze the broadcaster. His only concern was that the elderly man was getting proper attention.

Jim sweated it out in the nearly empty waiting area of the emergency room. A flow of mindless sitcoms paraded *ad nauseum* on the lone television set. The broadcaster had more than enough of Aunt Bea baking a pie for Sheriff Andy. *What's the matter? Doesn't anybody care about what's happening in the nation and throughout the world?* Jim had a mind to change the channel, if only he knew how. What news there was to be found was in a dog-eared copy of the day's local paper lying on an empty chair. No doubt the crossword puzzle had been worked. Besides, Jim had already read it.

He settled back for some people-watching. One woman was reading some trashy tabloid while her two young children, of whom one was presumably sick, were running around like little maniacs. One of them kept asking, "What's your name?"

Jim thought it was cute at the beginning. By the fourth time he answered, it had become annoying. Another woman, in her mid-thirties, was also in the waiting room, but she appeared to be healthy. Maybe she was waiting for someone, or perhaps she was a hypochondriac.

The waiting room had the typical smell of a medical center. The odors of rubbing alcohol and Band-Aids blended together in a perverse harmony. Traces of formaldehyde also wafted through the recirculated ventilation system. If you weren't ill to begin with coming into the place, the antiseptic stench certainly would've knocked you down.

The minutes continued to wither away, until a hysterical woman raced in. Taking in her silver hair and crow's feet, Jim pegged her to be about the same age as the man he had saved that evening. With her was a much younger man. Jim figured he was the son of the distraught woman. Deep fear was written on her features as she darted up to the front counter where the emergency room clerk was sitting.

"Please help me! My name is Joyce Langston! I understand my husband, Alan Langston, was rescued from Gillies Creek and was brought here. Is he all right? I must see him!"

"Please relax, Mrs. Langston," the clerk responded. "He is resting inside. I'll have one of the nurses or aides escort you there and then you can speak with the doctor."

"Oh, thank God! Thank God!" Mrs. Langston drew a deep sigh of relief. She appeared on the verge of fainting, but the man next to her held her up. "I rushed over here as quick as I could when I got the phone call from the police. This is my son. My daughter and her husband are driving down from Manassas." Her voice was calmer. The clerk had made them feel at ease with her pleasant eyes and warm smile. "How was he rescued?"

The clerk pointed over at Jim. Joyce slowly walked over to him, followed by her son. With tears in her eyes as well as in her voice, Joyce opened her arms up to the baseball announcer. Jim didn't know what to make of it at first, but soon realized she was making a gesture of gratitude.

"Oh, thank you, Sir! It's a miracle. God must've put you in the right place at the right time. How can we repay you?" And with that, Joyce gave Jim a heartfelt embrace. The son, who introduced himself as Michael, thanked Jim profusely as well.

"Oh," Jim replied with a smile, "it wasn't anything that any other decent person wouldn't have done, Mrs. Langston."

"Please, call me Joyce."

Just then a young blonde stormed into the emergency room waiting area. In her wake were two men: a bearded young man holding a large broadcast-style video camera, and a second, slightly older man carrying what appeared to be audio equipment.

Jim recognized the pretty woman with the straight, shoulder-grazing bob-style haircut as Amy Johnson, one of Richmond's local TV reporters. Apparently her station had picked up the police line news of the rescue of Alan Langston. Amy spotted Jim with Joyce Langston and pointed her right index finger at the baseball man.

"Diamond Jim Monahan, the Squirrels' play-by-play guy, right?"

Jim smiled modestly and nodded.

"Diamond Jim?" Michael interrupted, grabbing his hand to shake it again. "It's a privilege to meet you. I'm a big Squirrels fan."

Amy, looking from one to the other, asked, "What brings you here, Jim?"

Before Jim had a chance to utter a single word, Joyce quickly interceded. "He saved my husband's life."

Amy's jaw dropped and her eyes went wide as saucers. She gasped, as if it were her last breath. Then, gathering her composure, she smiled and turned toward Jim. "Well, well, well! Hey, don't go anywhere, buddy! You're part of the story!"

Joyce was puzzled. "Are you a wealthy person, Jim?"

"No," Jim replied. "I've been announcing baseball games for a long time, and baseball is played on a field called a diamond, hence the nickname *Diamond Jim*. It does go back years."

Jim was an instant celebrity, but still held a high degree of humility, not wanting to rate his deed up there with a soldier saving his comrades in battle, or a firefighter rescuing a family from a burning house. But Amy was adamant that Jim be given the recognition due to him.

One of the nurses from inside the triage area appeared in the doorway, calling out for Joyce.

7

"Hi, Mrs. Langston. I'm Nurse Nolan. Your husband suffered a hairline fracture of the right fibula and has a contusion on his forehead, but all of his vital signs are normal and he's fully alert. Please follow me."

"Thanks, but what about Jim? I want someone to take care of him immediately!"

Awkward!

Nolan twisted her lips and shifted her eyebrows. "I promise it'll be done promptly."

In the meantime, Amy was discussing various angles with her cameraman and soundman. "Hey, Jim, c'm'ere. I'm going to ask you what happened and how you went about getting the man to safety." Amy pointed to a secluded corner of the waiting area. "Uh, let's go over there. Are you ready with the lights, Chris?" The glare of the TV lights flooded the room. Jim winced at first from the sudden burst of light, but soon adjusted to it.

Joyce Langston continued to consult with the doctors and nurses in the triage area, standing next to her husband, who was lying on a gurney with various wires and an IV tube attached to him. Meanwhile, Amy Johnson peppered Jim with questions.

With no desire to be recognized, he was merely obliging a fellow member of the media and her role as a reporter. And as he gazed briefly at the waiting room clock, which had struck midnight, Jim knew later that morning everyone would become familiar with the face behind the voice of the Squirrels' announcer.

Chapter Three

There was hardly any rest for the victorious yet weary. Jim Monahan did not leave the Capital Medical Center until nearly two that morning. Just a minor scrape on his right forearm. Before he left the hospital, Joyce Langston had given him her home number, then taken his, and invited Jim to join her family for dinner at their home after Alan was released. Jim had smiled and told her he would be there.

Jim got about three hours of sleep. He hosted the morning-drive sports reports at the radio station, beginning at 6 and repeated every half-hour.

The bedraggled baseball man trudged into the building housing WRVN-AM at 5:47. He'd managed to slug down a cup of coffee on the way to the station, but actually felt like he'd need a whole pot to get him through that morning. There were more bags under his eyes than a Grand Central Station redcap could handle.

The moment he opened the doors to the studio, Jim was greeted by a blaring trumpet recording of the Star Wars theme. The sudden burst of music startled him at first as he looked around, thinking Darth Vader was going to show up. Instead, Station Manager Zach Moser, News Director Vince Wallace and News Editor and Traffic Reporter Lisa Hillenbrand emerged out of nowhere from different directions. Each one beamed, grinning from ear to ear, and applauded the resident hero. Jim thought their greeting was way over the top. He blushed and smiled at the grand reception, then shook his head in pleasant disbelief.

"I can't believe you guys staged all this." Jim laughed.

"Well, you deserved it, Jim," Zach replied. The white-bearded top man at the station continued, "It must have taken some doing getting that man out of the truck."

"As I told Amy Johnson, it was just a simple reaction to a situation that demanded quick thinking. Anyone else would've done the same thing."

"But *anyone else* wasn't around," Vince interjected. "Get your sports report done early, Jim, 'cause I want you on with me when I go on at six. You'll be my in-house guest the first hour. For a great change, we're not just breaking news, we're making news!"

"C'mon, hero," Lisa said with a smile, "I'll help you prepare your report so you can be out there with Vince on time."

Jim would've just been happy to give his sports reports that day, but the trio would not give in. On a day Jim should've been a twinge somber on radio with the Squirrels knocked out of the pennant race, the call was for the baseball man to be more upbeat on his rescuing heroics.

Chapter Four

The interview with his colleague went very smoothly as Jim answered Vince's questions with unassuming style. As he had with Amy Johnson, he downplayed his role in saving Alan Langston from sure death, but Vince embellished it in order to heighten the tension, not to mention the appeal of the listening audience.

The next three hours swung by quickly and it was just about time for Jim to do his sixth sportscast. The clock outside Zach Moser's office read 8:36 as his admin assistant Laura Mazursky trudged over to her desk to begin another day of work. Her auburn hair was slightly out of place as she plodded to her workspace with a modest slouch. Getting herself and her kids prepared each morning merited a day's paycheck.

During the summer Laura dropped off her two children with her mother and picked them up when she finished at five. But during the scholastic year, she took her children to school before coming to work. Her mother then picked up the youngest from middle school at three and waited for Laura to arrive after work to retrieve her. The elder of the two came home from high school by himself. Of course, a couple of times the routine was broken up and she received a call from either school concerning an incident involving one of her kids, although her husband Charlie had to intervene twice as well.

As was her custom, Laura plopped down her personal belongings on top of her desk. She always drew a deep sigh, for getting her two children ready to be sent to grandma's was a chore in itself. Now it came time to wage war with Zach and the countless number of tasks and floods of phone calls awaiting her. And with the sudden popularity of

Jim's feat of heroism, no doubt there would be many more calls than usual inundating the station.

As much as Laura wasn't looking forward to the unusually high demand that lay ahead that day, she took things in her stride. When she finished dropping her handbag and car keys on her chair, she took time to scan the large room to spot Jim at his customary desk. He was busy tweaking his next sportscast, not to make it sound like a carbon copy of the previous one. In spite of her early morning lethargy, Laura strutted over to him with purpose.

"Good morning, Superman!"

Jim looked up at Laura and released a short laugh. "Not you, too?"

"Well, not only has my family been hearing about you on our favorite radio station all morning, but we also caught you on the local news. I smell a book deal and a movie in the works!"

"I'll let my agent handle all that."

"I'm surprised the mayor hasn't called by now."

"He just did. I'm going to be at his office on Monday. You know, one of those fancy dedications politicians like to make. They wanted me down today, but I told them I have to drive up to Reading for the Squirrels' last weekend series of the season this morning. Uh, incidentally, your boss said he'll be there with me then, too. There's nothing like a photo op to boost the station's ratings and publicity."

Laura's phone suddenly began to ring. She had barely made two steps to her desk and already the projected high amount of calls had begun. She gave the caller her patented answer, "Mister Moser's office," but the call was for Jim. The person on the other end identified himself. Laura put the caller on hold. "It's Tony Salerno, Jim." Upon hearing Tony's name Jim rolled his eyes to the ceiling. But rather than creating an awkward moment for Laura, he waved to her to send the call through to his desk. Jim allowed the phone to ring twice as he steeled himself, for he knew the caller was his boisterous and irrepressible agent from New York. Jim offered a simple greeting before allowing the other party to pick up on the conversation.

"Hey, Mr. Big Shot, I saw you on CNN this morning! They showed the story. Whoa! Pretty awesome!"

"I don't know what I'm more impressed by, Tony. The fact that CNN carried that local story nationally, or that you watch CNN at all."

"Very funny, Shmarty," Tony said. "Say, you know who Dick Spencer is, right?"

"Dick Spencer? Oh, he's the play-by-play guy for the St. Louis Cardinals."

"Well, I have very reliable sources that after some thirty-odd years of meritorious service behind the mic, Spencer is going to hang it up. That means there's going to be a vacancy, Jim. What do you say you get a new audition tape for me and I'll peddle it to the Redbirds?"

"Oh, come off it, Tony. We go through this every year. First you tell me the Padres are looking for a new man, so I put a tape together for you. The next year you say Minnesota needs someone, so I go along with it again. Then the next year it's the Mets. Then the Orioles. Then it's Arizona. Heck, you even told me my childhood team, the Phillies, were looking for someone once. And every year I go along with it only to be disappointed. Not even the Squirrels' parent team in San Francisco wants me."

"That's because Joe Keegan and Bill MacGruder are an institution out there and you know it."

"What makes you think it's going to be different this time?"

"America loves heroes, Jim. And after that big story last night, I think it puts you in a whole new light. What do you say?"

Jim had heard this pitch from Tony before. As the calendars kept piling up, Jim grew more and more cynical of the chance for a major league job. But he then realized Tony might have a point on the intrepid angle. Perhaps his gallant effort in rescuing Langston from a watery grave could give him the edge he needed to push himself ahead of the pack.

"Okay, I'll get a tape together and give you a jingle once it's ready." He hung up the phone and began to dream once more. *Can I finally become a Major League Baseball club play-by-play man?*

Jim's head was swimming in delirium. He knew just about every major league ballpark, having been to a few of them personally; he'd seen the rest on television. Jim visualized himself up in the broadcast booth looking out toward Busch Stadium in St. Louis with the Cardinals on the field ready to begin a game. The roar of the crowd. The organist banging on the keys in rhythmic fashion. The smells and sounds of roving vendors parading the aisles, hawking their hot dogs . . .

Finally, Program Director Christine Haines walked up to Jim and nudged him on the right shoulder to let him know he was due inside the studio for his next sportscast. The pleasant dream inside Jim's head burst like a bubble. It was time for a reality check. Fortunately for the baseball man, he had already revised most of his copy for the next report. The rest he could easily improvise. It was time to get his act into gear for the final sportscast of the day before going home and heading up to Reading for that night's game.

Chapter Five

Although Jim wasn't looking forward to the last season series of the year, there was a side trip that he couldn't wait to make. The Squirrels were to play games in Reading that Friday evening, and then Saturday night before wrapping up the season on Sunday afternoon.

The Saturday night tilt was scheduled for a 7:05 first pitch. That allowed Jim to take a one-hour excursion down to Bryn Mawr to visit his 15-year-old daughter Madison.

He hadn't seen Madison since early July when the Squirrels last visited Harrisburg, and his time with her then was more brief than what was planned that Saturday afternoon. Jim hadn't even seen the young teenager he affectionately called Maddy on Father's Day because the Squirrels were at home that third Sunday of June against Erie, and he was under contractual obligation to broadcast the game.

Since his marital break-up three years earlier, the rift in Jim's relationship with Madison had grown as wide as the Grand Canyon, but that was in no part his fault. The baseball man had tried everything to convince his daughter he still loved her as any doting father would his child, but the aerial distance between them made it seem to her like he took a cavalier approach to the matter.

Jim painfully remembered how everything went wrong. It had been four years since the turmoil began, but to Jim it still felt like it had just happened the day before. He had remained in Richmond at the time to air the then Richmond Braves' games while his wife Maureen, then 42, took Madison with her to the Philadelphia area for a week to visit her relatives before Madison was to begin school again. While shopping up there at one of those factory outlet stores, Maureen ran into an old flame named Harley Bell. They had gone to school together at Lehigh Valley University years before. Whereas Maureen didn't apply much of her higher education to other things, Harley had gone on to the prestigious Wharton School of Business to obtain his Master's degree in finance. Harley had told Maureen he had worked for a huge commodities firm in Philadelphia and was doing very nicely.

In fact, Harley had told Maureen he was making more than ten times the annual salary Jim had been pulling down at that time. The infatuation with the Harley's large bank account made for a quixotic ambition. The next evening, Maureen had asked her parents to watch over Madison while she went to see a girlfriend from her past. The story had been nothing but a cover-up, for Maureen went to convene with Harley for dinner. Later that evening, Harley took Maureen back to his palatial home in Bryn Mawr. They had later engaged in passionate sex without protection.

A few weeks had passed since the affair and Maureen became ill. From her experience several years before with Madison, Maureen feared she had become pregnant again. She had visited her OBGYN and it was confirmed she was in the early stages of her first trimester. She couldn't hide the pregnancy from Jim and told him the news. While most men would be thrilled to learn they would become a father, even for a second time, Jim put a timeline together and deduced that the child-to-be wasn't his. That was when Maureen dropped the bombshell of her adulterous encounter with Harley on Jim. The revelation was a dagger to his heart. Maureen broke the sacred vow of matrimony she and Jim had made together on the day of their wedding nearly two decades before. Maureen's betrayal forced him into a decision that went against his own Catholic upbringing: divorce. There was no way he was going to allow an ill-conceived child into the household. That was fine by Maureen, for she preferred the elegant lifestyle Harley could bestow upon her, and she inevitably decided to move in with her new lover, taking Madison with her.

What followed were the divorce proceedings in Montgomery County, plus a nasty bit of contention. It wasn't over material items, but who got custody of Madison. Jim didn't want his daughter to be living with her mother and the terrible example she had set. But Pennsylvania was a no-fault state. All the family courts were concerned about was who could be more accessible to Madison with regard to schooling and all other facets of everyday life. Jim knew he was a loser because he was on the road half the time during the baseball season and that Maureen could always remain home in Harley's house and live off his bank account. The courts turned a blind eye to Maureen's lustful evening of debauchery and saw only the stay-at-home mom, rather than the sometimes-there dad. Jim was also forced to pay alimony and child support for something he did not create, which was another severe blow that ate at his gut.

Jim went into a deep depression soon after the judge's ruling. He could not afford a full-time psychologist to deal with his problems—not on his meager salary. But he did come across a local Richmond chapter that offered group therapy sessions for divorced men. It was there that he became good friends with fellow divorcés Marty Leary and Ed Holtermann, about the only good thing that came out of this personal tragedy.

The baseball announcer took a deep breath to muster up some energy and steady his nerves. He was girding himself to make a call to Maureen and let her know he would be taking Madison out for a few hours the following day before he had to drive back up to Reading to broadcast that night's game. Maureen had already known beforehand Jim would come by that day with the advanced schedule he had sent to her months ago. But there was the question of what time on Saturday Jim could show up.

Jim would have favored watching paint dry. But he knew Maureen was the obstacle to his securing Madison, for even just a few hours. The ogre, with spiked club in hand, was the decrepit gatekeeper Jim had to finagle around to get to the fair maiden. With a deep sigh he began punching in a series of numbers from his phone. It wasn't long after that the voice paramount to a truck horn came on. It was the sound of Maureen's caustic greeting to leave a message at the sound of the tone. As he was beginning to do just that, Maureen picked up the line.

"Yes, what is it you want?" Maureen's delivery was as cold and bitter as the woman she had become since the divorce.

"I just wanted to see what time I could pick up Maddy tomorrow, that's all." Jim was at a loss; he pounded his fist on the arm of his sofa when he heard Maureen's sharp statement. He then reminded his ex-wife of the timetable agreement. "You did remember the Squirrels were going to be up in Reading this weekend and that I was going to swing by Saturday to spend some time with Maddy, didn't you?"

There was a little hesitation. Jim wondered if the light bulb would finally flash inside her head. "Oh, yes, you're right. I had forgotten all about it. Sorry."

Maureen's apology was as shallow as a backyard stream. Jim wanted to vent at her, but thought better of it.

"Where's Maddy? I'd like to speak with her."

"She's out with friends."

Another damn excuse, Jim surmised. But again he was in no mood to argue over the phone, especially given his lack of sleep the night before.

Several seconds of dead silence ensued. Jim had been hoping Maureen might have heard the story of his rescuing Alan Langston from Gillies Creek. Heck, if Tony Salerno saw the CNN feed, surely Maureen would have done the same. He thought maybe she might bring it up. But if she knew about it, she wouldn't tell Jim. It wasn't that Jim was seeking a congratulatory statement from his ex-wife— just a little bit of recognition would have sufficed. But she wouldn't give him the benefit of such an accolade. This was another example of Maureen's apathy toward him.

Resigned to Maureen's indifference, Jim told his ex-wife he could be there as early as ten o'clock the next morning. Maureen shot back twelve noon. That would give Jim only three hours to spend with Madison; a time frame he knew was too short. He then countered with eleven. There was at last a compromise between the warring factions.

Jim ended the conversation with a sincere parting of the ways. Maureen, on the other hand, responded with an icy *bye* and hung up the phone. As he placed the receiver back on the cradle, he looked up at a corner in his living room of his modest one-bedroom apartment. The baseball man pouted as he shook his head in frustration. The tigress wasn't about to change her stripes. Rather than lament about Maureen's callous attitude, Jim simply rose from the chair he was sitting in and prepared to finish packing for his six-hour ride.

Chapter Six

The six-hour trip to Reading the day before was grueling, with one tree looking the same as the one he had passed. Yet Jim Monahan persevered to drive up there in time for the Squirrels-Phillies game, in which Richmond got clobbered, 11-2. With the team out of playoff contention and everyone focused on who was going to be called up to the big club in San Francisco for the latter's stretch run, there was no heart in the Richmond dugout that evening. Idle players were busy counting empty flower seed shells, catapulted from the mouths of teammates, and strewn across the floor like unwanted sandwich wrappers. This was what the vacuous mindset of the collective band of apathetic athletes had dissolved into.

By the next morning, Jim's latest debacle was ancient history. After all, his primary focus was seeing his beloved Madison and to spend some quality time with her before heading back up to Reading that evening. What precious little time he was allotted to be with her was like gold to him.

Jim's Honda Civic looked out of place in affluent Bryn Mawr. BMW, Lexus, and Mercedes ruled the roads in this land of million-dollar-plus homes. The area reeked of money with its well-manicured lawns and shrubbery, gilded front gates, lawn jockeys, quaint imitation gaslights, and Roman columned porticos.

Jim approached the huge Tudor-style home of Harley and Maureen Bell. Although he had been to the palatial house several times before, he still looked at it with resentment. It wasn't so much out of jealousy for the opulence it symbolized and the money he didn't possess. It was for the fact Maureen had shunned their wedding vows in exchange for greed. His stomach began to turn as if to reject the condescending bastion.

Jim pulled up in the semi-circular drive in front of the twenty-room mansion. After coming to a stop, he cut off the engine and took in a deep breath in order to prepare himself for whatever dirt Maureen was going to dish at him. As he got out of the car, the large, beautifully varnished, wooden front door opened. By the time Jim turned around, Maureen stood in the doorway. She was still quite slender and attractive in her mid-forties, wearing a pink t-shirt showcasing her frontal attributes and tight jeans to define her hourglass figure. Maureen's facial expression was passive, perhaps reflecting the same disdain Jim had for her, he thought. Although the sun was shining brightly on a beautiful summer day, Jim felt there was a black thundercloud over his head. He wasn't looking forward to this part at all, and he was praying that Madison was nearby so he could just whisk her away and spare an unnecessary swapping of barbs. The baseball man walked around his car and sauntered up to Maureen with suppressed feelings of hatred. There were no amenities exchanged between the two. Jim decided to cut to the chase.

"Is Maddy ready?"

"She'll be out in a minute," Maureen replied coldly. She looked down at Jim as though he were a vagrant. The sudden infusion of wealth into her bloodstream seemed to have forced Maureen's nose to jut upward. She looked at Jim's five-year-old Civic. He could easily tell by her expression that she was repulsed the car was stationed on her precious cobblestone driveway. Maureen made a biting remark about it. "So, are you still making payments on that poor excuse for a vehicle?"

Jim looked at Maureen with bitterness. "For your information, the car is fully paid for."

"You could've fooled me. Especially with the salary you make."

The baseball man shook his head in disbelief. "You know, Maureen, you never cease to amaze me. You never have anything positive to say. Even when I open myself up with a respectable greeting, you make it sound like I've got swine flu or something. You make me feel as though I'm something you accidentally stepped in on the sidewalk and then tried to wipe off at the curb."

"That's because you never amounted to anything. You're still languishing in the minor leagues. You're always chasing the dream, and you had me and our daughter tagging along for the ride."

"And I suppose this huge place gives you the security you never had."

"Damn straight it does! And I can always count on Harley to be home every night!"

"Oh, like I wasn't! Let me tell you something, Maureen! Except when I had to travel with the Squirrels and the other teams in the past on the road for away games, I was every bit there as a husband for you and a father for Maddy!"

"And let's talk about those road games! How do I know that you didn't try to shack up with some bimbo at a cheap motel in Buffalo or somewhere?"

"You should know because I always carried those framed pictures of you and Maddy wherever I traveled and I proudly stood them up on the dresser in my motel room so I could always see you two!"

"Oh, we're not bringing up that tired old story again, are we?"

"Damn right, I am! Do you think that, even if I had the audacity to do such a thing, I'm going to expose your pictures to some tramp? Get the fuck out of here!"

"You could've easily put our pictures away, you bastard!"

By now Jim had had enough of the argument with Maureen, to the point he was so hurt by her accusations that it brought him near to tears. "I have always been damn faithful to you and Maddy. I had gotten an eye from a woman or two but never did I stray from our vows. You, on the other hand, had that fling with Harley because you were attracted to his money. You ripped my heart out that night, Maureen, and you threw it on the ground like it was carrion for vultures!"

The raucous shouting match caused Harley to come from inside the house and join them. He looked very much like the banker, even on his day off, with his golf shirt, designer shorts, and wire-rimmed eyeglasses. And, ever the purveyor of market suppositions, Harley examined the episode like he would an article from the business pages of the Philadelphia Inquirer. He was holding his three-year-old son, Reed, in his arms, the innocent by-product of a night of betrayal. This was the child he and Maureen conceived together in their night of lust and passion. Harley's sudden presence caught Jim's eye. The baseball man decided to switch emotional gears for a bit of witty sarcasm.

"Oh, Harley! You're here! That's great, Harley, just great! Say. Listen! As you can see, Maureen and I are having this great fight together. Maybe you can pretend to be Don King or something and promote the fight! Huh, what do you say? I'll bet it'll sell a lot of tickets!"

"Of all the asinine things, Jim," Maureen jumped in. "You're behaving like an overgrown child!"

"Here's the challenger! From Philadelphia P A, at six-foot-three and weighing 202 pounds—now fighting out of Richmond—here's Diamond . . . Jim . . . Monahan!" Jim then started belting out the opening instrumental trumpet of Rocky. For added measure, he held up his arms in the air like he'd been introduced by a ringside announcer for a boxing match. He even threw a left jab, followed by a right uppercut.

As he carried on, Maureen continued to berate him for his immature behavior.

Harley's puzzled look was a sign of confusion. Suddenly Madison arrived at the open front doorway to the home. She saw her parents waging another one of their patented battles. The adolescent then gazed skyward as though seeking divine intervention to put a halt to the proceedings. When none was forthcoming, Madison took matters into her own hands.

"Enough! Both of you!"

For years until her parents broke up, Madison was used to being on the receiving end of a scolding by either of them. Now she was the one lashing out at them for a change to help put an end to their antics. Madison's scream worked, for Jim stopped his Rocky music and Maureen zipped her lips. Both were embarrassed by their behavior.

Maureen closed her eyes and rested her forehead against the outstretched palm of her right hand. Jim looked down at the ground and began to scratch the back of his head. If there were a hole to be found, he'd be in it. He attempted an act of contrition with his daughter.

"Look, Maddy. I'm ... I'm sorry."

"Never mind. Just ... let's go, okay?"

Jim replied with a soft yes. As Madison approached the passenger side of the Civic, Maureen icily gazed at him. She offered him a stern warning.

"Make sure you're back no later than four."

"Hey, I've got to be back in Reading by six tonight for a game, remember?"

And with that, Jim opened the driver's side door and sat down in the front seat. Once both he and Madison were securely buckled in, he drove off. The sooner Maureen's face disappeared from his rearview mirror, the better.

Meanwhile, Maureen glared at her ex-husband with disdain. When Jim's car was out of sight, she turned toward Harley. Still holding their son Reed, Harley thought it wise not to say a word. Instead, the banker shrugged his shoulders. Maureen then raced inside the house to vent.

Chapter Seven

Jim took his daughter to see a movie, but it was one of those teenage comedies that didn't suit him. He would have preferred an action film or a serious drama, but he wanted to cater to Madison and her tastes. That was the least he could do in light of his earlier embarrassing escapade. The movie wasn't that long, which was good for two reasons. First of all, Jim had little tolerance for a stupid flick; secondly, it allowed him a little more time to spend with Madison to take her to out for a snack.

The baseball man had gazed at his watch upon leaving the multiplex and figured he still had enough time to take her to one of his favorite haunts from his own teenage days—Pat's King of Steaks in Philadelphia. It was the birthplace of the cheese steak, the sandwich that made the City of Brotherly Love famous. Despite being modestly quartered on a small triangular parcel of land off 9th Street, Wharton, and East Passyunk Avenues, and with bigger brother Gino's across the street, Pat's still had a huge and loyal following.

Jim had the prime sub sandwich consisting of thinly sliced beef, grilled onions, peppers, and mushrooms smothered with Cheez Whiz sauce. It might not be great if you're calorie counting, but it certainly made friends with your taste buds. Heck, the mere inhaling of the aroma emanating from the heavenly hoagies until they held your olfactory senses captive was enough to send you to the gym later. Madison had a very modest version of what Jim was gorging on. Each washed down their delectable delights with an ice-cold beverage.

As Jim was chomping down his sandwich, he wanted to ignite a conversation with his daughter. They hardly spoke to one another as Jim was driving around earlier. He didn't want to bring up the rescue of Alan Langston because of his own modesty. That would have to be a topic strictly for Madison to start on. But there were other subjects he had wanted to discuss with his daughter, and the baseball man began to speak.

"So, you must be excited getting ready to go back to school, huh?"

"It's all right, I guess." Madison didn't make eye contact with her father in her reply. She just looked at what was left of her sandwich apathetically. Jim had to try again.

"You're going to be a sophomore. That's got to be thrilling!"

"Just another year of high school. More stuff about math I'm not going to use in life."

"Well, I bet you can't wait until April when you turn 16. Would you like a Sweet Sixteen party?"

"Maybe not. I don't really have enough friends in school to make it worthwhile."

Perhaps a change of topics was needed to stimulate their chat. Jim then asked Madison a question, broaching on the topic of long-range ambitions. "I know you're only about to enter your second year of high school, but have you given any thought to what college you'd like to attend and what you'd like to take up?"

"Not really. I may not even want to go to college."

"Maddy, a higher education is extremely important to have."

"Yeah, I see where that really helped you. You're still doing games in the minor leagues at near fifty."

Jim felt as though he'd been slashed with a razor. He figured a lot of Maureen's attitudes had rubbed off on their daughter. Then he realized once more how inappropriate his infantile behavior back at the house had been. He tried once more to make it up to Madison.

"Look. I'm truly sorry for the way I acted before with your mother. I promise, Maddy, to be better next time, beginning today when I drop you off. I'm going to do all I can to hold my tongue. Is that's what's eating you?"

"If you must know, Dad, I'm sick and tired of that house."

"What do you mean? Is your mother mistreating you?"

"Well, ever since she had that brat brother of mine, Mom's changed. She hardly even knows I exist anymore.

She spends all her attention on Reed, and even with him, only remotely. She'd rather have a nanny watch him while she plays tennis with friends of hers or, I should say, the wives of *Harley's* friends. I'm getting fed up with the whole thing."

Jim offered a solution. "You know, when we divorced, the judge ruled I couldn't have custody of you because you were so young. But now that you're fifteen, the courts will look at that differently. Perhaps you'd like to come live with me."

"And go back to Richmond? No thanks! Besides, Dad, what will the judge say when you're traveling with the team next year and I'm alone half the time? I'll be old enough to take care of myself, but they may not like the idea for several days in a row at several clips. Did you ever think about that?"

"No. You've . . . you've got a point. Let's finish eating. I've got to get you home and head back up to Reading."

Quietly Jim devoured the remains of his sub. Madison wasn't through with hers, but she was in no mood to eat. Jim turned to the counterman at Pat's. "Can you please wrap up her sandwich so she could eat it at home?" There would be no more talk of Jim wanting Madison to move in with him. What was the point? He quickly drove Madison back to Bryn Mawr before continuing his journey to Reading.

Chapter Eight

The Richmond Flying Squirrels had gotten scorched again by the Reading Phillies, losing 9-5, in a game marred by horrific defensive gaffes by the Squirrels' fielders and a couple of base running mistakes. On one play, leftfielder Ryan Cassidy, who had doubled home a run to pull Richmond to within 8-5 in the top of the eighth inning, thought there were two outs when Reading's Christian Borich caught a lazy fly ball off the bat of pinch hitter Francisco Calderon in centerfield. Cassidy had already been running on the flight of the ball. Third base coach Max Saunders had been screaming at Cassidy to get back to second base, because Borich's catch signaled only the second out of the inning. Seeing that Cassidy was practically down to third, Borich quickly threw to second baseman Dustin Hensler, who simply stepped on the bag after the catch to double up the embarrassed Cassidy to end Richmond's last threat. The loss had extended the Squirrels' losing streak to three and was indicative of the atmosphere around the clubhouse the last few days. Only a matinee the next day remained from the end of the season and a forgettable run down the stretch.

Nearly two hours had passed since the game ended. Jim was at the bar in the hotel where he was staying. He was nursing his second Samuel Adams lager, ruminating, not over Richmond's latest setback, but over the situation involving Madison at the Bell household. While he had done the broadcast, Jim happened to have noticed a family of four, consisting of the two parents and their young children. He recalled seeing the father and thinking how fortunate the man was to have his wife and kids with him, while Jim's own family was in tatters.

He slowly massaged the sides of his v-shaped beer glass, which was half-full of the brew. He stared at the line-up of liquor bottles ahead of him, but if you asked him on the spot what the brand name of the vodka bottle in his direct sight was, he would have had to take another look. Clearly his mind was elsewhere.

He was only kidding himself if he had thought for one moment there was a way to whisk Madison away from a home she was extremely uncomfortable with. The only way that would occur was if Jim had someone to watch and stay with Madison at home when he went on those arduous road trips with the team. He had contemplated the idea of Marty, who worked as an accountant and seldom traveled, moving in with him to keep Madison company. Then he mused how awkward it would appear for a friend to be at home with his daughter more often than he was. Besides, the courts might not look too favorably on having a male— relative stranger—at home alone with an adolescent female most of the time.

Another alternative Jim had entertained was to have a woman move in to offer Madison some matronly company. Jim laughed at the notion. *What a crazy idea that is!* Despite the fact that in present society it wasn't totally uncommon for a man and a woman to live under one roof, but not as husband and wife, the courts might prefer Jim be remarried to allow Madison to live with him again. However, the horrible experience with Maureen had made him extremely hesitant about taking the plunge again. Maureen gave women a bad name. Jim had to admit to the element of mistrust that he harbored toward members of the opposite sex now—that, and the fact he thought his best years were behind him. "What woman would want me anyway?"

Out of curiosity he perused the patrons at the bar. He noticed a number of women present, but they were either with dates or with other women. Not one of them knew he existed. That confirmed his theory of his own masculine magnetism, or more accurately, his lack thereof.

He went back to rubbing his beer glass, like Aladdin with his lamp. Then a genie appeared. Actually, a man a few years older than Jim, sat down at a bar stool next to him. The man looked a little disheveled and looked like he had made a few other tavern trips elsewhere earlier that evening. With bloodshot eyes to match his ruddy complexion under three days' growth of stubble, the man looked at

Jim rather oddly and began to strike up a conversation with the baseball man.

"Hey, pal," the somewhat inebriated man began, ". . . you look down. Can I get you a drink?"

Jim looked up and turned to his neighbor. He gazed at the man, who meant well, and smiled. "No thanks, I've already got one." Jim thought maybe the guy might just uproot and leave.

But the man insisted on getting him another beer. Again the baseball man politely turned down his would-be benefactor. All this was not going unnoticed by the bartender, who was familiar with the soused angel. It was time for the keeper of alcoholic concoctions to intervene.

"Oh, c'mon, Larry! Leave the poor guy alone, will ya?"

Larry was taken aback by the bartender's interference. "Aw, give me a break, Joe!" Larry then turned to Jim and placed his left arm around Jim's shoulders. "Don't worry about him, pal. Joe and I go way back. He's really a push-over." Larry then looked back at Joe with a goofy smile.

Jim wanted to humor Larry and agreed in allowing the fool to spring for his next beer. Joe wasn't all that pleased with what was going on, but Jim gestured to the barkeep that it was going to be fine. He quickly downed what was left of his current brew as Joe reluctantly drew another Sam Adams for the baseball man.

As he accepted the new beer from Joe, Jim turned to Larry. "Thanks again." Larry responded with a wink and a thumbs up sign. Jim then went to take a sip of the cold one. That was when Larry decided to probe the baseball man, asking him why he seemed to be down on his luck. At first Jim was hesitant to spill his problems to a complete stranger, but realizing that Larry went out of his way to buy him a drink, he conceded.

"Well, if you must know, Larry." Jim paused for a brief moment and then smiled. "I had a run-in today with my malicious ex-wife."

"Ah, say no more, friend. I know exactly how you feel. I had one once. Her name was Sally. Oh, what a fucking bitch she was! Nag, nag, nag! And she'd never give you a compliment. Nah, she'd always get on your case about something. Well, I'm glad those days are over! Good riddance!" Jim thought a moment. Perhaps he could learn a thing or two from the pickled patron. Larry paused briefly before asking Jim a question, "Say, pal, I didn't quite get your name."

"It's Jim. Jim Monahan."

"Nice to meet you, Jim. I'm Larry Wertheimer." Jim and Larry exchanged a hearty handshake. "You're new to the area, Jim, aren't you?"

"Actually I'm visiting here this weekend. I'm from Richmond, Virginia. But I'm a native Pennsylvanian. Grew up in south Philadelphia."

"Well there you go! I knew there was something I liked about you right off the bat! What are you doing up here?"

"I broadcast the Richmond Flying Squirrels games on radio. The team's up here this weekend to play the Phillies."

"No kidding! A genuine baseball announcer! You know, I had a nasty curveball when I pitched in high school. The batters couldn't touch it. I could'a pitched in the majors!"

"What happened? The scouts weren't impressed?"

"Scouts! Hah! What do those bums know? They couldn't recognize talent if they were drawn to it!"

The phone at the bar rang. Joe seized the receiver and covered his vacant ear to muffle the blaring music and boisterous barflies. He recognized who it was and then held the receiver close to his chest so that the person on the other end couldn't hear what was going on. Joe exercised his lungs to give Larry a stern message. "It's Sally!" The *supposedly* former Mrs. Wertheimer. The message she gave Joe for Larry was that she wanted him home immediately.

Jim looked at Larry oddly. The jig was up with the slightly drunken patron. He started to smile sheepishly and then covered his mouth, whispering, "It's a long story."

Jim thanked Larry for at least springing him for a brew and spinning a good yarn to ease his own pain. "Call me a cab, will ya, Joe?" Larry stumbled off of his bar stool. Jim was glad he had enough sense to hail a taxi rather than drive.

"Take care of yourself, Larry."

"You, too, my friend," Larry replied as he lumbered his way away from the bar.

Jim went back to his beer, placed in front of him courtesy of Larry. He shook his head and laughed at Larry's comedic act. Then Joe approached him to apologize for Larry's oddity.

"I'm sorry. That guy does the same routine every Saturday night. It gets tiring after a while."

"Hey, that's okay, Joe. Larry meant well."

With that, Jim chugged down the rest of the beer. He slapped down a five dollar bill for Joe's troubles and then slowly rose to head back toward the hotel lobby elevators, retiring for the evening. And while he had planned to channel surf on the room's TV, his mind was still anchored on the situation with Madison in the Bells' home. Evidently Larry's beer gesture wasn't enough to settle Jim's troubled brain.

Chapter Nine

The Squirrels ended their lost season on a positive note. Highly regarded pitching prospect Casey Farrings pitched a brilliant two-hitter over seven innings against the Reading Phillies. There was no doubt in anyone's mind that the magnificent lefthander would be recalled by the parent San Francisco Giants in a few days to help contribute to the major league team's bid for the crown of the National League West in their battle with the Rockies, Dodgers and Diamondbacks. Richmond went on to nip Reading, 3-2, thanks in part to Farrings' performance and timely hitting of Ramon Sepulveda, Todd Galecki and Ryan Cassidy. San Francisco had visions of Farrings joining the big club's 25-man roster the following year.

The win made the arduous six-hour drive back to Richmond tolerable for Jim. Funny how a victory makes looking at an endless array of highway signs less annoying and mind-distorting.

He didn't arrive back in town until late that Sunday evening. And there would be no rest for the weary. Jim had to get up at 4:30 the next morning for another round of sports reports during Vince Wallace's news-talk, morning drive show.

As if the grueling drive, shortness of proper sleep, and a seemingly endless number of reports weren't enough for Jim, he was obligated to attend a noontime meeting at Richmond's City Hall, held in his honor for his daring rescue last Thursday evening. For the occasion he dusted off a navy blue suit he hadn't worn in nearly a year.

The media was in full swing. There were two reporters from the *Richmond Times-Dispatch,* a couple of radio people including Kate Solaris from Jim's own station, as well as those who report for the local TV stations. None of the TV reporters was more noticeable than Amy Johnson, who was waving frantically at Jim. The baseball man thought Amy was attractive and entertained a wild notion that she was trying to win his affection. But he smiled as reality quickly set in. He knew Amy was just trying to gain an upper hand over her competition for another interview.

Also on hand for the festivities were Joyce Langston and her son and daughter.

And, of course, Zach Moser, Jim's irrepressible station manager, who was there more as a shill for WRVN than a morale backer for Jim. The baseball man posed with Mayor Reynolds as the African-American civic leader presented a plaque and the *keys to the city* to Jim. Oh, and Zach was in the same frame, too.

The crowd in front of the cameras soon swelled to include other political dignitaries: Governor Porch, Senator Caves and Congressman Borden. And then Jim and Zach posed with Joyce and her two grown children. The whirring cameras, popping flashbulbs, and bright lights of the TV cameras were an intoxicating elixir for Jim. Whereas at first he wanted to shy away from the attention, Jim was more than accommodating to please his fellow brethren from the media.

Still, he wanted to limit his day in the sun. The reporters gathered up around him and he answered their questions as best he could. Amy asked more questions than the other TV people, or maybe it just seemed that way, since Jim granted her a little favoritism. Besides being great looking, Amy was the first reporter to seek out Jim at the hospital, and he felt he owed her that privilege. Of course, a little wink and a flirtatious beaming of Amy's pearly whites helped her cause, too.

Twelve twenty-seven. The media people had their fill of Jim. The cameramen and photographers were packing their gear away. The reporters dispersed to their favorite watering holes, where imbibing was more sacred than describing. As for the politicians, they hightailed to evade the same reporters on other issues and not having to come up with their patented extemporaneous and ambiguous lines these grandstanders are noted for. And when the last of the glare of the TV lights was darkened, Zach took off back to the station.

Jim was about to head for home himself when he spotted Joyce and her son and daughter still hanging around. He was curious to find out how Alan was recuperating, so he approached the Langston matriarch.

"Hi, Joyce. How's Alan doing?"

"He's doing real well, Jim. His leg is in a soft cast. They wound up putting a long pin in him to set the bone right. As for the rest of him, doctors are saying he's doing okay. In fact, they believe he should be able to go home tomorrow. I'm just awaiting word from the hospital to verify that."

"That's terrific. I'm sure Alan will be looking forward to a home-cooked meal for a change. Did they say how long he's going to have that pin in him? I'm sure that won't make a great sight trying to go through an airport security checkpoint if you two plan to travel somewhere."

"No." Joyce laughed, in her cute Southern voice. "That won't be too pretty." The two shared a lighthearted moment before Joyce moved on.

"So, are you getting used to all this attention?"

"It's okay. I think my boss enjoys it more than I do, though. And aside from that feed to CNN the other day, all this hoopla is really being confined locally, which is fine by me. I don't need to be doing the talk show circuit."

"Well, you deserve all this fussin' and a heck of a lot more." Joyce paused briefly before continuing. "Listen, Jim. Our family tries to make a point for all of us to get together for Sunday dinner at our house. And with Alan back home by then, it'll carry a more significant meaning. I'd like for you to come join us. My son tells me the Squirrels played their last game of the season yesterday, is that right?"

"Uh, yeah, and they won, too."

"That's terrific! Nothing better than to end on a high note! But now that means you have no game to do Sunday."

"That's true. I don't have any plans at the moment."

"Well, then! That's all the more reason to come to the Langston house! Fried chicken with mashed potatoes and milk gravy along with string beans and, oh, gotta have those biscuits!"

"I'm putting on ten pounds just listening to you." Jim smiled.

"We eat more reasonably during the rest of the week. We try to be a little health conscious. But Sundays we go hog wild! How 'bout it, Jim? It'll sure be nice to see y'all and I know Alan won't take no for an answer."

Jim finally conceded. She then reached into her purse to pull out a small piece of paper and a ballpoint pen. She painstakingly wrote down her address for Jim so that the baseball man could read it clearly.

"We all get together promptly at three in the afternoon," Joyce continued, handing Jim the totally legible note. Jim studied the note as if he was going to swallow it and hide it from enemies.

"I will most definitely be there, Joyce."

Delighted by his acceptance, Joyce and the others bade him goodbye until then.

A shaking of hands with the son and daughter, but a soft peck on the right cheek from Joyce. And as he placed the folded note into the left breast pocket of the suit jacket he wore, he thought perhaps the visit for a grand meal from a grateful family would erase the problems Maureen had caused two days earlier. Even more than the photo op that had just taken place, Jim truly felt appreciated, thanks to the Langston matriarch.

Chapter Ten

Two days later, Jim spent a great deal of time compiling a new tape for Tony Salerno to peddle to the St. Louis Cardinals. He arduously selected a handful of key games and certain highlights to accentuate his play-calling capabilities. Jim wasn't satisfied with one sample, so he took out that selection. *Nah, this one isn't going to work either.* Then he reviewed the tape again, and still felt compelled to make even more changes. In total, he toiled until almost 4:30 that Wednesday afternoon in the station's production studio until he was satisfied he'd spliced the perfect combination of highlights.

Zach Moser frowned upon any of his announcers spending that much time on personal tapes at the station's expense. But he made a special allowance for Jim in light of his heroics and the publicity it brought his station. Also, a little more ad revenue for Vince's morning show and Jim's sports reports in particular didn't hurt either.

With finished tape in hand, Jim went to a nearby FedEx store to send it in a package destined for Tony's New York office. Jim looked at the box with guarded optimism as he handed it to the counter clerk. He then closed his eyes and asked for divine guidance to wish the parcel a safe journey to its final destination. It was more than just the parting of the box. It was praying for a good friend or relative to have a happy and sound trip. The tape symbolized perhaps his final hopes, aspirations and dreams of ever making it to the grand stage of Major League Baseball. It became the last dollar bet at the roulette table.

The moment he received his copy of the shipping slip, Jim walked out of the store to place a call to Tony. It was bordering on five o'clock, and Jim was hoping Tony was still in his office. After a few rings, he heard Tony's voice mail greeting to leave a message. Jim was frustrated he didn't reach his agent live, which forced him to start with his spiel. But after just a few words, he heard the line at the other end being picked up.

"Well, I'm glad to see you had enough time with all the media pounding down your door for interviews, that you were able to get that tape out to me," Tony opened.

"Don't forget, I had to go to Reading this past weekend to air the team's last three games of the season. Plus, I had that publicity thing with the mayor and governor along with a few other dignitaries on Monday."

"Somehow I can't see you hobnobbing with politicians, but what do I know? Oh, did you send that tape out overnight."

"Well, I sent it FedEx, Tony. You should get it sometime Friday morning."

"Excellent, Jimbo! Excellent! I'll review it on Friday. Unless I call you to polish it up a little, I'll send it out to the Cards. Now, I'm probably not going to hear from them until after their season's over in early October. Let's keep our fingers crossed, huh?"

"Yeah, whatever, Tony."

"Aw, don't sound so morose, Mister Monahan! Personally, Captain America, between you and me, I think we've got a winner this time! Yep, I really do!"

"Well, I find it rather ironic you'll be sending my tape to the Cardinals, because I feel I'm on the Missouri side of this."

"Hey, don't sweat it, Jimmy my boy! Ol' Tone here feels you're gonna make it! I'll keep you posted with a call, email and/or text on how we're doing. Ciao for now!"

Jim finished his call with Tony. He truly would like to believe his agent this time, but too many past disappointments had brought him down to come to grips for a reality check. This was to be his last shot at the bigs.

As Jim approached his Civic in the FedEx parking lot, his phone began to ring. He read the ID display and noticed it wasn't Tony. Instead, it was Marty Leary, one of the two men Jim had become good friends with after meeting him at several group therapy sessions for divorced men. He hadn't heard from Marty in a while, what with his busy baseball schedule. Pleased to hear from his fellow divorced friend, Jim answered the line without hesitation.

"Hey, Marty! Long time, no hear!"

"How's it going? Ed and I figured you were too busy with the Squirrels all summer. We didn't want to bother you."

"Well, the Squirrels had the occasional odd-day off in their home schedule. We could've done something then."

"That's true. Sorry about that. Say, how does it feel to be a big-time celebrity?"

"Personally, I'm getting a little tired of the hero tag. Since that presentation was made with Mayor Reynolds, I've suddenly gotten calls from all kinds of media people. It's driving me nuts!"

"It's the price of fame, my friend." Marty paused briefly before continuing. "Listen, Jim. In light of saving that Langston guy from the drink, Ed and I agreed to take you for a night on the town. Our treat."

"Oh, you guys don't have to do that."

"Nah, nah, c'mon! You deserve it. What do you say Ed and I pick you up from your apartment on Friday, say about six?"

Jim hesitated for a moment, but then accepted Marty's proposal. But for good measure he gave Marty his home address. "Three-Ten West Franklin, in case you misplaced the original slip of information I gave you some time back." He assured Marty he would be ready on time and then finished his call with his good friend. Just as Joyce's dinner invitation gave him a lift, so did the inducement by Marty and Ed to celebrate a repast with good company. More so than the media pandering, Jim cherished the lovely gestures made by people who wear their sincerity on their arms. He then got into his car and drove for home where he planned to have a light dinner and an early retirement to bed in order to battle that next day and its call to rise at four in the morning.

Chapter Eleven

Friday evening had finally arrived and, true to his word, Marty Leary picked up Jim at precisely six o'clock with Ed Holtermann in tow. Of the three, Marty was the flamboyant type as he showcased his sleek BMW Z4 sDrive35i convertible. The elegant burgundy-colored machine performance was as fierce as its dynamic, classy appearance. And it was a magnet for women, the very reason why Marty splurged on the sexy roadster. It was part of the spoils of a very successful accounting practice Marty had maintained.

Although he was four years older than Jim's 48 years, Marty appeared as someone no older than 40. He was physically fit, had an abundant, well-maintained head of dark brown hair. A suave moustache accented a face chiseled out of granite. Indeed, Marty's sporty lifestyle and distinguished looks made him a ladies' man. In fact, that's what led to the downfall of his marriage.

His former wife, Jennifer, was jealous with the way women gravitated toward Marty, and sometimes the other way around. Finally things came to a head when Jennifer caught Marty involved in an affair, with one of her best friends, no less. It soon became Splitsville for the flashy numbers man. The only regret Marty had was that he, like Jim, lost custody of his two children, both of whom had since grown to adulthood.

And to top it all off, Marty had since dropped Jennifer's ex-friend. As a matter of fact, Marty had had four relationships since. But the accountant didn't want to head to the altar again. He was more interested in how good these women were in bed. He certainly embraced the lifestyle of uninhibited promiscuity. Of course, Marty was one to talk. He had to take prescribed medication to deal with his own erectile dysfunction problems.

Ed was more like Jim; living under modest means. He was a fireman for the Richmond Fire Department, although at 50, Ed was on the verge of putting in for his pension. He was average-looking with a thin build and no hair on top of his head. About the only reason Ed stuck around Marty so often was because of the latter's uncanny knack of grabbing attention of those of the opposite gender. The fireman certainly didn't possess the ability to catch the eye of a wanting female on his own.

He and his ex-wife, Tara, broke up for peculiar reasons. They had gotten bored being with each other. And while at first there were no misgivings at the time of the rift, Ed in later years, rued the fact he and Tara gave up on each other so quickly. Fortunately for him, they had no children to divvy up. Like Jim, Ed drove a modest set of wheels; a Chevy Malibu.

Marty and Ed took Jim to Sam Miller's on East Cary Street, where the baseball man went totally seafood with a jumbo shrimp appetizer and a blackened Swordfish entrée, done to perfection. Marty wanted beef with a 16-ounce New York sirloin, while Ed ordered the bistro's famous seasoned crab cakes. Ed and Jim shared a bottle of Sauvignon Blanc to down their meals with, while Marty, the designated driver, stuck to sparkling water.

It was nearly eight o'clock when the men finished dinner. Even though he was being indulged, Jim only had room for coffee after such a sumptuous meal. Marty took care of the feast through his American Express card with an assist from Ed.

"Well, now that the tip's been taken care of, I'd like to make a suggestion to go someplace else," Marty began. "Are you game, Ed?"

"Yeah, sure."

Marty turned to Jim without asking the question again.

"Uh, I think you guys went above and beyond with the meal, to be honest," Jim replied. "I'd just as soon call it a night."

Marty's forehead furrowed. "What are you talking about? C'mon, let's live a little, will ya? And Ed, I'll pick up the rest of the tab this evening."

Jim wasn't going to argue, because he knew he would lose out. At that point the trio rose from the linen-topped table and forged ahead.

Marty drove his Beamer for twenty minutes toward the southern part of the city until he came to a stop. When Jim looked around the parking lot, he noticed an adjacent tall one-story building. On the side of it was a garish pink and blue neon sign that read *Sophisticated Lady Gentlemen's Club,* complete with the curvy outline of a woman holding a martini. Jim saw the sign and knew right away it was a strip joint. His visage manifested to one of utter disgust. He looked at Ed, who simply shrugged his shoulders. In the meantime, Marty was salivating over the place. He told his occupants to vacate and go inside. Jim was uncomfortable about entering and made it known to Marty, but the accountant countered with reasoning.

"C'mon, Jim, like I said before, live a little. Besides, I'm treating you, remember. George Maslin owns and runs this place, and he's one of my clients. I also happen to know the woman who manages the girls. Her name is Suzy, and she'll do anything, for me—within reason."

"I'm really not that keen about going in. I don't care who you know in there."

Marty was now the one whose face puckered as though he ate a lemon. His expression displayed disapproval over Jim's stubbornness. He then turned to the third member of the group. "Ed, will you convince this stuffed shirt that it's okay?"

"It's not so bad, Jim," Ed explained. "We may not be here too long, anyway. Isn't that right, Marty?"

"Of course! Of Course! C'mon, Jim. Let's go inside. I'll treat you to a lap dance. Where you go after that is your business."

Jim still wasn't thrilled about going in, but there was no way of getting around Marty's persistence. Besides, Marty was the driver and owner of that night's transportation.

After the cover charges were taken care of, the trio entered the bawdy establishment. When they got inside, Jim noticed it was dark, except for the lit runway the exotic dancers paraded up and down along. Cigarette and cigar smoke permeated the air to the point of near suffocation. Alcoholic beverages of all types were found everywhere, al-

though the club maintained a strict two-drink limit moni-
tored by a hole-punching system. Dancing music was blaring so loudly across the main speakers that one had trouble
trying to think.

In the dimly lit seating area Marty spotted Suzy. Who
couldn't? Although she was more than twice the age of
many of the dancers, Suzy still tried to pass herself as an
enticement for someone to score with as she frolicked in
her fake blonde wig and caked-on make-up. Her scrunched
up top made her appear very well-endowed. But with those
added years came experience. Suzy was tough when she
had to be and defended the dancers like a lioness would
her cubs. She was the ultimate den mother, although some
often referred to Suzy as more of a madam.

Marty waved at Suzy, to which the sprightly old vixen
waved back. He motioned to her to meander across the room
around the crowded tables. When she arrived Marty began
some dialogue. After a few pleasantries were exchanged, it
came down to introductions. First Ed was announced, and
then it came to the man being honored that evening.

"This is my good friend, *Diamond* Jim Monahan. He's
the voice of the Richmond Flying Squirrels."

"Well," Suzy said, smiling superficially as she gently
went to shake Jim's hand, careful not to dig her long, manicured and polished nails into his skin. "There's a heck of a
lot more action here than with the Squirrels you can supply
play-by-play for."

"You remember that guy being rescued from Gillies
Creek last week?" Marty then cupped his right hand around
Jim's right shoulder and gave him a vigorous shake.

"This is the guy who plucked that old man out of the
truck."

"Oh, I remember reading about it and watching that
ceremony at City Hall on the news the other day," Suzy
responded. She then turned to Jim and flashed her pearly
whites. "Hey, it's not every day we get a hero coming through
these doors!"

"Well . . . uh . . . thanks." Jim modestly smiled.

She sat the three men at a vacant table. Jim noticed
Marty giving the runway a long look. *Perhaps Marty would
have preferred sitting at a seat by the runway to look at the*

girls up close, Jim thought, but all the seats were taken. As he was being seated, Marty slipped a $50 bill to Suzy.

"See what you can do about getting us three seats up front, okay Doll?"

"Thanks, Hon," Suzie responded as she slipped the bill in her cleavage. "Give me a little time to work on that." She then sashayed away.

The electric music was still being pumped through the system. Strobe lights flashed every second from different directions focusing on the performing dancer on the runway as she slowly went up and down the pole in the middle in a suggestive fashion. A scantily clad waitress came to their table.

"What would you guys like to drink?" asked the perky young woman with the short black hair.

"I'm driving, so I'll have a club soda with a twist of lime," Marty answered.

"I'll have a bottle of Legend Porter," Ed replied as he handed her his card to be punched under the strictly enforced alcohol rule.

"Uh, make mine a club soda with lime, too," Jim requested.

"Thanks, guys! They'll be coming up shortly!" The waitress flashed a sensual grin and even bent over to promote her cleavage in the attempt to gain a grateful gratuity.

While he bided his time for the drinks to arrive, Jim looked down at the floor next to his seat. He wasn't interested in the practically naked woman prancing around looking for the wolves around her to lavish her with dollar bills. Jim wanted to be elsewhere, even back at his modest apartment watching an old movie on television. Marty was observing.

"Hey, cheer up, okay?"

Jim looked up at Marty with a halfhearted smile to assure the accountant he would. But he was only kidding himself on that matter.

Just then the waitress arrived with their drinks. But before any of the trio had a chance to take one sip, Suzy gestured to Marty that she was able to secure the seats he had requested by the runway. She rapidly waved at him to come over to the seats at that point or risk losing them altogether.

"C'mon, guys!" Marty ordered the others. "Grab your drinks and follow me."

While Ed showed interest in moving along, Jim was a little more reluctant. As Marty walked toward the new chairs, he turned around briefly and noticed Jim was making a halfhearted move to lift himself away from the old spot.

"Let's go, Jim!" Marty bellowed testily. The unenthusiastic patron conceded to walk over at a brisker pace.

By the time Jim settled into his new seat, the dancer who had been cavorting along the runway earlier had left. But just then, a young male near 30 years of age and sporting a black goatee began to make an announcement over the PA system. Getting his voice heard over the continuing electric music, the man introduced the next dancer.

"Ladies and gentlemen," the man began with verve in his voice, "here's our next lovely lady to grace the stage! Let's all give it up for the fabulous and vivacious . . . Sapphire!"

There were a few hoots and hollers sprinkled among the applause the patrons accorded the next dancer. Jim, however, just sat in his chair looking indifferently at the next woman to come out onto the runway. She was a stunning brunette, appeared to be of college age, and was bathed in a royal blue see-through outfit. Jim mused at the notion that perhaps this was her way of affording herself a higher education.

As the beat of the music became more pronounced, the stripper slithered her body up and down the pole in the middle of the runway. The male patrons around Sapphire encouraged her to go to the next step. She didn't disappoint as she removed her flimsy covering, making each new gyration of her enticing body more sensual than the last. All that covered her private areas were two pasties and a very thin g-string. A few of the patrons began to shower her with money. Sapphire seductively smiled at her willing contributors as she slowly peeled off the pasties to expose her breasts entirely. Some more yells and whistles went up as she approached Marty.

The accountant was grinning like a Cheshire cat. Sapphire gave him a beguiling stare and then slowly rolled her tongue around the circumference of her lips for good

45

measure. Marty caved in to Sapphire's sultry act and relinquished a $20 bill her way. She slowly retracted her nearly naked frame and seductively grabbed the note with her teeth. But Sapphire wasn't through yet. She was looking for her next victim and saw Ed mesmerized over the sight of her gorgeous, steamy body. Sapphire repeated the same routine but added a twist. She teased Ed by pulling down the right side strap of her skimpy thong. Ed placed a few bills between the strap and Sapphire's right hip. The vixen then released her grip to hold the money in place. Ed then gave Sapphire a soft pat on her butt. She smiled at Ed, but it was one of those *That's as far as you go, buddy* grins.

It then became Jim's turn. Sapphire applied the same charm to the baseball man. She showcased her left hip to him so that he might replicate Ed's gesture on the other side. She even went so far as to lower the left strap of her g-string and flash a little more of her private area than she did to Ed. But Jim would not have any of it. It wasn't for the fact that he didn't want to become another sucker to be enslaved by Sapphire's curves. He just didn't want to be at the seedy place, period. He politely waved his right hand at the stripper in a motion to have her move on. Sapphire was nonplussed by Jim's rejection, but she also knew there were plenty more saps willing to cater to her desire for more cash.

One of the other dancers was taking a break for herself and saw Jim's disapproval of Sapphire.

"Look at that guy, Buzz!" She gestured to the bartender. "That's bad for business. That creep told Sapphire to take a hike! I mean, what if that happened to me?" A scowl was etched across her face. "Excuse me. I'm going to give him a piece of my mind!"

The woman marched over to Jim from behind to make a comment. "Don't be such an asshole. We're all here to have a good time."

The idle dancer then went on to plant a kiss on the right side of Jim's face. Never had a woman's kiss seemed so hollow and fraudulent to the baseball man as that one. Not even Maureen was that phony. That was the nail in the coffin. Jim had had enough of the place and began to rise from his seat. He became more pissed than the woman, and began to move toward the front door, as if to exit.

Meanwhile, Marty and Ed enjoyed the show Sapphire was putting on with her sensual bumps and grinds. But when the accountant looked toward Jim, he noticed the baseball man was about to leave. His facial expression morphed to one of desperation. He quickly told Ed to hold their spots while he chased after Jim. The baseball man was inches away from the exit when Marty caught up to him.

"Hey! Where the hell are you going?"

"I've had enough of this place, Marty, if you want to know the truth. I never wanted to be here in the first place. This was your idea to satisfy your own sexual urges, wasn't it?"

"No, you've got it all wrong, Jim. Ed and I wanted to make sure you had a treat on us for the evening."

"Well, the dinner at Sam Miller's was more than enough."

"Was it that woman who came up to you? I did happen to notice her. What happened, Jim? What did she say to you? It obviously turned you off."

"Oh, she made a derogatory comment. I found it to be offensive. But it wasn't just her. I didn't want to set foot into this place when we were in the parking lot. I mean, look at these women." Jim gestured to the dancers for Marty's observation before continuing. "These girls are not that much older than my own daughter!"

"Oh, yeah? Well, I've got a daughter who's their age plus a couple of years. Hey, wake up, pal! These are not *our* girls on the stage!"

"It's more than that, Marty . . . more than that." Jim looked at the scantily clad women and confessed to his friend. "They remind me too much of Maureen—women who will have sex with you so long as you've got a fat wallet. That's what happened to me. Maureen was attracted to the money this guy has and so she slept with him and along comes their baby nine months later. These women are no different . . . only younger. Like Maureen, they've got no scruples. But, look. I don't want to be a wet blanket to you and Ed. You two guys have a good time. I'll just call a cab to take me home."

"I'm sorry you feel that way, Jim. I just wanted you to have fun, that's all."

"You meant well, Marty, and that's what matters most. Let's get together again soon. Just keep this place and others like it off the list."

Marty was disappointed Jim didn't want to stay any longer, but respected the baseball man's wishes. Hanging his head low, Marty returned to his seat by the runway.

Jim had one of the muscular bouncers call a taxi for him. Despite the very warm and humid conditions of the evening, he decided to wait outside for the car service to arrive, rather than stay one second longer inside the club. The place made Jim's skin crawl. What was his plan when he would eventually get back home? Probably either to watch a ballgame, a movie on HBO or an interesting and informative program. Perhaps even read a magazine article or two. Or maybe surf the internet on his computer . . . anything to get his mind away from Maureen and the strippers inside the club.

Chapter Twelve

Sunday afternoon. That meant dinnertime with the Langston family. Jim took a peek at the clock on the instrument panel of his Civic. Two forty-six. The beads of nervous perspiration on his brow quickly evaporated, for Jim was more than punctual. He had just arrived in the community called Glen Allen, a northern suburb of Richmond that served as one of the typical bedroom communities of the big town. Children were playing, neighbors were chatting, barbecues were going, and birds were chirping. Yellow daffodils surrendered their inner beauty for the local honeybees. Quite idyllic.

The GPS Jim used as his navigator advised him that he had arrived at his destination on Warren Road. What would he have done without the seductive female voice acting as his cartographic guide? He pulled up along the side of the curb and brought his Civic to a halt. Jim needed first to step back and smell the roses. He got out to observe the beautifully maintained exterior of the light blue Victorian-style house with white shutters. A long, old-fashioned white porch graced the entrance to the two-story home. Jim imagined members of the Langston household often sat there on many a summer evening with an ice-cold pitcher of lemonade to admire the red twilight.

The baseball man admired the well-manicured front lawn. And the shrubbery surrounding the sides of the property was perfectly managed, too. Even the driveway appeared to have been re-paved in recent times. The macadam was a contrasting ebony color and was still quite soft. Of course, the summer heat had a lot to do with that, but there was that scent of freshly-laid tar as a sign of fastidious upkeep.

As Jim walked along the stone-paved path to the front porch, the front door opened. It was Joyce Langston wearing a conservative burgundy dress and matching shoes, making her the epitome of the suburban matron. With the sun reflecting brightly off her silver hair, Joyce greeted Jim with open arms.

"Hi, Jim." Joyce smiled. "I'm so glad you made it! C'mon in!"

"Thank you, Joyce," Jim replied, and then looked around the outside of the house. "You've got a beautiful home!"

"Thanks! The whole gang's awaitin'!"

Jim carefully stepped inside, as if treading on hallowed grounds. Just as wonderful as the house appeared on the outside so was the interior. So rich and elegant. Jim marveled at the exquisite Colonial furniture in the spacious living room. There was a working fireplace in the middle of it for those chilly winter nights, although Joyce told the baseball man they hardly used it because of their central heating system, which was currently cranking out chilled air to battle the late August heat. A few paintings and pictures adorned the understated, but soothing earth-toned walls, giving the home a dash of elegance. A quaint glass-topped coffee table centered the L-shaped divan, end table and lounge chairs. The table itself rested atop a brilliant Persian rug, which graced the fine, gleaming oak wood floor.

Jim also noticed the richly stained, split-level wooden staircase leading to the second floor bedrooms. The stairs sparkled in the finish. Spotless crimson carpeting covered the middle portion of the steps to muffle foot traffic.

Before he had a chance to meet another human in the house, the Langston family dog came out of nowhere to greet the visitor. The dog's name was Barney and it affectionately began to get up on its hind legs to slobber Jim with a series of sloppy licks as it wagged its tail feverishly. Jim laughed at the love the big pointer administered. But Joyce became annoyed and yelled at Barney to go to another place in the house.

Obediently, the pointer got off of Jim and ran into another room.

"I apologize, Jim. Barney always craves attention. Go on! Get!"

50

"Hey, don't worry, Joyce," Jim laughed. "I grew up with dogs. I'm used to it."

The first person to greet Jim after Joyce was her son, Michael. For Jim, this was the third time he had met him, but now they had more time to chat and get to know each other. "I'm an electrician." A good profession to follow. The 43-year-old never married and, after a short while living on his own, Michael moved back in with his parents, only now he was co-owner of the house and stood in line to inherit it from Alan and Joyce when they passed on.

The next two to welcome Jim were Joyce's 46-year-old daughter Kimberly and her husband, Josh Cain, close in age to his wife. While Kimberly was the typical stay-at-home soccer mom, Josh worked for the Federal government up in Manassas, just outside of Washington. Unlike with Michael, this was Jim's second meeting with Kimberly, but it was his first with Josh. Kimberly then called in to the next room and summoned their two teenage children, Ashley and Jackson, both of whom scrambled into the living room, like Barney had dragged them in. Kimberly was embarrassed by her kids' apathetic appearance.

"I'm so sorry, Jim," Kimberly apologized. "Ashley. Jackson. Where are your manners?"

"Hey, it's okay, Kimberly," Jim replied. "My daughter Madison would have reacted the same way." Jim dismissed it entirely with a smile and a soft hello to the teenagers.

The whole crew proceeded into the adjacent dining room. There, Jim was captivated by the long table, covered by virgin white linen and graced with ornate china and silverware. An exquisite Waterford vase sat in the middle, filled with a stunning bouquet of freshly-cut flowers. A magnificently restored china closet stood alongside one of the walls, while a marble-topped credenza sat opposite it. A white, multi-paned window rose majestically behind the head of the table, thus giving that chair the regal appearance of a throne. And that seat was reserved for only one member of the clan—Alan Langston.

Jim was curious where Alan was.

"Grandpa's taking a dump," Jackson remarked sarcastically.

Joyce, Kimberly and Josh admonished Jackson for the uncalled-for comment. Jim simply raised his eyebrows and tilted his head downward, but still observed everyone's angry facial expressions.

Nearly a minute later the Langston patriarch appeared. Alan hobbled along on his banged-up leg, stabilizing himself as best he could with the cane the hospital provided for him. Although it was so good to see him back home again, Alan's recovery still had a long way to go. But for Jim it was great to see Alan up and about, period. The two men looked at each other with broad grins, like they hadn't seen each other in years. Jim waltzed up to Alan, and the pair gave each other a strong and warm greeting.

"Alan, it's great to see you again! And you're a heck of a lot better I might add!"

"Why thank you, Jim. If it weren't for you I might not be here at all, and I mean that."

Joyce, Kimberly and Michael went to the kitchen to gather food and beverages. Joyce gave Jim an option of four different items to drink.

"I'll have the wine, please."

The time spent by the others to garner the repast allowed Alan and Jim to chat a while. And the Langston patriarch wanted Jim to sit to his right so that he didn't have to shout across the table at him. Alan made it a point to give Jim his undivided attention.

It took five minutes for Joyce and the others to bring in the food and drinks. But before anyone had a chance to dig in at the scrumptious meal, Alan began a moment of prayer and thanks for allowing divine intervention to succeed in having Jim rescue him. Upon conclusion of Alan's blessing, Josh stood up.

"I'd like to propose a toast," Josh said. "To our distinguished guest, Jim Monahan. For saving Grandpa Langston's life. Here's to you, Jim!"

Everyone stood up with their glasses raised. It didn't matter if the beverage was alcoholic or not, everyone clanked their glasses with those closest to them.

It was time to eat and everything Joyce had promised several days before was delivered. Crispy fried chicken, mashed potatoes, milk gravy, homemade coleslaw, and string beans. Jim feasted on the delectable morsels. He made several comments on the chicken, gravy and coleslaw in particular. Michael responded by saying his mom had always been a great cook.

"She looks and talks a little like that Paula Deen on TV, but I think she cooks a heck of a lot better than her."

Joyce blushed, but thanked her son for the high praise. But Jim echoed the sentiment, contesting the accolade was well deserved.

The dining room table was more than a place where everyone gathered to eat. It also became a debating room where various topics from religion to politics to sports were discussed in an open forum. Then Michael brought up a subject that hit very close to home for Jim.

"I'm glad that I'm not married." He looked at his sister and parents as if an expected difference of opinion was forthcoming. "Oh, no offense to y'all, but that would not have suited me."

"Now, wait a minute, Mike," Alan objected. "You almost got engaged to that Patricia Turley girl."

"And, Pa, I'm glad I didn't. She got married, but she's now divorced and has to raise those three brat kids she has. And I've seen her drunk, too! I'm surprised she didn't have the law take her kids away from her."

"Well, she got mixed up with that abusive creep," Joyce added, "that Lenny character. Is he still doing time in the slammer?"

"Last I heard he is. At least you don't see divorce in this family."

"You forget about our dear lovely cousin, Pam," Kimberly piped in. "What's she working on, Ma, husband number three?"

"I reckon she is."

"At least ain't nothing like that happening here," Michael pointed out. He then turned toward Jim. He had already been told by Joyce that Jim was divorced. Michael then came out with a direct question. "I'll bet being divorced really sucks, Jim."

"Oh," Jim began as he looked around at everyone watching him for his rebuttal. "It's not something I wished upon myself, or anyone else for that matter. I still think the institution of marriage is great. But for some it causes friction. That's when it's better to part ways."

"Yeah, but then you gotta get these lawyers involved and decide who gets what."

"Yes, and that's no fun, let me assure you."

"Did you two have any children?"

"Yes, one daughter."

"She probably stays with your ex, too. That must tear at you, don't it?"

By now Joyce, Alan, and Kimberly were getting irritable at the way Michael was badgering Jim on the subject. Each one came to the baseball man's aid and scolded Michael for his grilling of their guest. But Jim waved at the others to convince them he could defend himself.

"Do you want to know something, Michael? I see your parents in front of me here. They're a sweet and devoted couple. Do you know why your mom and dad allow everyone to get together for this Sunday ritual? It's not an excuse to gorge on great food. No, they do it out of love. Love for you, love for Kimberly and Josh, love for their grandkids, and most of all, love for each other. I saw how frantic your mother was that night in the hospital. She was worried sick over what had happened to Alan. You remember. And I know Alan would react the same way if something happened to Joyce. From my brief encounter, I can see there's a strong bond between Kimberly and Josh. And although their kids put them through their paces—and I should know, being a parent of a teenager myself—I can see they truly love Ashley and Jackson. And they'll do everything to protect them. And you want to know what that's called, Mike? It's called love of family. Believe it or not, I've been brought up along those same sacred principles from my own parents. And I tried everything in my power to make it work, although sometimes I look back and wonder if I should've done a few things differently. I see how great your parents get along with each other and how your sister and brother-in-law show their devotion. But that's just it, Mike. You've got to have both parties involved. It's just like those old locomotive engines. Unless you've got someone stoking the flames with coal every so often, you go nowhere. For that reason I truly envy this family, because it's everything I wanted my own to be."

Joyce was so moved by Jim's speech to Michael that she had to reach for her napkin. The Langston matriarch's eyes welled up in tears and she couldn't control herself. She apologized for reacting the way she did, but then added a special comment.

"What you just said, Jim, is true. Alan and I certainly love Michael, Kimberly, Josh, Ashley, and Jackson. And, yes, we still love each other after fifty wonderful years of being together. That's the unity that holds the Langston family together. That's what keeps us going."

For at least ten seconds there was dead silence in the room. Then Kimberly spoke up to change the subject and enliven everyone's spirits.

"Y'all better save some room for Ma's pecan pie later. Jim, if you think her chicken was great, wait'll you taste her dessert! Mmmmm!"

"That's right," Alan seconded. "I'm surprised I'm as thin as I am with all of Joyce's great food!"

"My public has spoken," Joyce smiled.

Everyone broke out in laughter. The rest of the meal went without further incident. Jim and Michael exchanged dialogue later on, but the subject of divorce was strictly taboo.

The clock read 4:30 and the dining room table had long been cleared of the chicken and the rest of the fixings. A huge pot of percolated coffee was placed near the flowery centerpiece. Cream and sugar, plates and forks, saucers and cups soon followed.

And then came the aforementioned pecan pie with an abundant amount of freshly made whipped cream on the side to top it off. Jim was amazed at the rich dessert in front of him. He made a remark to Joyce and the others.

"Gee, I hope I can still sit behind the wheel of my car after all this!"

"Y'all can work out at the gym tomorrow." Joyce grinned.

The clock finally struck seven. Kimberly and Josh had to leave. Ashley and Jackson were about to start another school year the next day and Josh had to go to work.

The trip back to Manassas would normally take a little more than an hour and a half, but I-95 was prone to being loaded, especially with people returning to the Washington area from one of their last summer weekends at Virginia Beach.

That was Jim's cue to depart as well. He had to rise earlier than everyone else for his morning sports reports.

"Thanks for a lovely meal once again, Joyce, Alan."

"Oh, it was our pleasure," Joyce smiled. "Y'all gotta come back now!"

Jim then turned to Michael and extended his right hand.

"Hey. Let's stay in touch! On the light side, though." Jim's reference was to Michael's inquisition at the dinner table. The electrician laughed in agreement.

Jim walked out of the house and scanned the sky. Dark and ominous clouds were fast approaching, reminiscent of that night Jim had saved Alan from Gillies Creek.

He wanted to get back to his apartment in Richmond before it began to pour. But Jim had to take one more look at the Langston house. He waved at Joyce and Alan, who were standing on the front porch. The senior couple reciprocated and smiled in return. From out of nowhere, Barney made his last appearance with a loud woof of approval and wag of his tail. Everyone got a kick out of the pointer's sendoff. And all the while, Jim was thinking about the exchange between him and Michael and how fortunate the members of the Langston family were. As he opened the driver's side door to his Civic, he could only ask the question, "What if . . . ?"

Chapter Thirteen

Monday morning rolled around, and Jim was just two hours away from completing another round of his sports reports on Vince's program. He had just finished with his 8:40 report when Christine Haines caught up to him to give her own advice on what to change for the 9:10 report.

"I don't know, Jim," Christine commented. "Is it truly necessary to keep that tiny item of that minor fender bender of the Cavs' sophomore backup forward Dwight Vincent in the spotlight? I mean, nobody was hurt. He'll be fine for the upcoming basketball season in the fall. Maybe you ought to eighty-six it. Just a thought."

Although Jim was a seasoned sports reporter, he still took his program director's observations into strong consideration. Jim checked his pride at the door if only to enhance his reportage.

Jim was about ready to revise the copy he had just read on the air when suddenly the thoughts of the past weekend flashed in his head. His mind took a detour off a roadside cliff. Forget about what he had to say concerning the upcoming college football season involving the University of Virginia, Virginia Tech, William and Mary, and James Madison. All Jim could concentrate on was Marty Leary's wild idea to bring him to the strip club and Michael Langston's biting comment on Jim's marital life. And both had Maureen Bell as the common denominator, causing the reporter to think about his misgivings with his ex the week before and how he embarrassed himself in front of Madison. He shut his eyes tight for a moment in an attempt to purge the images from his mind. *Yeah, good luck with that.* Having great difficulty with it was an understatement. The recollections were so strong and vivid they were compromising Jim's efforts to channel his brain on the reediting.

Just then Laura Mazursky appeared. She said a brief hello to anyone she came in sight with. She even greeted Jim, but the reporter was unresponsive; caught inside the maelstrom of a convoluted vortex twisting his thinking capacity like a wrung-out wet towel. After placing her personal effects on her desk, she looked at Jim with a puzzled face. He needed to be rescued from his self-imposed gloom. But Laura had to get inside Jim's head first—a head weighed down by torment, resting on the outstretched palms of his hands. Laura tried again to get his attention.

"Hey, Jim, are you all right?"

Jim finally snapped out of his daze and responded to Zach's admin, like he'd been hit broadside by a two-by-four. He raised his head to look at her, like he had been in a deep trance. He quickly apologized for his inconsiderate behavior, but Laura responded by stating she was just concerned by his deep funk. Time now for Jim to fess up on the causes of his depression.

"Oh, I had these two friends of mine I met through this group I belong to take me out to dinner Friday night. That was great, but then one of them drives us over to this strip club afterward. I didn't want to be there in the first place. It was all for his pleasure. Then yesterday Joyce Langston invited me over for dinner with her family. Her husband, Alan, is now out of the hospital."

"How's he doing?"

"He gets along okay with a cane. It's going to take a while for him to mend. So, anyway, their son, Michael, bothers me on how terrible my life has been since my divorce. And all this reminds me of my episode with Maureen the week before. Needless to say, I'm not a happy camper."

Laura displayed a pensive look.

"Do you know what I think? I think indirectly your friend, Joyce's son and your ex want you to get involved with a woman."

Jim looked at Laura incredulously, "How in the hell do you figure that out?"

"Well, take your friend, for example. He brings you to the strip joint because he feels you miss the sensual intimacy a woman gives you. Now, as a woman myself, I commend you for not wanting to step foot in there from the outset and condemning it. But I think your friend, in his own twisted logic, wanted to reintroduce you to a woman's softer side and make you crave it. As for Michael, I just think he wanted to remind you that being divorced is lousy and to try to do something about it."

"And what about Maureen, *Dr. Ruth*?"

"I think she'd much prefer if you had a lady in your life so that you might not be so irritable when you see her."

"Well, Maureen married that rich bastard, but she's still an obnoxious bitch."

"That doesn't mean *you* couldn't change for the better, if you had a special someone to be with. And from what you told me, your daughter, Madison, seems as though she'd like to run away from that house. I think she would do much better being with you, but only if . . ."

"If there were a much better female role model to take Madison under her wing," Jim interrupted. He released a short laugh and shook his head while gazing at the floor. "Oh, I don't know if that's the solution to everything, Laura."

"I'll bet you miss having a woman to be with."

"There may be an occasion here and there when that's the case, but I really don't see myself getting involved in a relationship."

"Oh, c'mon, Jim!" Laura smiled while trying to coax a confession out of him. "Do you mean to tell me you don't miss being with a woman during intimate moments?"

"Okay! Okay! I miss the sex! There, are you happy? I miss the sex!" Laura laughed at Jim's sarcastic, but humorous remark after he finally caved in to her grilling. Then Jim became reflective and began to speak in quieter tones. "But more than that, I miss the little things. I miss the warm companionship: going out with her to dinner, seeing a movie, going on a trip. I miss coming home and being greeted by that subtle but effective little kiss to assure me that I'm wanted, and sharing the same feeling in return. I miss giving her flowers for no reason. I miss the friendly soft voice, the laughter and, yes, even her cries. I miss sharing the good times, and even commiserating each other through the bad and sad times. I miss the warm and tender embrace a woman gives. And I miss . . . I miss just the reassurance she gives you when you're down by saying, *Hey, honey. Everything's going to be okay.* You see, the little things, that, when you add them up all together, they far outweigh the big picture. That's what I miss the most."

Laura gave Jim a dreamy expression, apparently taken by his statement. She broke into a smile, as if hit with a startling revelation.

"Listen! I have a very good friend of mine. Her name is Anne Finley. She's 44, never married. As far as I know she's not seeing anyone. Why don't you, Anne, my husband Charlie and I all get together on Friday night for dinner?"

At first Jim looked at Laura like he thought she was crazy. Then he broke out with a short burst of laughter. "Are you trying to fix me up on a date?"

"Well, sort of. But I just look at it as an introduction. Maybe you can get to know Anne. She's really a good-natured person and fun to be with. Now I know it's the Labor Day weekend coming up, and unless you have plans to go somewhere . . ."

"College football starts this weekend."

"My god! Don't you have TiVo? Besides, the big games are on Saturday, if I'm not mistaken. This is Friday evening we're talking about."

"Okay, okay. You and Charlie pick the place. I'll be there."

"Great! Oh, and one more thing, Jim. Anne is very close to me, so you'd better treat her right."

"The one thing I was always taught by my family, Laura, is to treat women with the respect and courtesy they deserve, in spite of what happened in my earlier life."

"Well, I know who the culprit was there."

It was settled. Jim agreed to meet with Laura, her husband, and the mysterious Anne Finley. He wasn't looking to become involved with anyone, but figured it might just work out. Perhaps he might develop chemistry with Anne. At the very worst, maybe he and Anne could become very good friends whereby he could bounce ideas and topics off her to get a woman's perspective, rather than solely relying on the male slant people like Marty and Ed offered.

It had also been a while since Jim had courted a woman. Could it be he had forgotten how? By his own admission, he had taken his relationship with Maureen during their last few years together for granted, although she didn't do much to rekindle the spark they once had either.

Now he would have to start over from scratch. But who or what could he turn to for advice without the slightest bit of embarrassment?

The clock was approaching nine. Jim suddenly realized he had to go over his old copy with the proper revisions he had planned to put in. As wonderful as the thought of meeting a new love interest and recapturing the glory days of years past was, he had to explain the new spread offense highly ranked Virginia Tech planned to employ during the upcoming college football season, for his next sportscast, which was due in ten minutes!

Chapter Fourteen

The rest of the week went without any fanfare, which suited Jim just fine. All he wanted to do was focus on his present job as a radio sportscaster Monday through Friday until the following April when the Richmond Flying Squirrels' new season came around. That is, unless the St. Louis Cardinals hired him, of course.

Speaking of which, Jim hadn't heard from his agent Tony Salerno in New York. That was actually good news, because that meant the tape Jim had sent Tony the week before was worthy of being heard by the Cardinals' brass for review. The wait was on until October rolled around for a serious showdown.

Jim stood in front of the Tobacco Company restaurant, not far from Sam Miller's on East Cary Street in Downtown Richmond. He was watching the traffic, both vehicular and pedestrian, race by to and fro. Everyone was focused on getting out of the city for the holiday weekend and darting in different directions.

As he did the week before, Jim wore a crisp light blue dress shirt, only this time he wore a sharp red tie with a medieval crest design running throughout, a light gray sports coat, and black pants with shoes to match.

He gazed at his watch. Five forty-eight. He was early by twelve minutes, but it was better to be ahead of schedule than behind. It wasn't for Laura and Charlie's sake. Jim had met Charlie several times before anyway. But the baseball man wanted to make a good impression on Anne Finley.

A commercial truck caught Jim's eye as he bided his time. As the vehicle raced down the street, he heard his name being called out, causing his head to freeze. He turned around and saw Laura strolling toward him, wearing a snazzy black dress. The admin waved and smiled. Walking next to her was her husband Charlie, who like Jim, was clad in a blazer, slacks, shirt and tie.

"Hi, Jim," Laura beamed. "I hope you weren't waiting too long."

"Not long. I'd say about five minutes or so."

"Well, that's good. Of course, you know Charlie."

"Hey, Charlie! Long time, no see!" Jim shook hands with Laura's husband.

A woman, who was standing almost in the shadows of the couple, stepped into full view. She wore a pink business suit consisting of matching blazer and skirt with pink pumps to round things out. Underneath the blazer, she wore a white chiffon blouse.

"Jim," Laura continued, "this is my good friend, Anne Finley. Anne, this is *the* Diamond Jim Monahan!"

Jim and Anne exchanged a subtle handshake and simple pleasantries. Jim couldn't help but notice Anne and was amazed at how attractive she was. Was she a spectacular knockout? No. But there was a wholesome beauty about her. And just by the mere touch of her hand, Jim could feel the vibration of someone good, someone kind—someone with a warm heart. From her beautiful soft green eyes and infectious smile, to her flowing locks of medium brown hair, Anne's appearance captivated Jim no end. His eyes remained riveted to hers.

Laura beamed as Jim and Anne showed some admiration toward each other. Time to move the show inside.

"Uh, hey guys! I don't know about you two, but Charlie and I are starved!"

Jim and Anne all at once got the hint. They broke out of their trance. Each apologized to Laura and Charlie for their stare as the quartet proceeded to walk inside.

Reservations had been made by Charlie, who approached the host to give the party's name. All the while Jim began to admire the décor of the former four-story, tobacco warehouse. He had been in the restaurant before, but it had been some time ago. He appreciated its quaint antique furniture, the alabaster chandeliers, remarkably restored brick walls, and magnificent atrium allowing daylight to illuminate the middle interior of each floor. There was even a spectacular fireplace nearby, although it wasn't being used during the waning summer days.

A young waitress guided the foursome to a turn-of-the-century metal caged elevator, where they were promptly whisked away to the second floor. The blonde then led everyone to their table, next to a wooden railing overlooking the atrium. After the party was seated, the waitress eagerly mentioned a few of the specialties for the evening and then asked if anyone would like a drink before dinner. They all agreed on two bottles of wine—one chardonnay, and one merlot. Everyone needed a little time to mull over the menu. Clearly understood. She then walked away to retrieve the wine.

As each began to read through the menus, Laura slapped hers shut so hard that all heard it. Jim observed Charlie's stunned look of disbelief.

"So soon?" Charlie asked. "This has to be a record." Perhaps Laura was the type who notoriously took her time to decide on what to have for dinner. The quick decision took Charlie by surprise.

Laura then opened her purse and began to search for an item in it. She appeared frustrated, as if she had forgotten to bring something with her. *Damn! Where is it?* Laura then rose from her seat.

"Excuse me, everybody, but I think I've misplaced my cosmetic case," Laura apologized to the rest of the group. "I'm wondering if it may have fallen out of my purse somewhere. I'll be right back." Laura then looked at Charlie, who by now was again looking over the menu. "Uh, Charlie, why don't you help me look for it?"

"Hmm?" Charlie was still glancing over the list of entrees.

Laura appeared annoyed that he was practically ignoring her. Time to raise the volume to get his attention. "I said, Charlie, I want you to come with me and look for my cosmetic case." Laura then jerked her head away from the table.

Okay, Charlie got the hint this time. "Uh, yeah, right, Sweetie."

Charlie smiled and got up from his chair to join Laura in the *hunt* for the elusive cosmetic case, if it had been missing to begin with. That left Jim and Anne alone for a moment. Jim was still looking over the roster of dinners. He started a conversation with Anne by commenting on the variety of meat entrees. Anne countered that she rarely ate meat, but if she did, it would be limited to poultry. *I guess I won't be able to get Anne to cook a steak,* Jim thought to himself. The baseball man then shifted gears.

"So, Laura tells me that you're an office manager."

"That's right," Anne answered. "I work for Kleister Services. We're one of the largest human resource consultants in the country."

"You mean employment agency."

"Not really. Employment agencies' main focus is on getting secretaries work. We deal with executives in management and sales professionals. We're a little more upscale."

Jim didn't want to make Anne sound like a snob. He tactfully came up with a clever response. "Gee, I didn't know there was a difference. Shows you what I know."

Now Anne didn't want to appear condescending either. She smiled and offered a well-crafted reply. "That's okay. Everybody says the same thing." Anne paused briefly before commenting on Jim's line of work. "You know, I often hear your reports on radio when I go to work."

"Oh, really?" Jim was surprised that Anne had an interest in sports; perhaps it was because of his own chauvinistic beliefs that women are not generally followers of athletic competition. "Do you follow sports a lot?"

"A little. Just enough to know a few things here and there."

"You probably know that I also do the play-by-play for the Richmond Flying Squirrels."

"Yes. I've actually heard you a few times when I've changed stations in the car."

"Are you a baseball fan?"

"Probably more so than any other sport. I grew up in Brewster, New York. My folks still live there. Most of my family members are die-hard Yankees fans, but I followed the Mets. I was always favoring the underdog."

"I was born in Philadelphia, so naturally I rooted for the Phillies. But here I am broadcasting games for the top minor league affiliate of one of the Phillies' rivals. Go figure. And now I'm being considered for the St. Louis Cardinals' top play-by-play position. I don't know. My agent really believes I can do it this time. To tell you the truth, I think it's more because I had saved Alan Langston from possibly drowning in Gillies Creek."

"Right! I saw you on TV with Mayor Reynolds, Governor Porch and Senator Caves! Wow! That must've been exciting!"

"Oh, it was okay. I'd just as well not have bothered with all the attention, to be quite honest. That's just not me."

Anne appreciated Jim's low-key response. Whereas many people would've taken up the spotlight and gloated over their own heroics, Jim took a backseat. And he could tell just by looking at her that Anne admired those qualities. Just then the waitress returned with the bottles of wine. She proceeded to uncork them and decant the chardonnay for Anne and the merlot for Jim.

Jim knew Laura and Charlie would return from their *search* soon. It would have been awkward to ask Anne out in front of the Mazurskys, so he had to make the move right then. He politely asked Anne if she were doing anything the next evening.

"I don't have any plans," Anne responded.

"How would you like to go out for dinner and a movie then?"

"I'd love that," Anne smiled. "That would be great!"

They each exchanged phone numbers and addresses and agreed that Jim would stop by Anne's apartment around five.

Just as Jim and Anne were putting away their pieces of paper, Laura and Charlie reappeared. Jim then looked at Laura.

"So, did you two find your cosmetic case?"

"My cosmeh . . ." Laura began with bewilderment. "Oh! My cosmetic case! Well, it turns out it must have slipped out of my purse downstairs. The host found it for me."

Jim and Anne then looked at each other and smiled. *Uh huh. Sure.* They knew it was all a ruse by Laura and Charlie to allow the baseball man some time alone with Anne.

In quick order each person decided on what they wanted. Anne opted for grilled swordfish. Jim was originally going to order the prime rib, but then he factored in Anne's comment for her disdain of meat, and red meat in particular. He decided upon the Company chicken, sautéed with artichokes, sun dried tomatoes and shiitake mushrooms and a creamy sherry sauce. Charlie, on the other hand, had no guilt in ordering the prime rib for himself. He didn't have to placate Laura after so many years together. His wife opted for the lamb chops. The blonde waitress took their orders and sprinted off to the kitchen.

The rest of the dinner was spent in small chatter. As he and the others were leaving the restaurant, Jim addressed Laura and Charlie.

"Hey. Thanks for the night out, you two," Jim said, although he and Charlie split the costs.

He then turned to Anne with broad grin. "I'm looking forward to seeing you tomorrow night, Anne."

Jim had his back turned to Laura as he said this. Laura looked at Anne, raised her eyebrows, and puckered her lips to mouth out *oooh*. She shook her right hand up and down vigorously to dramatize the effect. Anne had smiled at Jim in return, but then she caught Laura's act. The office manager broke out into a short laugh. Jim was quizzical about what was causing Anne to chuckle. He turned toward Laura, who by this point had stopped her playful gesture. She simply flashed a wide grin at Jim. Then the baseball man looked over at Charlie. He just rolled his eyes, scratched the back of his head and looked away.

The handshakes and soft kisses marked an end to an enjoyable evening for everyone. But for Jim, it was the beginning of a new chapter in his life.

Chapter Fifteen

Jim wanted to make a good impression on Anne. He wanted to make sure he had allowed himself time to get to her apartment, so he made sure he left his pad by four o'clock. For good measure, he purposely set his watch five minutes into the future in order to keep one step ahead of time. That still enabled him to catch the Virginia-Georgia Tech game in its entirety, which had a noontime kickoff. Jim wanted to make notes on the game to include in some of his Monday morning sportscasts to remark on the Cavaliers' tough 27-23 loss to the Yellow Jackets. Taking a cue from Laura, he had set his TiVo to catch the highly anticipated Virginia Tech-Florida State prime time tilt later that evening.

The baseball announcer had to make two side trips before heading to Anne's apartment in the Gayton Pointe Townhomes complex, which was located in the trendy West End section of the city. But his stops did not include a florist or a confectionery store.

The moment he had approached Anne's apartment door, he checked himself out. Brand new IZOD royal blue golf shirt, khaki slacks and loafers. Jim looked down at the gifts he had in hand for Anne to make sure they were appropriate. There might have been a sliver of trepidation, especially now going one-on-one, but he took a deep breath to allay any lingering hint of self-doubt and fear. Satisfied with his choices of offerings and wardrobe, Jim pressed the buzzer. The button felt formidable, as though it was the only object standing between Jim and the launching of nuclear ballistic missiles—another sign of intimidation perhaps? As he waited for the door to be opened, he nervously checked the time on his watch. Four fifty-one. Like the night before, it was better to be a little early than a little late. He became a prisoner to father time.

Anne opened the door and greeted him with a warm smile. Like Jim, she was casually dressed in a light blue button-down blouse, black pants, stockings and sandals. Jim was happy to see the office manager, too. He then offered his presents to Anne. They were an odd pair, which threw Anne into a tailspin. Clearly an explanation was in order.

"I know you're going to think I'm a little eccentric with what I brought you, Anne, but allow me to explain." Jim first offered a book containing love poems from classical poets such as Elizabeth Barrett Browning, Robert Frost, John Keats and Percy Bysshe Shelley. "I know a box of candy is nice, but it adds calories and promotes tooth decay. This book has a lot of classical love poems to expand the mind. I guess you'd thought the only thing guys like myself read was Sports Illustrated, huh?"

"Oh, no." Anne smiled. "I never thought for a moment you were one-dimensional."

After Jim handed Anne the book, he gave her two large scented candles, and then gave his rationale for the candles.

"Flowers are pretty, but they die after a week and a half. I figure these candles will last a heck of a lot longer. Besides, they offer a wonderful strawberry fragrance and are charming to grace any table." Jim saw there was a little hesitation in Anne's demeanor and he was beginning to wonder if he had made bad choices. "I hope you don't mind what I got."

"Oh, no! That's fine, Jim. It's just a little . . . unusual, to say the least."

"I'm sorry, but I had wanted to be a little different, that's all. I mean, flowers and candy are natural selections, but I just wanted to throw a curveball. Ugh! There I go again! Always getting a baseball metaphor mixed in somehow."

Anne laughed. "That's okay. And do you want to know something? I'm beginning to appreciate what you got me. That shows ingenuity on your part. I like that."

Jim was glad Anne grew to appreciate the book and candles. After she had placed the items on a nearby counter, she stepped out with Jim. The game plan was to eat first and then catch a movie later before calling it a night. The two took Jim's car as they sped away to an eatery.

Chapter Sixteen

There was no need to go for an extravagant meal like the one the night before at the Tobacco Company restaurant. That was intended as their *first date* dinner, even though they had shared it with Laura and Charlie. Jim and Anne decided to shift downward and chose a TGI Friday's location on West Broad Street. The casual theme allowed each to be themselves and release any inhibitions their more corporate attire the night before might have restrained.

After a nominal fifteen-minute wait, Jim and Anne were seated by the hostess at their booth. Anne opted for the honey pecan salmon. Jim wanted to choose the baby back ribs, but then remembered Anne's disapproval of over consumption of meat.

"Is that okay?" Jim asked. "I don't want you to feel strange seeing me eat them, knowing your dislike of them."

"No, please! Go ahead! I'm fine with it. I mean, I respect other people's wishes, even though I might not agree with them."

Permission granted. As for beverages, Anne opted for a white zinfandel while Jim selected a Sam Adams lager. The waiter then took their menus and sped off to obtain their drinks.

Despite the fact that it was in the middle of the Labor Day weekend, Jim was surprised at how busy the bistro was. Patrons and servers were busy going to and fro. The hustle and bustle that was the bistro was in evidence. Full plates going in one direction, empties the other. And the cacophony of mixed conversations made it hard to focus. Yet amidst the din of the diners was the soothing Sarah McLachlan song *I Will Remember You* playing over the restaurant's overhead speakers. It wasn't long before the waiter returned with their drinks, but it would be a while before they would eat. This gave Jim and Anne ample opportunity to get to know each other more intimately than the previous night. And this time they wouldn't have the Mazurskys to worry about.

"So," Anne began. "What's life like as Jim Monahan? I mean, not when you're *Diamond Jim Monahan?*"

"Well, I don't know how much Laura told you about me, but I'm 48 and I live near Downtown." Jim hesitated for a second to reveal the next item, almost as if he was ashamed. "I'm also divorced."

"I'm sorry to hear about that. Laura did tell me, though. I mean about your being divorced and all."

"You don't seem to mind about that."

"Oh, not in the least. Hey." Anne smiled at Jim and placed her hands over his right hand. "We all make mistakes in our lives."

Jim smiled in return and gently tapped Anne's right wrist with his left hand. "I'm glad you're an understanding person."

Anne retracted her hands before continuing. "Do you mind telling me about it, or would you prefer not to?"

Jim raised his right hand so that the palm of it faced Anne. There was going to be no holding back. His forehead wrinkled as he answered her question. "No, I don't mind one bit. It all began four years ago when my ex-wife Maureen was visiting her folks up in the Philadelphia area. One night she met an old friend who made it big as an investment banker. They had sex and out came a boy nine months later. And, before you ask, no it is *not* my child. A timeline and DNA test will prove that."

"That's horrible! Having an affair is bad enough. But having a child with someone other than your spouse . . ." Anne shook her head in disgust. She then looked up at Jim before continuing. "Did you two have any children together?"

"Yep," Jim answered proudly. "One daughter. Her name is Madison, and she lives with Maureen and her new husband and their boy up in Bryn Mawr. That's just north of Philly. Here, I've got some pictures of her."

Jim pulled out his wallet, opened the billfold to a compartment and pulled out two photos.

"This is a picture of Madison when she was five. This was taken in dance class at the time." Jim proudly handed the picture over for Anne to get a closer look.

"Oh, she's so adorable!" Anne said this with a broad grin and a slight song in her voice.

"Here's one taken recently. Madison is now 15."

"Well," Anne remarked impressively. "Madison has grown up to be an attractive young lady. She must take after her father."

Jim almost buried his head in embarrassment. Now he wanted to learn more about Anne. "Okay, I know you're originally from Brewster. What made you come down here?"

"I had worked for a huge company up in Westchester County. Then one year they relocated down to this area, so I came with them. Since then the company has gone bankrupt. I was considering heading back north to my family, but I like it down here. The winters aren't as severe. Lo and behold, I got interviewed by Kleister, and here I am today."

Jim gave Anne an admiring look. "You're such an attractive woman, Anne. I hope you don't mind my asking, but did you ever come close to getting married yourself?"

"Well, I've had my share of relationships in the past and, yes, I did come *this* close to getting married," she said as she held her right thumb and index finger a quarter of an inch apart.

"What happened?"

"It's a long story. I guess I should start out with something I had learned when I was 14, a year younger than your Madison. A physician I had seen at the time told me after an extensive examination that I wouldn't be able to bear children. I didn't care at the time. What did I know? Of course, as time went on, I learned of girls I grew up with becoming pregnant as women and having babies. And I kept getting depressed about it, because I knew I wouldn't be able to have one."

"I don't get it. What does that have to do with you not getting married?"

"I went out for a time with this guy named Steve. He was really handsome, and had a strong muscular build and all. He had a very good job as a forensics lab technician with the Brewster Police Department. One day he actually proposed to me." Anne looked at Jim with pride as she said this. "When he talked about us having children eventually, I had to confess my dark secret to him. Steve became enraged and decided to call it off."

The smile Anne had earlier had quickly morphed to a frown. In fact, a tear emerged when she mentioned the halt to the wedding plans. Jim pressed forward.

"What about adopting?"

"Oh, no, that wasn't good enough for Steve. It had to be his genes being passed down. And before you ask me about artificial insemination, forget it. Steve was one of those ultra-high conservatives and had religious reservations toward that. We had to conceive naturally." Anne sighed and looked off into the distance. "So, you see, that was my claim of nearly getting married. Since then I pretty much resigned myself to never tying the knot."

"That's pretty awful. And I think it's downright selfish of this Steve character, treating you as nothing more than a breeding factory."

"I suppose you're right, Jim."

"And another thing, I think it was ver . . ."

Jim stopped mid-sentence. Something he heard caused him to halt his train of thought. Over the speakers, there was a familiar repetitive scale of piano notes being played. The same notes then changed pitches from F diminished seventh to B-Flat diminished seventh. It was the beginning of the song *Color My World* made famous by the rock band Chicago.

Jim's eyes began to bulge as pent-up rage started to come to the surface. He tried to suppress his anger by violently clutching the red and white plaid table cloth with his fingers. Anne observed his odd behavior and became worried. But he did not address her. Instead he began to hyperventilate and started turning his head from side to side.

"Tell them to stop it! Tell them to stop it!"

"What's the matter, Jim?" Anne frantically asked. "Stop what, the music?"

"Yes! Tell them to stop it!"

At this point Jim sprang from his seat and grabbed the attention of the first server he came across, one who wasn't tending to their table. He vehemently ordered the startled young waitress to see the manager on duty. Before she had a chance to do so, the manager entered the picture. By this time, Jim was creating such a scene that several fellow patrons were staring in his direction curiously. Anne meanwhile was somewhat embarrassed about the situation. But there must have been something about the song that was driving Jim nuts.

He finally got the ear of the manager on duty. "Listen! You've got to stop the music! I can't take it anymore!"

"Sir," began the puzzled manager, "that music gets piped in here. I mean, I'll see what I can do to possibly tone it down, but other than that, I have no control over it."

At this point Jim couldn't wait for the manager to act. He bolted out of the restaurant toward the parking lot. Anne and everyone else saw Jim run like a bat out of hell. Still deeply concerned over his reaction, Anne made a gesture to the manager and the servers that she would return. She had to go to Jim's aid and probe what about the song caused him to react in such a way. She sprang from her seat to join him in the parking lot.

Meanwhile, Jim tried to calm down. He was still breathing heavily, but not as pronounced as when he was inside. He looked in different directions as another sign of coping with his anxiety.

Finally, Anne exited the restaurant. She scanned the lot, but her search for Jim didn't take long. She raced up to him.

"Jim, what's the matter?" Anne asked nervously as she tried to console the baseball man by placing her hands on his upper arms. "What was it about that song that made you act like that?"

Jim didn't express it, but he was appreciative of Anne's concern and her attempt to comfort him. Slowly he composed himself. When he finally felt a sense of serenity from within, he answered her question.

"That song, *Color My World,* it was . . . it was the song Maureen and I danced to as our first dance together at our wedding reception!"

Jim then looked away from Anne and began to bury his face in his hands. A few seconds later he moved his arms down. Anne detected a tear or two on his face. She put her arms around him and held him tightly. She closed her eyes and pressed the left side of her face against his left shoulder.

"I'm so sorry, darling."

Jim reached around Anne and cupped his right hand against the exposed right side of her face. He was at peace with Anne's gentle kindness and comfort. "Thanks," he answered quietly. "I purposely don't listen to easy-listening stations just so I can't possibly hear that song. I trashed all my Chicago LPs and CDs after Maureen and I broke up as a result."

Anne raised her head away so that she could look at Jim dead-on. "Listen, if you want to, we can go eat somewhere else."

Jim looked at the restaurant. "No, it's okay. I'm . . . I'm feeling a little better now, thank you. Besides, it's a short song. I'm sure it's over by now."

Anne looked at Jim and smiled. She was relieved to see he had a more relaxed demeanor about him once again. He even sported a slight grin in return, just to show her he was now a better man. Anne hooked her right arm around Jim's left. She reached across with her left hand to give him added assurance that she was behind him; leaned her head against his left shoulder and the couple slowly walked back toward the bistro.

Once inside, Jim apologized profusely to the manager and any staff member he came across for his earlier outrageous behavior. As Jim had predicted, the Chicago song that caused him heightened alarm had long since ended. Melissa Etheridge's *Come to My Window* was now ruling the restaurant's air waves. There would be no further incidents as Jim and Anne took back their seats. By this time their meals had arrived.

Chapter Seventeen

For the second time in two weeks Jim went to see a movie other than the type that would interest him. When he took Madison to see a film, it had to be a teenage comedy that appealed to her. This time he placated Anne's tastes by watching the latest Jennifer Aniston chick flick. But that didn't dampen the growing affection he was having toward Anne.

As a way of showing he had put the restaurant episode behind him, Jim performed a playful act with Anne as they were waiting for the film to start. He had bought some popcorn for the two to share, along with two soft drinks. He took one of the popped kernels and tossed it in Anne's mouth. She played along with the gag and consumed it. Then he repeated the act a second time. Again, Anne opened her mouth and ate the morsel. Then Jim revealed the college boy in him. He took a big handful of popcorn and was about to toss it all into Anne's mouth. Realizing he had gone overboard, Anne raised her hands to wave Jim off. Of course, Jim had no intention of jamming the popcorn into her. They then broke out in laughter over the humorous moment.

Long after the movie was over, Jim drove Anne back to her home. Ten-thirty. Still relatively early. But for the first time around, maybe it was best to call it a night. As they approached the front door of her garden apartment, he thanked his date for the time they had together.

"Listen, Anne, I just want to say that I had a wonderful time tonight."

"So did I," Anne smiled.

"And I just want to apologize for my behavior in the restaurant. It was embarrassing."

"I'll tell you what. Next time you come over we can listen to Ozzy Osbourne. I'm sure he doesn't give you any trouble."

"Whoa! No, but that is a great departure!"

Jim asked Anne if she would like to get together for lunch one day during the upcoming week, to which the office manager accepted. He then leaned in and gently touched her upper arms. She reciprocated with a light kiss on the lips.

Suddenly a sensation overcame Jim. It was a feeling he hadn't experienced in nearly twenty years, back when he first dated Maureen. He felt his blood circulating throughout his body. Numbness overpowered him as he became a little giddy. He felt extreme warmth, but it wasn't from the early September evening. Yes, those feelings Jim once had, feelings he thought were lost forever, were now returning. In just 24 hours Jim was falling in love with Anne. He wanted her. And he could see in her eyes that she was willing to accept, albeit to a point.

Jim and Anne embraced each other strongly. They gave each other a long, luscious tongue kiss. After several seconds of their heated lip lock, Anne broke away.

"If it's okay, Jim, I'm getting very tired. I'm going to retire for the night. I'll talk to you soon about getting together again, okay?"

Jim nodded in agreement. There was one golden rule of protocol and conduct Jim had always followed when it came to women. Out of respect, he would never push the envelope when it came to any sexual relations. As far as that was concerned, he believed women should be in control to make the call, when it came, for intercourse, not men. Any man who forces the issue upon a woman can make things very uncomfortable. In a relationship, the female significant other should hold the cards and will let her soul mate know when it's time.

Each smiled at the other and offered soft goodbyes. Jim then turned away to walk toward his car. Anne stared after him with affection as she was starting to feel some hormonal vibrations of her own. And as she turned around and opened her front door, she saw the book and candles on her coffee table in the living room. She decided to light the candles and read some of the poetic selections. She wanted to perpetuate the evening, but in a controlled setting.

Chapter Eighteen

Laura Mazursky had time off for Labor Day. Unfortunately, for Jim it was a regular workday. But he did his normal sports reports, just like he did on any typical Monday. That was a reflection of the time, effort and pride he placed in his profession. The show must go on.

The very next morning, Laura arrived looking exhausted, as if the three-day weekend wasn't enough respite for her. But her tiredness had everything to do with getting herself and her two children prepared for school and then dropping them off at their respective institutions of learning.

Laura looked across the room and spotted Jim reediting his copy. He was too busy to have noticed Laura's entrance moments before. A loud-enough greeting was in order to break his concentration, to which he answered in kind.

"I'll have you know, Jim, that I spoke with Anne over the weekend," Laura said.

"And?"

"Well, she gave you a lot of high marks. Excellent job, Mr. Monahan! You must've made a good impression on her!"

"I'm glad I passed the litmus test. What else did you two gossip about?"

"Gossip? Now, I'm ashamed of you, Jimmy dear boy. Anne and I didn't trade hot juicy details. You know me better than that."

"Hmmm. By the way, did Anne tell you anything that happened at the restaurant we ate at?"

"No," replied Laura quizzically. "Did something go wrong?"

"Uh, not really. It was just a little confusion with the bill."

Jim thought to himself that Anne was kind enough not to mention the incident inciting Jim to leave when he heard *Color My World* being played. That put Anne in a very good light with Jim. She had proved herself as a woman Jim could trust with just about anything. It was either that, or Anne did tell Laura, and the latter was putting on a good act to sound surprised when he brought it up. But the baseball man had known Laura too long for her to put up a façade successfully. Jim was convinced Anne could keep a secret and that he could confide in her.

The phone on Laura's desk began to ring. She raced back to pick it up and discovered it was Jim's agent, Tony Salerno, calling for him. Although he still had to do more editing on his copy, he told Laura to switch the call to his desk phone. He wanted to hear any news Tony had for him. After the two exchanged pleasantries, Tony continued with the purpose of his call.

"I had a call over the weekend from Sam Waldman, Jimbo. He's the VP of Marketing and Broadcasting with the Cardinals. He heard your demo and he was hot for it!"

"That's great, Tony! Wow! What's the next step?"

"Well, you know the Cardinals are currently in a pennant race? Unless they make the postseason which'll delay things, Waldman wants you on a flight to St. Louis to meet with him and a few other biggies on Tuesday, October 3rd. They want you to audition using footage of Cardinal games to announce. What d'ya say about that, pal?"

"This is fantastic! Tony, you really came through for me this time! I don't know what else to say! Thank you very much!"

"Whoa! You haven't got the lead role yet, buddy. I'd advise you to get a media guide on the Cardinals and brush up on their players. Become familiar with their names. You might catch them on some game on either ESPN, MLB Network or TBS. Know these guys better than your family, Jim. That'll put you ahead of everybody else."

Jim agreed to Tony's directive. He had his homework cut out for him if he wanted to achieve his ultimate goal. Tony ended the conversation by stating that he would be in touch with the baseball man about the plans on the meeting.

Jim hung up the phone and began to daydream again. To heck with the editing of his copy, Jim allowed himself to be absorbed by the mere thought of the red-capped players charging from the dugout for the first pitch. The one job he had aspired to all his life seemed within his grasp if he played his cards right.

Zach Moser happened to be walking by. He was mulling over some papers in his hand and appeared too preoccupied with them, taking a blind eye to Jim and even Laura. That was when Jim snapped out of his trance to stop the station manager.

"Hey, Zach, have you got a minute?"

Zach broke his fixation on the papers to give his attention to Jim. "Uh, sure. Is it something you want to talk about in private?"

"No, no, I, uh . . . I can talk to about it out here." Jim paused for a moment, but was a little unsure of himself of the venue for the chat. "I think you know I have this agent, Tony Salerno, based up in New York, who has promised me the moon when it came to me getting a major league announcing gig. Well, he just called me to say the St. Louis Cardinals are very interested in me, to the point where they want me to fly out there next month to audition. It's the job I've coveted all my life."

"Gee, it sounds like you're giving me your two weeks' notice."

"Well, I know there are no absolutes in life except death and taxes. But I do need to take a couple of days off in early October to meet with them."

Zach gazed at Jim at first with a furrowed brow. Afraid of losing his sports director and the man who made headlines with the daring rescue of Alan Langston the month before caused him great concern. But then the station manager broke out in a smile. "Hey, far be it from me to stand in your way, Jim. You've done so much for us over the last several years and with the Squirrels. And your act was a shot in the arm to the station's ratings. More than you'll ever know. But you'd be a tough act to follow. Sure, go for it. And good luck."

Jim was somewhat surprised at Zach's decision to give him the green light to take off for a few days for a job interview, especially since ad revenue had jumped during the last several weeks, due, in part to Jim's sudden rise to notoriety beyond the ears of Squirrels fans. Maybe it was payback for saving the station from anonymity in the community.

As Zach walked toward his office, Jim went back to putting finishing touches to his copy. That was when Laura called over to him to say he had another call. It wasn't Tony again. This time it was Anne. Despite the fact he had wanted to make a couple more revisions in his radio script, Jim didn't hesitate for one second and told Laura to send the call to him.

"Hey, I didn't quite expect a call so soon," Jim opened.

"Well, I hope I caught you at the right time."

"I don't go on for another ten minutes. Oh, by the way, thanks for not talking about the . . . you know . . . incident in the restaurant with Laura. I appreciate that."

"Some things are best not said. That's one of them." Anne hesitated for a brief moment before continuing. "Listen, I sometimes go to this sandwich place for lunch. I've got a thing for their salads. I was wondering if we could meet there, say one o'clock."

"Sure! Where is it?"

Jim wrote it down and then softly ended his conversation with his newfound love. After hanging up, Jim closed his eyes briefly to allow Anne's soft voice to place him in rapture. Instantly, her dazzling image burned inside his brain, searing it like a blistering branding iron. Between Tony's big announcement, Zach's blessing to pursue the Cardinals' job, and Anne's sweet lunchtime invite, it had turned out to be one of the best mornings Jim had had in a long time.

Chapter Nineteen

The weather that Thursday was wicked. Tropical Depression Inez pummeled the greater Richmond area with a deluge of rain and horrendous gale force winds that made walking across the street and driving an odyssey. Inez had been downgraded from a Category One hurricane when it first hit land off the Georgia coast the night before. But its fierce winds and rage made one's body contort to hold fast. If you hadn't read the headlines that day, don't worry. The front pages, swirling in the torrent, would smack you between the eyes as they blew at you.

Despite the severe weather conditions, Jim made it a point to meet Anne once again for lunch at the sandwich place they had been to just two days before. That was when he had asked her out for a picnic on Saturday, when the forecast was promising a beautiful sunny day, a complete 180 from the present day. She gleefully accepted his invite.

Nearly three o'clock. Jim was resting in his apartment, working on his computer as he scanned every bit of Cardinals minutia the internet could provide him. Besides wanting to brush up on his prospective employers, there was not much else to do with the wind and rain Inez was packing.

Suddenly his home phone began to ring. By the time he had gotten to it, the answering machine had kicked in. The caller ID pegged the caller as Marty Leary. The accountant was about to leave a full-scale message when Jim interrupted the speech by picking up the receiver.

"Hi, Marty. I'm here."

"I figured you would be. I couldn't honestly picture you going out in this weather. Boy, it's raining cats and dogs out there! Oh, man, it is brutal!"

"That it is. So, what's happening?"

"Well, you've heard of Dr. Seymour Klein, the plastic surgeon?"

"Who hasn't? His TV commercials run non-stop."

"Klein is one of my clients. He invited me to his cabin cruiser down by Virginia Beach this Saturday. I heard the weather is supposed to be good, so I accepted. He said if I wanted to bring along a couple of people that'd be fine. I had already asked Ed Holtermann and he said yes. So, how about you coming along, too? Maybe we can catch some blues from the ocean."

"Uh, I don't think I can make it, Marty. I've already asked my girlfriend if she'd like to go on a picnic that day and she said yes."

"Girlfriend? You didn't tell me you're seeing someone."

"Well, I just started seeing her. Her name is Anne Finley. She's a very sweet person, warm and attractive. I'm growing very fond of her."

"Oh? How good is she in bed?"

"She's *not* that kind of woman, Marty. She wouldn't be your type."

"Hmmm. Well, listen. If she's the kind of woman I'm envisioning, then she wouldn't mind if you told her that you'd like to postpone the date for another day. Klein's a big baseball fan and he has season tickets for the Squirrels. He'd like to meet you, Jim, especially in light of the big heroics last month."

"I don't think that's the right thing to do."

"Aw, c'mon! It's a little male bonding. I'll bring along some beer and food. They're calling for calm waters, so you won't have to worry about getting seasick. Besides, Seymour told me he never takes it out more than a mile or two anyway."

"How the hell am I going to tell Anne this?"

"Will you listen to me? Just tell her who's inviting you and she'll know and understand. And I promise, Jim. No raucous women like last time, especially now that you're sort of, excuse me, taken. So, how about it?"

Jim wasn't thrilled, but he didn't want to make Marty look bad in front of Klein. He reluctantly agreed to go with Marty and Ed on the cruiser. Marty was ecstatic that Jim went along, albeit with some reservations. The accountant said he'd pick him up Saturday morning around eight o'clock. End of conversation. The baseball man was feeling a touch remorseful and began ruing his decision.

The rain was still pelting down menacingly against the windows in his living room. Jim looked up and walked over to peer out. He began to stare out the window, but he wasn't captivated by the torrential downpour. No, it was the call Jim had to make to Anne to inform her of the sudden change of plans that had him tied up in knots. Not good.

He turned away and looked at the phone resting on the cradle atop the end table next to his sofa. The instrument might as well have been a rabid raccoon, for Jim had a deep fear of picking it up. He began to formulate a few words for practice. At first the words just didn't sound right. But rather than trying to agonize over the correct phrasing, Jim threw up his hands. *Screw it!* He decided to go over to the phone and wing it.

Three-seventeen. Jim knew Anne was still at work and that would be the best number to call. After being welcomed by the automated greeting that Kleister had programmed, Jim punched in Anne's extension. Her admin came on the phone first. The delay bought him a few extra seconds. After Jim asked for Anne and identified himself, the secretary placed him on hold for a brief moment. *Okay, work up on the nerve.* It wasn't long after that Anne picked up her line.

"This is a surprise," Anne commented. "Is there something wrong?"

"Uh, no, not really." Jim was still fumbling for the right combination of words to use. "Uh . . . you've heard of that plastic surgeon with all those ads, Dr. Seymour Klein, haven't you?"

"Yeah, I've seen them. Where are you going with this, Jim?"

"Well, Marty Leary, he's that accountant from that support group I belong to that I told you about on our way to the movie theater the other night. Well, Marty just called me. It turns out Klein is one of his clients and is a big baseball fan. Marty said Klein invited us on his cabin cruiser."

"Hey, that's great!"

"Unfortunately, the outing is for this Saturday."

"Oh, I see."

Jim detected dejection in Anne's voice. Saturday was meant for the two of them. Jim had to stop the bleeding.

"Listen, I understand the entire weekend is going to be fine. They're not calling for rain again until late Sunday night. What do you say we postpone the picnic by one day? We'll go out Sunday. Is that okay?"

"Sure," Anne answered. "Hey, put in a good word for me with Klein. I may need his services someday."

"You certainly don't need Klein now."

Anne laughed at Jim's sweet reference to how attractive she was to him. They agreed on a noontime rendezvous at Anne's place on Sunday. Jim offered a tender goodbye before hanging up the phone. After he had placed the phone back down upon the end table, Jim looked off into the distance. He smiled at the way Anne agreed on the delay of their date, although she wasn't totally thrilled at first. There weren't too many times that both he and Marty were in agreement on things, but the accountant hit the nail on the head knowing that Anne would understand Jim's asking for a *boy's night out.*

However, Jim didn't want to make date switching a habit. He cared about Anne so much that he didn't want to disappoint her again anytime soon. Jim planned on letting Marty and Ed know where he stood on the subject when he saw them that Saturday. The baseball announcer cared about Anne so much that he didn't want a sudden fishing trip to interfere with their relationship in the future. Not even Maureen in her prime captured Jim's heart the way Anne did. Indeed, Anne was one special lady.

Chapter Twenty

As miserable as Thursday was, so delightful was the weather that following Saturday. Temperatures were expected to be near 80 degrees with abundant sunshine and low humidity. A deep blue punctuated the morning sky.

As he said he would, Marty picked Jim up from his apartment that morning at eight prompt. They in turn picked up Ed Holtermann along the way and proceeded down I-64 for the two-hour journey to Virginia Beach, where they would meet the waiting Dr. Seymour Klein.

It was nearly 10:30 by the time the trio found Dr. Klein at the Long Bay Pointe Boating Resort where the plastic surgeon kept his vessel. Forever the boating man, the fifty-something Klein sported a navy and white striped shirt, white pants and a pair of white deck shoes. In honor of Jim, Dr. Klein also wore a Richmond Flying Squirrels baseball cap.

Jim and the others marveled at the sleek 35-foot Bayliner 340 cabin cruiser, which Seymour proudly proclaimed as his second home. The engine of the nautical beauty purred like a kitten when Seymour revved up the motor once everyone was on board.

After unleashing the rope from its dockside moorings, Seymour slowly wheeled the craft out of the port and toward the open waters of the Atlantic. Ripples licked the body of the craft. And just as Marty had told Jim two days earlier, Seymour went no farther than about a mile off shore.

Seymour handed each of his guests a rod and reel. The plastic surgeon landed a 26-pound yellow fin tuna, while Marty caught one of comparable size and weight. Unfortunately for Jim and Ed, the only things they were able to catch were rays from the sun, which suited the broadcaster fine. Seymour had brought along a huge chest full of ice to keep the prized possessions fresh.

One o'clock rolled around and there was a consensus among everyone to call a temporary halt to the fishing exercise. Seymour broke out an assortment of pre-made sandwiches and various beverages, both alcoholic and non-alcoholic, although Seymour and Marty stood away from the beer, what with them being designated drivers of either aquatic or land crafts.

As Jim was chomping down his ham and Swiss sandwich, he couldn't help but marvel at the magnificent catch Seymour had made.

"Wow, I still can't get over the size of that tuna, Seymour."

"Oh, that? That's nothing. I've caught stripers bigger than that one. I can't wait until November. That's when the stripers really run big down here."

"November? Don't you keep this boat in dry dock in the winter?"

"Yeah, but not until mid-December. And then I'm back at it in late March."

"How the hell do you get your wife to cooperate?" Marty asked as he appeared stymied how Seymour was able to amass much free time for the seas.

"I invite her along a lot of times. And let me tell you something, guys. She knows how to handle a rod. She's put me to shame a couple of times."

Seymour's line drew some laughter among the men.

After everyone was just about finished eating, Seymour posed a question to Jim. "So, Marty has no doubt told you, Jim, that I'm a big fan of the Squirrels."

"Yes, he said you're a season ticket holder."

"Yeah, that's right. By the way, I happen to notice that Casey Farrings pitched for San Francisco the other night."

"That's right. He tossed five innings against the Padres. Gave up only one run on three hits, four strikeouts and no walks. Don't look for Farrings to be back in Richmond next year, Seymour. I think he's going to stay up with San Francisco."

"Well, good for him! He deserves it." Seymour paused for a moment before offering a proposition. "Listen, Jim, is there any chance that I might be considered as an investor for the Squirrels with the current owners?"

"The Dalmut brothers?" All of a sudden Jim noticed all eyes were upon him. "I don't know that they're in the market for any partners. What makes you think they might be?"

"Oh, I don't know. It's just a hunch. But I do know they ran into some trouble legally over some shady real estate deals."

"Oh, well, that was well over a year ago. The Dalmut brothers have got their lawyers working for them. The District Attorney even dropped the charges. Nothing ever went to trial."

"Yes, but I'm sure to keep those lawyers happy and keep the law at bay, it has to have taken a toll on their bank account. Just put in a good word the next time you see either Aaron or Jared Dalmut. Tell them I've got a group of investors interested in buying a piece of the team. We've got the capital. Okay?"

"Fine, Seymour. But now that the season has been over for a few weeks, I may not be seeing them for some time. Heck, with any luck, I may not see them again. Ever."

"I don't get it."

"I think what Jim means, Seymour, is that he is strongly being considered for the top job with the St. Louis Cardinals," Marty interjected.

"Is that a fact? Well," Seymour added as he hoisted his glass of lemonade in his right hand and spirit in his voice, "this calls for a toast! To Diamond Jim Monahan! May he achieve that big job with the Cards!"

The four men clanked their respective glasses together. That was when Ed suggested a game of poker. He had brought a deck of cards with him in the event things became dull. Everyone agreed to play, but with limited funds and no ATM machine floating aboard a buoy on the high seas, the wagering would be extremely limited. As an added treat, Seymour brought out a box of fine Cuban cigars he was able to get his hands on through some high-placed connections.

The game went on for a couple of hours until it was time to head back to land. And when they did reach port, Jim, Marty and Ed thanked Seymour for the invite. Marty was ill-prepared to take his tuna home with him and he didn't want to have his car reek of the dead fish. Seymour was more than happy to take it back home with him, along with the one he had caught. He and his family were big fresh seafood lovers. But before they parted company, Jim promised Seymour that he would put in a good word with the Dalmut brothers for him.

And as Marty began to speed back up toward Richmond, Jim sat in the front seat thinking about Anne. He'd wanted to speak with her earlier, but thought it wise to hold off until he got back home. His true feelings toward her were private and not intended for someone like Marty to hear. Jim still held an ounce of guilt for calling off their original picnic date to be with the guys, and he hoped to make it up to her the next day.

Chapter Twenty-One

Although the temperature wasn't as high as it was the day before when Jim went on the fishing expedition with the guys, it was still quite comfortable in the mid-seventies on Sunday. Only a few cirrus clouds dotted the blue skies. Rain wasn't expected until late that night, and that wasn't going to deter Jim from his promised picnic date with Anne.

Twelve noon. Jim picked up Anne and then sped off to a couple of shops to purchase a bottle of cabernet sauvignon, brie, crackers and some fruit. Upon his urging, Anne brought along the book of romantic poetry he had bought her the weekend before.

They later drove over to Maymont Park, where they settled under a shady elm tree overlooking Shields Lake. Jim used a spare blanket he took from his apartment to spread over the grass so the two of them could sit without getting their clothes dirty.

They drank the wine from two wine glasses Jim had brought from home, and indulged themselves on the cheese, crackers and fruit. Each took turns reading various poems to the other. Anne especially cherished one piece by Emily Dickenson. Upon completion of the poem's recital, she closed the book and held it close to her body. Anne closed her eyes and smiled sensuously. At that moment Jim softly brushed the strands of her hair with his left hand. The sensation felt like cool zephyrs on a warm summer day running through his fingers. And Anne wore a perfume that was seductively intoxicating, acting like an aphrodisiac, heating up the passion. Jim delicately moved his left hand until he cupped it around Anne's left shoulder. She woke out of her trance to realize what Jim was doing. Anne admiringly looked at Jim as he returned her gaze. The two slowly moved toward one another until the moment came when

Jim and Anne were about to exchange a long kiss. He could feel his blood rushing through his veins. Right away, their eyes closed as Jim and Anne engaged in their passionate embrace. Their lips locked and their tongues entwined.

The two eventually came up for air and temporarily halted their sultry exchange, only to go back to it shortly thereafter. There would be a few more seductive encounters before they agreed it was time to leave the park. As the clock struck two, Jim and Anne gathered their personal effects and headed back toward the Civic. As they meandered through the park arm-in-arm, Anne asked if he would mind taking her to a few shops to browse. Jim wasn't the shopping type, but conceded to her request nonetheless. There was still a sense of guilt on his part for initially abandoning their date to be with Marty, Ed and Seymour Klein.

Jim drove Anne downtown where she strolled into a boutique. Anne looked over some fall attire. But then a summery wide-brimmed straw hat caught her attention. It was reduced for clearance and so she modeled it atop her head. She looked at herself in a full-length mirror to see how it would look on her. A store clerk walked up to her from behind.

"Oh, that really says you," she said.

But Anne was still looking at the hat atop her head backward, forward, and sideways. Jim was growing a little impatient with her indecision toward buying it. He finally walked up to her from behind and jerked the front of the brim over her eyes. Anne turned around and playfully slapped Jim on his right shoulder. She got the message. Anne laughed at Jim.

"I want to buy it, Jim," Anne commented.

Before she could make an attempt to buy it on her own, Jim reached into the front of his pants pocket for his wallet.

"I'll take care of this please," Jim happily told the clerk, handing her his debit card. He then turned to Anne. "Your money's no good here."

"Uh, if you say so," Anne shrugged with a smile, not offering any resistance.

The clerk gladly handled the transaction and carefully placed the new hat and the receipt in a bag, handing it over to Jim. Anne couldn't thank him enough for getting her the chapeau. The clerk appreciated the couple for their patronage, and the pair wished the clerk a good day as they made their way out of the store.

Jim drove Anne back to her apartment complex. He pulled up in front and escorted her to her front door. He'd resigned himself to calling it a day with Anne after handing over the bag containing the hat. As Jim was about to give a final kiss, Anne surprised him.

"Would you like to come in for some coffee?" she asked.

"That sounds great. Sure!"

Once inside, Anne prepared a pot of coffee for the two of them. She had kept some oatmeal raisin cookies in the refrigerator to preserve them better and offered them to Jim to have with the cup of Joe.

To pass the time, they played a few rounds of poker. He was amazed how good she was at cards and eventually had to call it quits before embarrassing himself further.

After the last drop of coffee, Jim and Anne teamed together to take care of cleaning the dishes. Anne washed while Jim dried. And after the last plate was put away, Jim turned toward her; each galvanized their eyes on the other. They slowly embraced until they finally connected in a gripping kiss. The passion and fire built within as both Jim and Anne appeared not to want to give up their tongue and lip fusion.

Finally they came up for air. Jim lifted Anne off the floor and slowly spun her around. She giggled with delight, and Jim smiled in return. Their love was so pure, so strong. They were acting like high school sweethearts.

Anne was ready. With a sparkle in her eye and a smile that could warm anyone on a cold January evening, she reached out and clutched Jim's hands. She slowly tugged him toward her bedroom as she went along. When they got inside, they engaged in another heated embrace. Each went wild as they rapidly planted kisses on each other's faces and necks. Anne reached for Jim's crotch and could feel he was getting aroused. She began to unbuckle his belt to release his heat. Jim returned the favor by removing her top. It would be another two minutes before each had disrobed the other of clothing.

Anne seductively unfurled her bedspread and sheet as she and Jim lay down together. Jim made passionate love to Anne, from various angles. He admired her naked body and even remarked how firm her breasts were. Her skin was like silk to the touch. And Anne delighted in absorbing his masculinity in return. She couldn't get enough of his solid muscular shoulders and arms. Finally Jim climaxed as Anne released a loud cry of orgasmic pleasure.

When copulation was completed, Jim lay on his back. Anne reclined on her right side and nestled next to Jim's left flank. She snaked her right arm behind his neck while gently stroking his chest hairs with her left hand. Jim secured Anne from behind by latching his left arm around her back. It was then time for reflection.

"Wow," Jim opened the dialogue. "It's been a long time . . . a very long time."

"Oh?" Anne was intrigued. "How long ago was that? Was it since your time with Maureen?"

"Well . . . yeah. It has been a few years."

"Of course, I wasn't there when you and Maureen last got it on, but judging from what I experienced just now, I'd say you haven't skipped a beat."

Jim smiled and thanked her for the wonderful comment. He then kissed her softly on the forehead. Anne was on the fast track to becoming Jim's new soul mate. Then he began to think of the possibility of him signing with the Cardinals and moving out to the Midwest. His sex drive lowered as he conjured up the thought. But he felt he needed to ask Anne an indirect question to see how committed she was to making their newfound relationship work.

"That company you work for . . . Kleister. You say it's a national company, right?"

"Mmm hmm. Over a hundred offices throughout the country."

"Even an office in St. Louis?"

"Yep, even an office in St. Lo . . ." Anne suddenly stopped. "You think the Cardinals may hire you, huh?"

"Well, it's a possibility. I mean, I still have to audition for them. My agent set me up to meet with a couple of big wigs once the season is over in October." Jim paused briefly before continuing. "I'm falling in love with you, Anne. With each passing second my burning desire to be with you grows. I'm also going to level with you. Yes, the Cardinals are going to interview me. And if they offered me the job, I'd be foolish not to accept. It's the dream every baseball play-by-play man from every two-bit ball field in the country covets. But then, what would happen to us?"

"I'll have to admit it, Jim. I've grown very fond of you, too. But I think it's a bit presumptuous even to think of you moving halfway across America."

"I suppose so, but the likelihood still exists."

Anne smiled nervously at Jim. "Look, let's savor this moment together. We'll cross that bridge when we come to it, okay?"

Jim grinned and agreed to stow the talk of moving to Missouri. He was staring intently at a small birthmark Anne had just below her left shoulder. At first she was curious why he was so mesmerized. She glanced down in the direction of Jim's stare and saw the blemish. She then looked back at Jim.

"You seem fascinated by my birthmark."

Jim broke out of his gaze to channel his vision at Anne's soft eyes.

"Well, it's one of the things that make us all different." Jim then mused over his comment as he looked back at the birthmark. "You know, that reminds me. Maureen has this birthmark. It's in an unusual spot. It's right next to her . . . uh . . . right next to her . . ."

Anne gasped, although there was a trace of a smile. She then started to scramble. "Oh, my gosh! I'd better get dressed! There's no telling what else you'll find on me!"

Jim reeled Anne in as he broke out in laughter. "Hey, c'mon, relax! I promise not to tell!"

"You'd better not!" Anne then playfully slapped Jim and laughed with him. The pair snuggled together as they lay peacefully in each other's arms.

Chapter Twenty-Two

A few days had passed since his steamy encounter with Anne, yet Jim still carried fond memories of it. More and more, he believed that if ever a woman were ever going to take his heart again, it would be her. But then there was the hint of Anne's possible unwillingness to go with him to St. Louis if he were to land the Cardinals' play-by-play job. Gee, that dampened his mood somewhat.

And even more important was the further distancing himself from his daughter Madison. It was bad enough to have 250 miles wedged between them. To nearly quadruple the mileage would be a heavy burden. But even more important was the fact he needed to pry Madison away from Maureen in a seemingly unwanted household.

He also needed someone like Anne to convince a judge to get Madison to him. Jim, however, did not want to use Anne as a means to an end. He had true deep feelings for her and wanted to be careful not to have her thinking she was a pawn in a custody case. These thoughts were tearing Jim up, causing him to have many sleepless hours at night. Migraine city.

Jim did harbor some thoughts about possibly marrying Anne to perhaps achieve his overall objective. But before he even thought about popping the question, he wanted to have Anne meet Madison and see how the two of them would get along. Convincing Anne to agree to such a meeting might not be too difficult. Getting Madison to play along might prove the hardest part.

Jim wanted to get everyone together the upcoming Saturday. He had to gird himself because that meant a phone call to Maureen. Castor oil was easier to take than speaking to her. With a deep breath he began dialing the Bryn Mawr residence. Hmm, the answering machine. Not that he actually wanted to speak to his ex, but he needed to find out if Madison would be available that day. After hearing Maureen's taped greeting and the accompanying beep, he began leaving a message. As he got halfway through it, Maureen picked up the phone.

"Hello," Maureen answered coldly. "I'm sorry, but Madison will not be available this Saturday. She has some sort of function she volunteered for with her high school. That's going to prevent her from seeing you."

Jim was a little incredulous, but he played along with Maureen's game. He then countered with the following Saturday.

Maureen offered a very weak, "We'll see."

Oh, no you don't! Now Jim was simmering like an overheated car radiator. He had enough of Maureen's flimsy excuses and her caustic behavior.

"Listen, it's been almost a solid month since I last saw Madison. The Squirrels' season has long been over. I don't think I'm asking too much. I would like to see my daughter!"

Maureen didn't say a word for at least eight seconds. She then sighed and conceded in allowing Jim to come up and visit with Madison the weekend after next. He was relieved that the exchange with Maureen wasn't going to be protracted and any more heated. He told Maureen he'd call again soon to finalize a time.

Jim hung up and relaxed back on his living room sofa to jettison his tension. He began to rub his eyes, since even dealing with Maureen for just a few minutes took a lot out of him. What a mental workout. Jim looked up toward the ceiling as though in search of some answers on how to handle this live hand grenade of an ex. His phone rang. Breaking his concentration. It couldn't be Maureen. As for Anne, he was on the phone with her less than an hour before. Jim investigated who the caller was by answering with a simple hello.

"Hi, Jim! It's Joyce Langston!"

"Hello, Joyce! How are you doing?"

"Oh, I'm doing the best I can. What about you?"

Jim didn't want to weigh Joyce down with his problems with Maureen, so he switched gears. He blinked for a second to expunge Maureen from his memory. "Fine! How's Alan coming along?"

"He's doing spectacular, which is why I'm calling you. Alan would like to know if you'd like to come have dinner with us again this Sunday."

Jim readily agreed to Joyce's invitation. But then he thought of Anne and politely imposed a question. "Would you mind terribly if I bring someone, Joyce? Her name is Anne Finley and she's a very friendly, warm person."

"Why, sure, Jim! Look, you go tell Anne we'd love to have her come over, too!"

Unlike the previous phone call he had, Jim smiled from ear to ear and thanked Joyce for inviting Anne. He then ended his chat with Joyce and told her he was looking forward to seeing the Langston family again.

The next call was to his sweetheart.

"Hey, I just got a call from Joyce Langston to come over to their house again on Sunday for dinner. You're invited, too. How about it?"

"Sure! What time?"

He made arrangements to pick her up knowing Joyce's Sunday dinner bell. Jim then affectionately offered a soft good bye to Anne, and she did the same in return. As he hung the phone up for what would be the final time that early Wednesday evening, he began to think of his quest to get Madison away from Maureen and entertained thoughts of the possibility of starting a new family.

Chapter Twenty-Three

Rain was forecast that Sunday, but it didn't deter Jim and Anne from their appointed rounds with the Langston family. Although Joyce and Alan were not blood relatives, their clan had evolved into a surrogate family for Jim. For that reason alone, Anne was nervous about trying to make a good impression on them, as if meeting potential in-laws. However, Jim kept reassuring her everything would be fine and she was to relax and be herself. Anne just offered a halfhearted smile in return, as she was still querulous about what appearance she might manifest.

Still ten minutes away from the Langston house. From his casual observation of Anne as he was driving, Jim could tell she was still uptight about the meeting. Jim had to say something to make her feel a little more at ease. He had noticed her navy blue sleeveless dress and wanted to make a comment on it.

"That dress looks great on you."

Anne looked at Jim. "Do you really mean that, or are you trying to make me feel better?"

"No! No! I'm dead serious! It really looks fabulous. As does that pearl necklace. Of course, you'd look great even if you were wearing a burlap sack."

"Or if I wasn't wearing anything at all, huh?"

Jim just laughed as he continued to drive the remaining mile. Anne giggled a little, too, if only to relieve her pent-up fears of acquainting herself with the Langston family.

As Jim finally pulled up into the driveway, there waiting on the front porch to greet them was Alan. The Langston patriarch was still hobbling around with a cane, but his mobility was a little better than Jim had remembered from the previous visit. As they left the car, Alan welcomed both with open arms.

"Jim! How the heck are you, son?"

"I'm doing okay, Alan. How are you doing with your leg?"

"Oh, it's coming along. Doc said I might be ready to go dancin' soon!"

"That's great! Oh, Alan, I'd like you to meet my new girlfriend, Anne Finley."

Alan was pleasantly surprised that Jim unexpectedly had a new love interest in his life. The old man extended an open hand to Anne and she warmly accepted the courtesy in return. Just then there was a loud woof. It startled Anne, but Jim knew right away who that voice belonged to. Barney the pointer had gotten loose and raced up to Jim. The dog was eager to greet the baseball announcer with a series of slobbering licks. Jim vigorously petted Barney as Anne took a step back in order not to be tackled by the overzealous animal.

In the meantime, Alan wasn't too keen on Barney's gregarious reception. He yelled for his son, Michael, who raced out of the house to quell the obstreperous animal. Michael briefly smiled at Jim and his date, but never had a chance to introduce himself. His main concern was corralling the cavorting pointer. Once he got hold of Barney's collar, he escorted the pooch inside the house. All was safe. Jim and Anne were good sports about Barney's overzealous show of affection, but Alan simply shook his head. Without hesitation, he persuaded the couple to come inside.

Anne admired the interior of the Langston home. For Jim, it seemed old hat, since he was there only three weeks earlier. Michael had the Washington Redskins' game on the big flat screen television in the living room. With Richmond's close proximity to the nation's capital, it was no wonder that the rooting interests among the Langston family members sided with the Redskins. Jim noticed the game and was pleased to see that the Philadelphia Eagles were beating Washington 24-13 late in the third quarter. He didn't make a big issue over it, so as not to roil up any fan animosity.

Presently, Joyce emerged from the kitchen to greet her guests.

"Well, hello, Jim!" Joyce beamed and gave him an open-arm embrace. "It's great that you could make it!"

101

"Thanks, Joyce. This is my sweetheart, Anne Finley. Anne, this is Joyce Langston."

"It's a pleasure to meet you, Anne!" Joyce gave her the same warm, hospitable greeting she had given Jim. "Oh, Jim told me all about you! Nice things, of course!"

Anne laughed. "I'm glad to meet you, too, Mrs. Langston."

Joyce looked at Anne strangely. "Now, c'mon, Anne! It's Joyce! You're part of the family here!"

"Okay . . . Joyce!" All shared a laugh. Anne then handed the hostess a weighted plastic bag. "Jim and I brought along a couple of bottles of wine for the occasion."

"You didn't have to do that. But thank you just the same. Come! Sit down and relax."

"Are Kimberly, Josh and their kids here?" Jim asked.

"Well, Kimberly is helping me with the cooking in the kitchen. Josh is taking care of personal business in the bathroom. As for Ashley and Jackson, they're busy with those Wii games upstairs. Don't ask me how to play them, I haven't a clue. Listen. If you two need anything, just give me a holler."

Joyce gathered the bag containing the wine as Jim and Anne sat down with Alan and Michael in the living room. And while the guys were riveted to the TV set watching the football game, Anne was more interested in admiring the décor of the home. She rose from her chair to get a better look at the arrangements made in the room.

"I love the Colonial furniture and the way you furnished everything," Anne mentioned to Alan. "Where did you buy it?"

Alan just shrugged. "You'll have to ask Joyce. She makes the decisions there. I just provide the money."

Just then Josh and Kimberly entered the room. A few more introductions were in order before everyone settled down—everyone except Kimberly. She was summoned by Joyce to prepare to remove the items from the kitchen to the dining room table. Anne volunteered to help, which Kimberly appreciated. Kimberly then asked Josh to call their children down for dinner.

It was time for everyone to come to the table. But just before Michael shut off the set, he watched the Redskins quarterback make an attempt to throw downfield to an open receiver, who just missed the connection. "Oh, damn!" Michael groaned as he turned off the TV.

Ashley and Jackson joined the others as the food was being placed. There was a delectable glazed spiral ham, which Michael was in charge of carving up and distributing. Joyce also had sweet potatoes along with a spinach and cheese casserole. The Langston matriarch even made cornbread to accent the meal. Anne was going to force herself to take one piece of the ham, even though she'd rather not.

As for the dinner itself, everyone feasted on the sumptuous food. Idle chatter was mainly heard around the table, although there were a few questions of curiosity directed at Anne, to which she answered with aplomb.

Then Michael asked a question which struck a nerve. Although it wasn't on the same wavelength as the salvo he fired on Jim's last visit, it did peak interest among those present.

"You and Anne seem to be a great looking couple, Jim," Michael began. "When are you two gonna get married?"

There wasn't the same controversy as the last time, but there was some nervous laughter at the table.

"Well, Jim and Anne have barely gotten to know each other," Joyce responded. "To make a strong commitment like that at the present stage of their relationship isn't something they should be worrying about."

But Jim came up with a whimsical response. "Gee, Mike, I knew you had a trade. I didn't know you had a side business as a wedding planner."

Everyone got a kick out of Jim's answer, but Michael came up with a rejoinder to justify his remark.

"Well, I just figured that perhaps if you and Anne had gotten married, maybe y'all might have a better chance to get your daughter away from your ex-wife. I mean, you did mention at the table last time that with you being away and all with the baseball team a lot, having someone home most of the time might make it easier for the courts to accept you getting your daughter."

All eyes were now on Jim, particularly Anne's. The subject never reached discussion in their brief moments together. Yet it was a point Jim had been thinking about for a long time, knowing that Anne becoming his wife could facilitate a decision to having Madison live with him. But it was a subject he had wanted to discuss with Anne in his own time, not at a time where he was being prodded by an outsider. He was a little bent at the instigation initiated by Michael. Still, he did put his best foot forward in trying to dance around the query.

"You bring up a very good point. But it's something Anne and I didn't think of. Perhaps that might be an item of discussion down the road, just not right now."

From that point on there was no further talk about the future plans of the couple. The rest of the time was spent enjoying the meal and eventually the magnificent peach cobbler, which Joyce had made from scratch.

Finally it came time for Jim and Anne to leave. Anne thanked Alan and Joyce for their gracious hospitality and exquisite cuisine. Jim did likewise, but Joyce was compelled to make a statement to the baseball announcer.

"Y'all better take good care of Anne, Jim. I think she's a keeper!"

"I think you're right. Thanks once again for a great dinner, Joyce."

Parting pleasantries had been exchanged as the couple proceeded to Jim's Civic. Hand waving was in full force. Even Barney made one last appearance with a loud bark of approval as if to invite the couple back soon.

As they began to drive away, Jim and Anne engaged in a thoughtful conversation.

"Michael was too much with his comment," Jim began. "Oh, you should've heard him the last time I was there. That was even worse."

"Oh? What was that about?"

"Well, he was getting on me about being divorced and all and the fact that my daughter was still bound to Maureen in spite of what she did. He was a little tame today, but he does have a tendency to pry into one's private affairs."

"And how do feel about what he had to say?"

"Freaky. It was like he was reading my mind." There was some pause before Jim continued. "I'll be quite honest with you, Anne, because every relationship deserves that. I am feeling more and more deeply for you. But I do not want to abandon Madison. In fact, I would still like to get her back. I want the two of you to meet each other and get to know each another."

"I don't know, Jim. Don't you think it's a little too soon for that?"

"You sound like you'd rather not get involved with Madison."

"No, no! Absolutely not! I mean . . . ugh . . . we're just starting to get to know each other, and now you want to bring your daughter into the equation? These things take a little time, that's all."

"And time is something that may not be on our side. She told me she'd like to run away from that house. I need to prevent that from happening, Anne, and fairly soon."

"You're not using me as a means to get Madison, are you?"

"Of course not. Each moment I spend with you I am growing more and more fond of you. My love for you is strong, Anne." Jim hesitated before adding more, formulating the proper blend of words and sentiment. "You know, I originally wanted to have us see Madison yesterday, but Maureen gave me some lame excuse why Madison couldn't be available. She finally conceded in letting me see her this coming Saturday. How about it?"

"I'm still not sure this is the right decision . . ."

"Hey," Jim interrupted. "If I recall you gave me an impassioned speech at that restaurant on our first date together about how you envied women you grew up with from childhood and how they became mothers and you couldn't. Just think of Madison as the child you could've had. Be a little open-minded."

Anne gazed at Jim and smiled. She agreed to come up with Jim to Pennsylvania the following weekend. *Wow! That hurdle is cleared,* Jim thought. But the crucial test was yet to come.

Chapter Twenty-Four

Two days later found Jim relaxing in front of the TV watching the San Francisco Giants battle the Milwaukee Brewers. His main reason for seeing this game was that Casey Farrings was making his second start for the Giants since being called up from Richmond.

He was about an inning and a half into the match when it finally dawned on him that he had to talk with Madison to get her take on allowing Anne to meet her on Saturday. Although Anne was somewhat agreeable to the meeting, Jim wouldn't take Anne with him if Madison disapproved.

Jim dialed the Bell residence, which still caused self-inflicted abdominal pain, for he had to battle Maureen from the start. Just his luck, he happened to get the answering machine. *That figures! Got to leave a message.* But then Maureen picked up the phone on her end while he was in mid-sentence. She was as cold as a fish lying over a bed of chopped ice at the market.

"What is it that you want?"

Jim was taken aback at first by Maureen's question. Then reality set in and he figured she was just acting her usual bitchy self.

"In case you've forgotten, I'm driving up this Saturday to see Madison. I just want to ask her a question concerning my being there. I mean, if that's not too much to ask."

"She's doing her homework. You'll have to call back some other time."

"Doing her home . . . Look, I just want to ask Maddy a few questions. I promise it'll only take a couple of minutes. I'm sure she wouldn't mind pulling her head away from a biology textbook for a little while. You know, take a break and all."

"I don't think it would be appropriate at this time."

But Madison was eavesdropping. She was listening to Maureen's end of the conversation. Madison pouted and was not pleased for Maureen to dictate terms to him on her behalf.

"Let me speak with Dad, okay?"

Bitter that Madison was nearby, Maureen was even more annoyed that she had to relent. There was no way of her getting out of this lie. With great reluctance Maureen handed the phone to Madison.

Before she began to speak to her father, Madison glowered back at Maureen.

"Do you mind? I'd like a little privacy please!" She displayed an evil eye toward her mother. Maureen became indignant that she was being pushed out of the room, but decided to vacate the area nonetheless. Once she knew her mother was completely gone, Madison opened the conversation with Jim.

"Hey, Sweetie," Jim said before she had a chance to say anything. "How's the weather up there?"

Jim actually couldn't care less about the climate in Bryn Mawr. It was merely a question to check to see if Maureen was lurking around. Jim and Madison had made a pact between the two of them to use special codes when communicating to prevent Maureen from picking up their chat.

"The weather here is clear."

Jim knew he was now free to talk. Up next were a barrage of questions by him, to which Madison would answer tersely, again a pre-arranged code. For the most part these would be simple yes or no answers, without too much explanation behind them.

"Listen, Madison. As you know, I'm coming up on Saturday to see you and be with you. That should be about noon. What I want to let you know is that I recently started seeing a wonderful woman. Her name is Anne and I have told her all about you. I would like very much to bring her along with me so that you can meet her and get to know her. But I'm not going to bring Anne with me if you feel it might be a little awkward. So, with that in mind, I ask you, would it be okay if I brought her with me, yes or no?"

There was some hesitation at first. Madison displayed a look of confusion, not knowing what to make at first of her father's new romantic interest. But she soon said yes. Jim deduced by his daughter's delay in answering his question that she might have preferred a little more one-on-one time with him, so he wanted reassurance.

"Are you sure it's okay?"

"Yes."

"Great! I'll see you on Saturday at twelve. Take care, Maddy. I love you."

"I love you, too, Dad."

Jim hung up the receiver. He was grateful that Madison agreed to his taking along Anne, although he appeared bemused by her hesitation. *Oh, what the heck.* Now it was time for him to call his love and tell her everything would be all right for the Saturday visit.

Chapter Twenty-Five

Lovely day for such a long drive. Jim had picked up
Anne at precisely seven Saturday morning. Despite the
longwinded drive on the Beltway around Washington creating a little circuitous route to Pennsylvania, Jim was making good time managing to get to the Bell residence punctu-
ally.

"I still have a little anxiety going up, Jim," Anne commented.

Jim rolled his eyes and drew a deep sigh. "Will you relax, Anne? Everything's going to be all right."

To make her feel at ease, he had brought along some
CDs featuring The Beatles, Billy Joel, Bruce Springsteen,
Elton John and Hall & Oates to listen to. But not even the
myriad of great tunes by these artists erased the deep-root-
ed fears Anne was still harboring about this meeting. And
Jim could tell this just by looking at her along the way. The
initial Langston visit the weekend before was a picnic com-
pared to this trip.

But then came the arrival to Maureen's home turf and
Anne's countenance had changed drastically. She stared
in awe at the exclusive neighborhood and the opulence of
the various homes. Jim noticed her gawking at the properties. He didn't want Anne to become fixated on the gorgeous
homes. After all, that was how Maureen got sucked in. He
made a comment that the houses were out of their league,
which Anne confirmed to be true. She was just browsing.
Was there anything wrong with that? On the one hand, he
was relieved that she didn't allow the decadent allure of
these swank homes to get the better of her; on the other, he
wasn't pleased that she was still captivated by them despite
that.

Jim drove his Civic onto the semicircular driveway. Anne was impressed by the spacious home, but Jim once more placed Anne back into reality.

"Money doesn't always buy you happiness, as you'll soon see."

Jim told Anne to wait in the car while he went and got Madison. He rang the doorbell and waited nearly a full minute before the door finally opened. *About time!* Maureen stood in the doorway, but gave Jim a halfhearted greeting. Jim returned the favor, although not as caustic in tone. He politely asked if Madison was ready, to which Maureen replied she was and that she was about to get her. Maureen was about to turn her back away when she unexpectedly spotted Anne in the car, despite the fact that she was not up close. A scowl soon emerged over Maureen's face as she angrily pointed at Anne.

"What's that?" Maureen testily asked, demanding an explanation.

Jim was not pleased with Maureen's phraseology and quickly corrected her. "Excuse me, but I believe the term should be *Who is she?* if I'm not mistaken."

"Whatever! What is the meaning of bringing along that woman and, yes, I would like to know her identity."

"*That* woman happens to be my girlfriend. Her name is Anne Finley. She is sweet, warm, affectionate, and caring. Basically she's everything you're not."

"You've got some nerve bringing her here when you should be focusing on seeing Madison!"

"Oh, I've got some nerve?" Jim responded in astonishment as he pointed his right hand at his chest. "Au contraire, let's see if I get this straight. You shacked up one night with Harley and you essentially stole Madison from me to have her live in this ostentatious place so Madison can see her mother every day with her new lover! What, you think you're the only one who can play this game, Maureen?"

"Oh, so this is your idea of retribution, is it? Well, I'm going to tell you right now, Jim Monahan, I am not going to stand for this! Do you hear me? You might as well drive away right now, and take that tramp with you!"

"Now you listen to me! Don't you ever, *ever* call Anne names! You of all people have no fucking right to do that!"

"And I suppose you asked Madison if she was okay with this arrangement, huh?"

"As a matter of fact, I did. And do you want to know something? Maddy was cool with it!"

Maureen glared back in disbelief. She and Jim continued to argue for nearly a minute longer until their daughter finally surfaced.

"Stop it! The two of you," Madison pleaded with her parents. Jim and Maureen conceded to Madison's wishes. Despite their differences of opinion, both Jim and Maureen knew it wasn't productive to vent at each other in front of their daughter. Jim didn't want a repeat of the last visit as he easily recalled how ashamed he was then. Maureen, though, gave Madison a curious look.

"Sweetie," Maureen began, with no smile to match the term. "Did your father ask you if he could bring along that," Maureen gestured in the direction of Jim's Civic where Anne continued to sit embarrassingly in the front passenger seat with contempt, "woman?"

There was some hesitation on Madison's part, like she wasn't allowed to tell a secret. But the adolescent confessed to her mother that she told him it would be fine to bring Anne up for the ride. Jim made a remark with an *I told you so* undertone. Maureen gazed at Jim with question marks written all over her face, but saw no point in arguing with Madison. Just by her countenance she was not pleased that Madison yielded to her father's request, but there was no sense in carrying on an argument with her daughter, too. Maureen then relinquished Madison to Jim and sternly reminded him to be back by five that afternoon. Still with a hint of anger in his voice, Jim assured Maureen that he would.

Anne was waiting patiently in her seat as Jim and Madison approached the car. She couldn't believe the spectacle she had just witnessed. Anne wanted to hide under a rock. Just then Madison opened the driver's side rear door as Jim entered the vehicle at the same time. Anne looked bothered over the incident and made it known to Jim when he sat in the driver's seat.

"I knew this was a terrible idea," Anne said with conviction.

"Relax," Jim countered. "That's just Maureen's way of saying, *Hi! It's so nice to meet you!* Oh, speaking of introductions, Anne, I'd like you to meet my daughter, Madison. Maddy, this is my very special friend, Anne."

Anne gave Madison a halfhearted smile as she was still looking flustered over having been caught in the middle of Jim and Maureen's confrontation. While Anne gave Madison a full sentence in greeting, Madison was terse in reply, along with a lack of sincerity. Jim felt Anne wasn't actually welcomed after all. She made an attempt to try to win Madison over, at least for the next few hours.

"So, your dad told me that you're a sophomore in high school," Anne cheerfully noted.

"Yeah, it's all right," Madison deadpanned.

Anne tried to keep her side of the conversation upbeat, although it looked like a losing battle. "Gosh, I remember it like it was only yesterday when I was your age and still in high school."

"Did you have any boyfriends back then?"

Jim was now curious as to how the chat with Anne was going. He was beginning to believe that perhaps Madison had a boyfriend. While this would normally be a sign of coming of age for the adolescent, Jim was starting to wonder if Madison would get mixed up with the wrong type of guy, given her strong desire to break free from her mother's home.

"Not really. I was a little heavier then. You know what boys are like."

"You look pretty good now."

"Why thank you, Madison! I do try to eat right and exercise."

Jim sped the trio away for their rendezvous at the bowling alley. It would be a short drive to the lanes in nearby Ardmore. Further discussions in the car were then kept to a minimum.

Chapter Twenty-Six

Several minutes later in nearby Ardmore, Jim maneuvered his Civic into the parking lot of Wynnewood Lanes. He was looking forward to playing a few games, having not played a frame since the last presidential election. He was hoping Madison was in the mood for it, too. The adolescent enjoyed bowling with her parents years earlier, but with so much on the troubled mind of the youth, it was difficult to place one's finger on the pulse of her level of enthusiasm. As for Anne, she hadn't bowled in such a long time that she admitted she had forgotten how. But Jim reassured his girlfriend that it was like tying one's shoe. Once you've done it before you never forget. Jim's remark boosted Anne's confidence and thusly raised her eagerness.

It seemed like a lot of people had had the same idea. The parking lot was teeming with vehicles of all types. The closest Jim could get to the entrance was a hundred feet away. He wanted to cruise around some more in order to gain a better spot, but knowing his time with Madison was limited, it was important to get her out of the car and into a fun atmosphere quickly. Jim offered a simple apology for not parking a little closer, but neither Madison nor Anne seemed to mind.

He brought the car to a halt. Before she was able to get out of the car, Madison gazed at Jim. She saw that her father was attracted to Anne a lot. Was marriage between the two in the offing? From their last encounter, Madison knew that Jim wanted her to live with him, but was also aware that it couldn't happen under the present state of affairs. Anne would solve that problem instantly. But was Anne interested in her? Were Anne's earlier comments genuine or fake? Madison focused on Anne through the squinted eyes of curiosity. There was no telling when she would meet

Anne again and she had to have an answer fast. Could Anne become the mother Maureen was once? The teenager appeared pensive, as though scheming a plot.

As all three got out of the Civic, Madison decided not to wait for Jim and Anne to stretch their legs. She began to wander off toward the front entrance of the bowling alley without them. The baseball announcer began to yell at his daughter to wait for the two of them, but his pleas fell on deaf ears. Jim became frustrated and hastily asked Anne to walk with him to catch up to Madison.

All at once, the right situation presented itself to Madison. She had seen an SUV moving at a slow but steady pace along the front of the building. That was when she pulled a daring and perhaps deadly stunt. She walked into the path of the oncoming vehicle. The driver of the SUV was completely taken by surprise. It wasn't known if the driver had seen Madison beforehand or not. But if so, he didn't have much time to react to stop safely in advance. The front of the vehicle bumped Madison, causing the adolescent to tumble to the ground.

Jim and Anne gaped at the incident from a short distance away in horror. The baseball man screamed Madison's name in shock as he raced to his daughter's side with Anne in pursuit.

The driver leapt out of his vehicle quickly to join the others. He, too, was in stunned disbelief about what had just happened. The short, baldheaded driver, who appeared to be ready to collect his first social security check, was shaking like a leaf and white as a sheet. He groveled to Jim to give his side of the story.

"Oh, God! Honestly, mister, I didn't see the girl! It was as if . . . as if she appeared out of nowhere! Oh, Jesus!"

Jim wasn't sure whether he would have to tend to the shaken man as well. He gestured to Anne to calm the driver down, because he was making Jim nervous. In the meantime Madison was lying on the ground, apparently unconscious. Jim noticed his daughter was breathing and checked for some vital signs. Yet Madison remained on the ground, as if she were asleep. Jim told Anne that he would need to call an ambulance. That was when Madison came out of her stupor and told her father not to bother. Jim was taken off guard by Madison's sudden recovery.

"I'm all right, Dad," Madison insisted as she cracked her eyes open and slowly began to rise up to a sitting position. She gingerly rubbed the left side of her torso prompting Jim to beg a question.

"Honey, are you hurt? I mean I ought to take you to a hospital to be examined."

"I said I'm okay! If anything, I might have gotten a small bruise, that's all."

The thinly framed driver was relieved that Madison seemed to be in good health, but he told Jim that he wanted to cooperate and help any way he could. He was willing to volunteer name, rank and serial number.

"Listen, mister, my name is Ted Neskalko. I live not too far from here. I'll wait here if you want to call an ambulance or the police."

"That's quite all right, Mr. Neskalko. But I don't think that's going to be necessary."

"Look, I insist on giving you my driver's license and insurance card information to write down. Please let me do it."

Jim asked Anne if she had some paper and a pen in her purse, to which she told him she did. He asked her to jot down the information that Neskalko was freely willing to surrender. In the meantime, to everyone's amazement, Madison began to rise up on her own two feet. Still a bit wobbly, she stood up and managed to take a few steps without much discomfort. Jim made the sign of the cross, a reflection back to his Catholic upbringing, as he released a huge sigh of relief and closed his eyes. But now that Madison appeared to be fine, it was time for Jim to go on the offensive and chastise his daughter for not being observant of the oncoming SUV.

"What the hell was going through your head, Maddy? Don't you realize that you could've gotten yourself killed? Didn't you see that vehicle coming? What the hell is wrong with you?"

With just one look one could see that Madison was ashamed for making a grievous mistake. But she didn't need the harsh scolding her father administered either. She forlornly looked at Jim as if seeking solace and comfort knowing that she was okay.

Anne had finished gathering the information that Neskalko had given her. While she thanked the driver for volunteering the data, she was listening in on what was transpiring between Jim and Madison. Despite the fact that Madison committed a severe lapse in judgment, Anne didn't appear pleased with the vehement reprimand the adolescent was being given by Jim. The office manager interceded.

"Oh, please, Jim," Anne pleaded as she wrapped her arms gently around Madison's shoulders. "Madison has gone through enough as it is. I'm sure she understands her transgression. Let's be grateful nothing terrible happened, okay?"

Jim yielded to Anne's request, but not without it leaving a bitter taste in his mouth.

Meanwhile, Madison didn't say a word. She shut her eyes and displayed a grateful smile that Anne came to her defense. However, there was something else. By virtue of Anne's expression for compassion and forgiveness, Madison established a line of trust between the two. She looked back at Jim's girlfriend with admiration. And if Jim ever decided to take his relationship to the next level, it would seem that Madison wouldn't hesitate for a second to campaign vigorously for her dad to get her away from the Bryn Mawr prison shackling her.

In light of the situation, Jim thought best to do something less physical than lifting a heavy bowling ball and rolling it down an alley. However, Madison contended that she was fit to go bowling. Jim and Anne looked at each other and each gave a gesture to allow Madison to play. Jim made it clear that if his teenage daughter expressed the least amount of discomfort, he would call a halt to the proceedings. And he also made it a point that he wasn't going to rule out the notion of taking Madison to the nearest emergency room to get checked out. That was when Anne volunteered to examine Madison inside the women's restroom.

"I'll check her out, if that's okay," Anne said. Jim gave his girlfriend a nod of approval.

The three walked into the bowling establishment without any further incident. Anne expressed a look of relief that Madison appeared none the worse for wear. Jim wasn't entirely thrilled and was closely monitoring the situation.

As for Madison, she may have connected to a new ally and confidant in Anne.

Chapter Twenty-Seven

Jim, Anne and Madison managed to bowl four games. Throughout play, Jim repeatedly asked his daughter if she was all right and not feeling any pain from the parking lot fiasco, and each time Madison insisted she was fine. To make her point she actually beat Jim and Anne in the last game. It appeared whatever ill effects she incurred from being bumped by the SUV in the parking lot, had dissipated. They even enjoyed a bite to eat from a local diner.

All good things had to come to an end, though. Jim drove his Civic around the semi-circular driveway of the Bell home. Maureen had been standing outside with her arms crossed. As Jim came closer toward her, she looked at her watch. Her lips were pursed and contorted sideways. Jim knew he was a few minutes late, but the delay was due in part to the parking lot mishap. Maureen did not appear pleased with the slight tardiness.

Jim knew he would need to give Maureen a solid explanation for being late. He figured he couldn't hide Madison's fall from Maureen, so he decided to confess.

"Listen, I'm sorry we're a little late, but there was a problem in the parking lot of Wynnewood Lanes over in Ardmore. Madison ran from us when we arrived in the lot and an SUV struck her."

"What!" Maureen was both shocked and furious at hearing this. Her eyeballs bulged. Her arms flung open. Her nostrils flared. And her voice went up several decibels Jim never thought Maureen was capable of.

"It's all right! It's okay. Madison appears to be okay. The vehicle wasn't moving fast. I even had Anne check her out thoroughly in the women's restroom at the bowling alley."

"And you didn't check this out yourself?"

"Oh, what the hell would that look like, Maureen? Pardon me ladies, but I'm just checking out my daughter in here if you don't mind. Are you for real? I'd be locked up! Besides, I trust Anne, and she told me Madison was fine except for a small bruise on her left side."

"And you just think it's perfectly natural to have a complete stranger eyeball our daughter?"

"Maybe Anne seems like a stranger to you, but I know her enough to trust her. Who did you want me to have Madison checked out by, Maureen? I didn't know any women in there. I do know Anne. And please don't use the term *eyeball*. Jesus, you make it sound like Anne is some sort of pervert or something. The correct term should be *examine, okay?"*

"Whatever! I don't want that woman getting anywhere near Madison, do you hear me?"

"And you think it's perfectly okay with Madison in that house with Harley? How do I know he isn't some sicko? Madison is becoming a young woman soon, you know. I'm her father! And I have every right to be suspicious!"

"How dare you! Harley is a respected businessman and a moral citizen!"

"Moral citizen, huh? Oh, he just went and screwed some poor slob's wife and had a baby with her nine months later. You call that moral? How do you know he doesn't have the October issue of Penthouse tucked inside his Wall Street Journal? Or if he's surfing the net for porn when he's saying he wants to check out the overseas markets?"

"You know, you are a pathetic creep that needs counseling! Seriously! You are nothing but a . . ."

"Please! Stop it, the two of you," Madison vehemently interjected. "Just shut the fuck up!"

Maureen and Jim were shocked at the salty language emanating from Madison. Maureen went so far as to shake her right index finger at her daughter angrily, while addressing Jim with what she had to say.

"Oh, this is really disgusting using such vulgarity! No doubt your locker room vocabulary has rubbed onto her!"

"And like you haven't dropped a few F-bombs in your time, Sainte Maureen."

Maureen was tired of carrying on. She placed her right hand across her forehead and closed her eyes. Maureen

119

told Jim just to go. She even said the word *please*. He was more than happy to escape the diatribe that was unleashed upon him. Turning 180 degrees, he gave Madison a warm and sincere caress and kiss, to which the adolescent responded in kind. And then came a remarkable twist.

"Can I say goodbye to Anne?" Madison asked.

Jim was pleasantly surprised. "Yeah, go ahead, Maddy."

Maureen, on the other hand, wasn't particularly fond of the idea, judging by her scowl, but there wasn't anything she could do. If it meant Jim and Anne would leave quicker, then so be it. Madison approached the passenger side front door. Anne looked amazed that the teenager was making an effort to go beyond the obligatory wave and came up to her. She smiled at Madison as the latter walked up to the open car window.

"I want to thank you for coming to my aid before."

"Hey," Anne responded warmly, "no sweat!"

"I mean, you could've agreed with my dad and yelled at me, too, because I didn't look where I was going."

"Well, I want to tell you my simple philosophy about that, Madison. It's easy to find fault in someone's mistake and drive it into the ground. It's another thing to step back for a moment and look at the bigger picture. We all make mistakes in our lives at one point or another. But sometimes . . . sometimes you just need that consoling pat on the back and to be grateful for other things around you. Everybody tends to harp on the negative when things go wrong. What about thinking positive and looking on the brighter side? That's all."

Madison's grin was evidence that she appreciated Anne's wisdom. The adolescent reached inside the car to give Anne a warm hug. Anne reciprocated. Finally they loosened their grip on each other as Madison backed away slightly.

"I hope I get to see you again soon," Madison said.

"I'd like that, too, Madison," said Anne. "I'd like to get to know you better. And thank you for your nice comment. That really made me feel special."

Madison was about to respond to Anne's comment when suddenly Maureen called her name to put a halt to the drawn-out farewell. She wasn't happy being yanked away, but Anne politely encouraged Madison to obey her mother's wishes.

Jim observed the exchange between Madison and Anne. He was pleased that the two of them hit it off big on their first encounter, but tried not to gloat to show up Maureen. Madison came up to him. The doting father, in spite of the earlier incident, embraced his daughter affectionately and gave her a soft kiss on the cheek. Jim released his hold on Madison as the latter slowly walked back to the house. Jim stared at her until she was no longer in sight. He then turned his attention to Maureen.

"Well, I guess I'll be seeing you soon."

"Next time, leave her behind," Maureen replied through clenched teeth.

"Maybe you ought to allow Madison give you her thoughts on the subject before you make that ultimatum. Just an idea."

Jim retreated to his car and quickly got into the driver's seat. He slowly drove away and headed back south.

As the Civic pulled out of the driveway, Maureen looked at Anne with contempt. She couldn't help but notice the way Madison and Anne had carried on before, in such an amicable fashion. Perhaps Maureen saw Anne as competition for the love of her daughter. She looked back at the house angrily, knowing Madison was inside. All at once, she felt vulnerable, and it wasn't sitting too well with her. She needed to speak with Madison immediately to get the record straight and reinforce the rules of the house.

Chapter Twenty-Eight

Only a few minutes elapsed since Jim and Anne had left Bryn Mawr, still far away from the open road of I-95 South. They were free and clear of the lurching shadow of Maureen, so it was time to review what had just happened and exchange views.

"Well, now you know how vindictive and paranoid Maureen is," Jim began. "She just wants to continue to make my life miserable."

"If it makes you feel any better, I'm not keen on her either," Anne replied. "I mean, first I'm being referred to as an object, then I'm being accused of molesting Madison. And then she accuses you of being weird in allowing me to check Madison out. There's something wrong with Maureen, Jim. Seriously." Anne paused for a moment before adding a second comment. "You know, if I hadn't seen it for myself I'd swear I'd say you were exaggerating things when it came to describing your ex-wife to me before. But now . . . now I'm convinced."

"She is one sick puppy."

Jim drove a little farther until he reached the inner heart of Philadelphia. It wasn't long before they would latch onto the interstate for their five-hour sojourn back to Richmond. Anne spoke up once more.

"Madison is an amazing young woman, Jim. You ought to be a proud father."

"Oh, I am. But I wasn't too keen on the parking lot fiasco."

"Well, the main thing was that she wasn't seriously hurt." Anne paused again before continuing. "You know, I think she really likes me. I mean with the way she came up to say goodbye to me. I was really flattered. And I like her, too."

"I'm glad for that, although I noticed Maureen wasn't too thrilled. I believe she thinks you were trying to win over Madison's affection from her."

"If that's the case she's more psychotic than I thought."

"I don't know. Maybe Maureen sees you as more of a motherly figure to Madison."

"Well, I don't know what goes on in that house of theirs day in and day out, but if Maureen thinks I'm a threat to her, maybe she ought to improve on her parenting skills with her own daughter. Perhaps Madison wouldn't be so troubled."

Jim didn't respond to Anne's opinion. Instead, the baseball announcer was beginning to imagine a scenario. What if he decided to propose marriage to Anne? What if he then asked if she'd allow him to pursue wrestling Madison away from Maureen, considering he would have an ideal arrangement that would be looked upon by the judicial system as highly favorable with Anne present much of the time? He didn't want to sound too aggressive on the subject. He didn't want a repeat of what happened after he and Anne had left the Langston house the Sunday before. It was an idea, though, that Jim was giving serious thought to. But it would have to be drawn out slowly and carefully and handled with kid gloves. *Powder keg issue.*

Anne couldn't help but notice that Jim was being very pensive. Not a word was coming out of his mouth.

"Is anything wrong, Jim? You seem to be a little agitated about something. What's the matter?"

"Huh?" Jim had to act quickly and come up with an excuse to deflect his real feelings. "I, uh . . . I was wondering what Virginia Tech was doing. They're playing Notre Dame today in South Bend. Hey, maybe I can catch the game on the radio somewhere."

Her quizzical look indicated that she didn't totally buy his answer, but she decided to give it a rest. The gist of the conversations for the rest of their trip would be focused on idle points. There would not be any further discussions about Maureen and what was best for Madison. And for Jim, that was preferred.

Chapter Twenty-Nine

Jim had finished the last of his reports that following Monday. Program Director Christine Haines buttered Jim up when she commented on another series of excellent pieces. Ah, but there was an ulterior motive.

"Listen, Jim," Christine began sweetly, "could you be available to do a few more commercial voiceovers for a couple of advertisers? Please?" Christine even batted her eyes and spoke in song to coax him to do it. Jim saw through her fawning with skepticism. He wasn't overly excited about doing them, but being the good company man that he was, he agreed to it. Christine flashed a broad grin in appreciation; as it gleamed against her dark mocha complexion, she happily thanked him.

Jim was going over a few items left in his *In* box when Laura Mazursky announced there was a call for him. Tony Salerno. With the St. Louis Cardinals' gig as chief play-by-play man hanging in the balance, Jim was eager to take the call.

"Good morning, Tony. How's it going?"

"I am fantastic! So, how's my number one hero?"

"Okay, but I think the story behind that rescue effort of Alan Langston is beginning to fade. I'm back to being good ol' Diamond Jim Monahan that everyone knows and loves. To what honor do I owe this call?"

"Interesting bit of news I have for you, Jimmy my boy. It appears the Cards want to audition you as soon as possible."

"I thought you said they were going to wait until after the regular season was over, and that won't be until this Sunday."

"Yeah, but the Cards are finishing the season in Houston and Cincinnati. They want you over there pronto. How fast can you grab a flight to St. Louie?"

"Well, I guess I can go right after the last of my sportscasts tomorrow morning. Let me check what flights are available. Tell them I could be out there tomorrow afternoon, but let me call some airlines before you do."

Tony yielded to Jim's wishes. The baseball man moved on and began making a few calls to find out that U S Airways had available room on a flight to St. Louis at 12:40 the following afternoon with an arrival at 4:10, with a change in Charlotte. The late arrival time might not sit well with Cardinals brass, but delaying another day might show disinterest on Jim's part. He was just as eager to meet with representatives from the St. Louis ball club as they were with him. And so Jim looked at the airline's website once more to check for earlier flights.

He discovered there was an 8:05 flight in the morning, which would eventually take him to St. Louis at 11:55, thus leaving him enough time to sit down with the Cardinals bigwigs.

The only problem was that he would have to abdicate his morning's sportscasts for the next day. Whoa! That's going to force Jim to tell Zach Moser that he wasn't coming in Tuesday. But just what should he use as an excuse? He sighed and frowned, stupefied about how he could cleverly mask the real purpose of playing hooky. Perhaps he could use some family emergency as the reason without going into specifics. At any rate he had to tell Zach something just before he left for the day, out of fairness. He walked over to Laura and asked her if Zach had a minute to speak with him. After a brief exchange with her boss, Laura gladly told Jim to go right inside and see Zach.

Jim had been in Zach's office many times, but not recently. Things still hadn't changed, however, since his last visit. There were the numerous plaques hanging up on the walls for the various achievements the station had attained during Zach's tenure at the helm. And there were those personal trophies which Zach showcased along the top of the credenza behind him, some perhaps to feed his own ego. But there were also objects even more precious than the glistening silverware. Zach had various pictures on his desk of his family, which included his wife of nearly forty years, Barbara, two sons, a daughter, and five grandkids. The station manager would trade any of the awards if the price was right, but the members of his family were off limits.

Jim spotted Zach entrenched behind his desk scanning over some papers. The station manager was brushing his white beard with his right hand in a sign of studiously reading the material in front of him. Jim decided to clear his throat to get his boss' attention. Zach broke out of his trance and peered at Jim over the top of his horn-rimmed spectacles.

"Oh, I'm sorry, Jim," Zach apologized as he placed the papers to the side and removed his glasses to give his guest his undivided attention. "Please have a seat."

Zach gestured with his open left hand toward one of the two chairs opposite his desk. The baseball man felt a bit awkward. At first Jim just sat in the seat offered by Zach. In a sign of nervousness, he rhythmically tapped his fingers on his lap. His face appeared deadpanned, but when Zach looked at him with curiosity, Jim offered a forced smile. Zach was puzzled by Jim's silence, after having at first inquired about the station manager's audience. That was when he decided to open the dialogue.

"Well, Jim, what's on your mind?"

Jim had to respond. He did so apprehensively. "Uh . . . well . . . it's like this, Zach. There was something I had been aiming to talk to you about when you first walked in at seven o'clock. Unfortunately you were busy and I, of course, was tweaking and fine tuning my reports for the air. A sudden family situation came to my attention. My sister called me up last night to say our mother had gotten ill and had to be hospitalized. She told me she didn't know how long Mom was going to be laid up. Heck, I've discussed Mom's deteriorating condition with Diane and our brother Dan on numerous occasions. We feel Mom may need to be placed in a nursing home, but we're trying our best to avoid that. She and Diane live together back home in Wayne. Dan and Diane don't know what we're going to do."

"I'm so sorry to hear that, Jim."

"Thanks. Quite frankly, I don't know what we're going to do either." Jim hesitated for a moment before asking a favor from Zach. "I was wondering if I could take off tomorrow and be back here on Wednesday. I can get the weekend guy, Scott Larson, to sit in for me. He can usually do it for me, especially since he's in semi-retirement. What do you say, Zach?"

Zach sat back in his high executive chair to absorb Jim's request. He knew Jim's mother and sister lived together, but Jim didn't discuss much about the elder Monahan's health. After a moment, Zach's visage of concern disappeared, like it had been unmasked. Zach then countered Jim's request with a direct question.

"Listen, the reason you're wanting off isn't because you have an interview with the St. Louis Cardinals, is it?"

Suddenly the jig was up and Jim sat in front of Zach with a stunned look. He thought perhaps Laura might have told Zach. But how could she? Laura only knew that Tony Salerno called and spoke with Jim a few times in recent weeks, but she wasn't privy to their conversations. Then it dawned on him that he had told Anne about the possibility of the Cardinals' gig and that she might have told Laura, who then spilled the beans to Zach. Curiosity caught the better of Jim; he had to inquire how Zach knew of the job opening.

"The Cardinals called the Richmond Flying Squirrels and asked how long your contract was with the team. Russ Sands from the Squirrels then called me about it. Besides, we did discuss this possibility just recently, remember?"

While Jim wasn't happy that Zach knew about the Cardinals' job possibility, he was relieved to know Anne hadn't mentioned to Laura that he might be calling games in St. Louis next spring, thus keeping Zach in the dark. There was no need to keep the news suppressed any longer. With the revelation of the prospect to broadcast games for the Cardinals, Jim had to confess the situation.

"Yes, Zach, the reason I need to take off tomorrow is because the Cardinals want to audition me for their number one play-by-play position with them next year. I didn't want to tell you until they offered me the job. I mean, c'mon. How would it sound to you when an employee tells his boss, *Oh, I need to take off tomorrow for a job interview?* That would be crazy."

"The trouble is I already knew the Cards were pursuing you. Using your *ill* mother as an excuse was not fair."

"I'm sorry, and you're absolutely right, but how the hell was I supposed to know you knew about that?"

"This is true. But you did forget about it." Zach drew a deep sigh, rubbed his eyes and stroked his beard. "That unfortunate incident involving Alan Langston was actually a blessing in disguise for us. If it weren't for that rescue effort you did, thus making not only local, but national headlines, Vince's morning show would still be mired where it was. But thanks to your heroics, Vince's show took off to where we're number one in morning drive. We've been knocking out ad sales at a generous rate, especially your segments. And it has had a carryover effect on the rest of our programming. And we have you to thank for this boon. Believe me, this station is eternally grateful to Diamond Jim Monahan."

"Well, I'm glad to hear that, Zach. I've had my fair share of promos to do recently for sponsors, so I know something is going well. Heck, Christine approached me earlier about doing some more voiceovers."

"As much as I hate the prospect of losing you, Jim, I know you've always had this dream of being a major league baseball announcer. It's why you've languished in the minors for so long. I want you to succeed, because I don't want to see you asking the nagging question, *what if?* You don't need to be in the minors forever and end up mired behind a small desk the rest of your life. And so, in closing, I just have two words for you regarding your audition with the Cardinals: kick ass!"

And with that Zach broke out in a broad grin one could easily make out through the cover of his white whiskers. Accepting his boss's beefy right hand, Jim was pleasantly surprised to learn he had Zach's blessing to do well in the audition, possibly because the station manager didn't want to stand in the way of Jim's last good chance of fulfilling his lifelong dream. *Nice gesture.* Jim heartily accepted the goodwill with a sincere debt of thanks.

Jim quietly walked out of the office. Time to bust a move and book that earlier flight. "Hello, Tony?"

Chapter Thirty

Jim was resting comfortably in his apartment that afternoon. He had already booked his early flight the next day to St. Louis and informed Tony when he'd be there to meet the Cards' top people. He wasn't going to stay overnight, so there was little packing to do. Just wear a very good suit, dress shirt, tie and shoes. *Simple enough.* As determined as he was not to prolong his visit to the Midwest, the baseball man had already booked a flight back to Richmond the following evening. He wouldn't have much sleep to prepare himself for Wednesday's reports, but he would have to deal with that when the time arrived. It was a meager price to pay in exchange for spending money unnecessarily on a hotel room, not to mention running the chance of irking Zach by trying to get a second straight morning off.

The game plan was for him to review more media information on the club and watch a few tapes of Cardinals' games to familiarize himself with the players. But that was for later. At that moment he spent time calling his brother and sister in Pennsylvania, who wished him well. And there was a call to Marty Leary, and even a call to his daughter, Madison, who cheered him on, although it would probably mean even lesser moments together than the few he had. Maureen, on the other hand, couldn't have cared less.

And then there was the call to Jim's beloved. He had to wait for a few minutes because Anne was on an important call regarding a client. But when the moment presented itself, he and Anne had a chat.

"I got the call from Tony Salerno this morning. The Cardinals want to audition me ASAP. So, with the green light from Zach Moser, I'm taking tomorrow off and flying out to St. Louis to meet with them."

"That's great!"

Jim hesitated for a moment. He distinctly recognized by the sound of Anne's tone that her response was more bittersweet than congratulatory. He then probed her on how she really felt.

"C'mon, Anne, you can't hide it from me. I can tell you're really not thrilled about my auditioning out there tomorrow. It's because you're afraid that we might drift apart, is that it?"

"Well, the thought did cross my mind."

"Hey, I haven't been handed the keys to the kingdom yet. And wasn't it you during our moment of steamy intimacy a couple of weeks back who said if the opportunity came around, *Let's cross that bridge when we come to it?*"

Anne sighed. "Yes, I admit I did say that."

"We haven't approached the bridge yet, but the highway signs are posted for it." Jim paused for a second before continuing. "Look, let's see what happens tomorrow before we both start jumping to conclusions. Who knows? I may wind up falling flat on my face."

While Anne wasn't excited over the prospect of possibly losing Jim, unless there was a commitment between the two, she didn't want to discourage his audition either. With deep sincerity in her voice, she wished him well. A noticeable change in tone. He thanked her for the words of encouragement, then softly hung up the phone. He sat in silence and looked into space, mulling over his relationship with Anne.

If the opportunity with the Cardinals presented itself, he knew he would have to act fairly soon. While there were eligible women in Missouri to be sure, there was only one Anne Finley. And the camaraderie she had developed with Madison seemed solid.

Jim snapped out of his dream to focus on articles and videos of Cardinals' games; his intent was to impress the club's hierarchy the next day. It was reminiscent of cramming for a college exam, and Jim was determined to ace the test.

Chapter Thirty-One

US Airways flight number 248 was running on time. Jim could feel his stomach float in his body, a sign the aircraft was about to descend on its final approach. As the announcement was being made by the flight captain that the 737 he was riding was about to approach Lambert-St. Louis International, Jim couldn't help but stare out of his window. He saw the St. Louis skyline, dominated by the famous 630-foot Gateway Arch overlooking the mighty Mississippi. He admired the majestic silver edifice and thought of taking a ride up in it if he had the time. Of course, with a return flight pegged for early that evening back to Richmond, the prospects of such an excursion appeared dim.

The plane touched down without so much as a jolt, like the landing gear consisted of soft, round pillows. Jim had only his briefcase with him, which was up in the overhead compartment, so the agony of going through baggage claim was eliminated.

Several minutes later, he grabbed a cab parked alongside the terminal entrance and had the driver take him to Busch Stadium. As he gave the cabbie the instructions, he looked at his wristwatch. Twelve forty-five. Jim had an interview at two with the team's Broadcast VP Sam Waldman, but he didn't want to take a chance of being late. He decided to forego lunch, rather than risk being tardy—coupled with the fact he had too much nervous energy inside him to warrant even a morsel of food.

The ride along I-70 swung Jim near the Gateway Arch again, only this time he saw it from ground level. The colossal structure appeared more imposing from land than it did from the sky, with its steel frame glistening in the Missouri sunshine. Twenty-five minutes were spent combating the traffic on the highway, but Jim eventually made it curbside of the Cardinals' ballpark with more than a half hour to spare.

His fare taken care of while exiting the taxi, Jim took a long look at the side of the ballpark to drink it all in. He marveled at the exquisite charm of the brick and steel structure. A smile creased his lips in awe of the stadium. There was the imposing bronze statue of former Cardinals' great Stan *The Man* Musial. And then he reflected upon his past and how many times he had visited the former Veterans Stadium in Philadelphia as a boy, and then as a young man attending Phillies games along with a few other major league parks as well. But this time he would not be treating it as a spectator. This time he envisioned himself working in Busch Stadium for a change, as well as in other National League venues. Memories he recalled of watching games in person were just one test away from capturing new ones with his voice. It took him a few seconds, but he finally came to his senses and began to seek out the entrance to the executive offices.

Jim walked through the front glass doors and made his way up the elevator to the executive floor. There was still a little bit of eagerness inside, but he approached his meeting as a calm professional. A lovely young receptionist greeted Jim the moment he stepped off the elevator. She even wore red hair, and why not? The Cardinals are also known as the Redbirds. She cheerfully greeted him.

"Yes. My name is Jim Monahan. I have a two o'clock appointment with Mr. Sam Waldman."

"Great!" The woman beamed. "Please have a seat, Mr. Monahan, while I summon Mr. Waldman."

While waiting, he looked around the walls and gazed at the various pictures displaying former Cardinals' heroes in vintage action shots. Besides Musial, there were photos of legendary starting pitcher Bob Gibson, outfield great Lou Brock, and fellow Hall-Of-Famer Bruce Sutter. In fact, the Cardinals prided themselves as one of just a few teams to have sent a multitude of former players to baseball immortality in Cooperstown.

After a nominal wait, a jovial middle-aged man with dark swept-back hair appeared in the reception area. He approached Jim with a meaty right hand and a smile as wide as the outfield scoreboard.

"Hi, Jim! I'm Sam Waldman."

"It's a pleasure to meet you, Mister Waldman," Jim greeted as he shook hands with Sam.

"Please call me Sam. My father was Mister Waldman."

The two shared a laugh. It also made Jim feel more at ease about the encounter with Sam's inference of the family-type atmosphere the club had.

Sam first escorted Jim to the broadcast booth to view the layout of the ballpark from that perspective. The panoramic display overwhelmed Jim with the elegant old-time construction of the upper deck and a view of downtown St. Louis, and yes, even the famous Arch in the distance past right-center, beyond the outfield fence. Jim was also captivated by the scoreboard and all the other accoutrements, giving the stadium a classic throwback look to the way ballparks once were decades ago. It was a far cry from the round, cookie-cutter and fully enclosed old Busch Memorial Stadium.

Sam noticed how mesmerized Jim was in his observation of the park.

"Quite a sight, huh, Jim?"

"Oh, yeah! It's truly awesome!" Jim then realized this realm could be his if he aced the audition. That task was about to come.

Sam gestured to follow him to the hallway behind the booth. They walked down the corridor to a single glass-paneled conference room. In it sat a long wooden desk with its glowing finish glistening with the overhead track lights shining on it. At the head of the room was a huge flat screen HDTV.

Sam then asked him to take a seat in one of the luxurious padded executive chairs where he could view the screen in comfort. *Very relaxing.* Jim was asked to wait there for a minute or two while Sam stepped away.

Waiting for Sam to return seemed an eternity to Jim. He was slightly intimidated by the mere fact he was inside Busch Stadium and seeing the arena from a broadcaster's perspective. The 73-inch television also looked imposing. All Jim could think to himself was just to act relaxed and let the flow of the videotaped play appear, like he was watching things live and assume he was back in his perch at the Richmond Squirrels games. *If I'm going to fall flat on my face during this audition, then so be it. I'm going to give it my best shot. Just let it flow naturally, Jim.* He closed his eyes for a brief moment with that thought seared on his forehead. But if his stomach had a latched door, he would release the butterflies held inside.

Abruptly, the door to the conference room opened. Jim's attention riveted toward Sam, returning with two others following him. *Uh oh,* Jim thought, *more trouble!* He took a big gulp of nerves and readied himself to meet the strangers. Jim somewhat recognized the first man. He was in his early-to-mid sixties and wore a Cardinals' red blazer over a navy blue golf shirt to go with a pair of beige slacks and white golf shoes. His hair was nearly all white and swept back.

"Jim, this is Royce Fenton, the team's owner," Sam said as he introduced the first man.

"It's a pleasure to meet you, Jim," smiled Fenton. "How is that man you saved?"

"Alan Langston? He's coming along very well," Jim cheerfully responded as he shook Fenton's iron vise of a right hand.

The second individual was the head of press and media relations for the Cardinals, Dom Castiglia. Dom was much younger than Fenton. In fact, he was even younger than Jim by a few years. Unlike Fenton, Dom wore a conservative gray pinstripe suit similar to the one Jim wore. Dom couldn't stay too long, because he had to fly out immediately to Houston to join the Cardinals before their game with the hometown Astros that evening. After an exchange of handshakes and formalities, Dom placed a few media pages in front of Jim. To the baseball man, it was like the proctor handing out exam papers. Jim stared at the files as if the pages were going to roar back at him. The PR director then had to make his quick exit.

This left Sam and Royce with Jim. The Q and A session was over with quickly, and then the meeting came down to the purpose of Jim's visit.

Sam had given Jim a briefing of the tape he was about to see, a game played back in June. There were two outs, and speedy outfielder Armand Hillaire was at first base. The Cardinals were down a run in the bottom of the eighth inning to the Los Angeles Dodgers. There was a 2-1 count on second baseman Pete Heilmueller. LA had their big set-up man Tim Wilson on the mound. It was up to Jim to make the call as the tape played.

"The 2-1 offering by Wilson. Change-up misses low and inside and now the count is 3 and 1. Fans here at the Busch are getting antsy. Meantime, Dodgers' manager Bill Dinsmore has his ace closer, Jorge Castro, throwing darts in the LA pen. Hillaire represents the tying run."

As Jim adjusted to the tape and play calling, Fenton gave a slight impressive nod toward Sam concerning Jim's handling of the play. Jim then continued to talk some more.

"Dinsmore is now motioning his right hand fingers to his catcher, Alfredo Toro, to chat with Wilson in order to buy some time for Castro as the fans begin to boo for the stall tactics. Despite Hillaire's speed, I think it's rather doubtful if Cards' skipper Lou Anzalone is going to have Hillaire running on the pitch down a run."

Sam looked astonished, apparently blown away by Jim's knowledge of the game and anticipating a non-running situation in this instance.

"Home plate umpire Mike Salmon started advancing toward the mound to break up the conference, but now Toro has retreated back to his position behind the plate. Wilson now looks in on Toro. Gives a side glance at Hillaire, who has a modest lead off first by his standards. Wilson makes a slight head gesture, forcing Hillaire to rush back to first. Fans are booing, thinking a balk is in vogue, but clearly Wilson did not make any false movement."

While Sam and Royce wanted an announcer to be enthusiastic, especially if the Cardinals made a great play or won a game, they didn't want a shill for the team. Jim's explanation of the non-balk call might not sit well with St. Louis fans, but it was the correct call, nonetheless. Again, Jim earned some more big points for being impartial.

"Here's the 3-1 to Heilmueller. Fastball low and outside. Good eye by Pete, and now the Birds have the go-ahead run on first with home run leader Trevor Salazar up. And that's going to be all for Wilson, as Bill Dinsmore elects to bring in Castro to try and get a four-out save."

Sam told Jim to take a breather for a minute. A release of a sigh and a slight relaxation of the neck muscles were all that Jim required to rejuvenate his brainwaves and body gestures. Sam then said the tape would resume with the continuation of the game. Sam wanted to make sure Jim was ready to take up the call, to which Jim gave a confident nod.

"So now we come down to heat versus heat. LA skipper Dinsmore opting to go put his closer, Jorge Castro, in the game now, despite the fact that the flame-throwing lefthander is going against a right-handed batter. But this just isn't any batter. Trevor comes into tonight's action batting .342 and leading the majors with 24 homers at this stage and 61 RBI. And this is only late June! Salazar already has a double in the fourth inning and later scored. Here's the first offering by Castro. Swung on and hit *deep* toward the left field fence. Lance Preston is going back and he's going to run out of real estate! She's gone! A three-run blast off the bat of Trevor Salazar has put the Cardinals ahead for the first time, 5-3!"

Jim elevated his level of excitement to match the game, but not to the point of being obsequious and overbearing. Sam and Royce were astounded greatly by Jim's delivery of the Salazar shot. Sam informed Jim of the next segment. It was the same game, only this time it was the top of the ninth. The Dodgers had managed to get a run in the inning to cut the Cardinals' lead to 5-4. There were runners on first and second for LA with two out. St. Louis closer, Blake Collins, had to get out hot-hitting Kevin Teller to preserve the win.

"Two on and two gone. It's a 3-2 count on Kevin Teller. And now it comes down to this one pitch by Collins. Runners will be going with the pitch. Here's the offering by Collins. Swung on toward second. Heilmueller scoops it up and quickly tosses it to Contreras as they just get Morales! Put a padlock on this one! The Cardinals win!"

Sam and Royce had seen enough. They came away with nothing but praise for Jim's play calling. Royce then approached Jim as Sam turned the TV off.

"You did a heck of a job, Jim! Say, what time is your flight back to Richmond?"

"Not until 7:30 this evening."

"I'll bet you didn't have time to have lunch before coming here."

"Well, come to think of it, Mr. Fenton, I haven't had time. I might as well head back downtown to look for a bite to eat."

"Nonsense! Sam, I want you and Jim to join me for lunch in the Cardinals' Club. I'll make sure you don't walk out of here hungry, Jim!"

Jim was pleasantly surprised by Royce's enormous hospitality. It was more than just an invite to dine on culinary cuisine—it was a warm security blanket enveloping Jim. He hadn't expected the offering of an executive-style meal from Fenton and took it as an outward sign that the top boss was impressed by his audition. But Jim wasn't going to take anything for granted. He would spend the lunch with Fenton and Sam getting to know his prospective employers better; and they, better acquainting themselves with him.

Chapter Thirty-Two

Ten days had passed since Jim had the audition in St. Louis, and he hadn't heard a word from Tony Salerno. Perhaps the Cardinals chose someone else to replace the retiring Dick Spencer. Perhaps the club was too preoccupied with the closing of the season the past Sunday in Cincinnati to be bothered. Then again, maybe the search for Spencer's successor was still ongoing. Nevertheless, Jim had been on pins and needles for a week and a half in anticipation of *the call*. All this time he nervously stared at phones or scoured his emails in anticipation of any hint by Tony.

During the interval, Jim had been asked the big question of whether the Cardinals had offered him a contract countless times. *Nothing yet, Laura. No word so far, Marty. I haven't heard anything, Joyce.* And he'd even said the same to his beloved Anne.

Friday morning. Nine fifty-seven. Jim had only one more scheduled sportscast nearly 20 minutes away on a dreary, rainy day in Richmond. As he was tweaking his script, Laura Mazursky told him that he had a phone call from Tony. Jim's eyes lit up and the adrenalin began to rise from within. Perhaps this was it. The baseball man girded himself before accepting the transfer from Laura. When he felt somewhat composed, he gave Laura the signal to switch Tony over to him.

"Hey, Jimbo! What's happening? How's the weather down there?"

"Lousy. It's raining like cats and dogs."

"Don't sweat it! We're getting the same in the Big Apple."

"I'm sure you didn't call me for a weather report, Tony."

"Oh, you are on the ball, Diamond Jim! I can't put anything past you! As a matter of fact, I called to tell you about that audition you did for the Redbirds last week. How does this sound to you, my friend? Diamond Jim Monahan, the radio voice of the St. Louis Cardinals!"

Jim nearly fell out of his chair. He released such a loud yell that it alarmed both Laura and Christine Haines. Jim's scream even forced Zach Moser out of his office. The new Cardinals' play-by-play man then composed himself to allow Tony to continue.

"This is not some prank you're pulling, is it, Tony?"

"Jimmy, I would never kid you on something as big as this! Sam Waldman called me a few minutes ago. He and Royce Fenton loved the way you handled certain situations in the tape and the fact that you did your homework on the players, even on the Dodgers. You really wowed them last week. Congratulations!"

Jim still had to pinch himself into believing what he was hearing.

"What's the next step?"

"I'll be negotiating a contract today. I can fax or email the contract when it's done, and then we can go over it before signing your John Hancock."

"What if I were to come up to New York?"

"Sure, you can do that. But what about your present commitment with the station down there? I don't think your boss would be too keen on letting you up here."

"No, you raise a good point, Tony." Jim paused for a moment and then came up with a solution. "How about I come to your office tomorrow? I mean, I know it's Saturday, but this way you and I can go over the contract face to face, without either of us worrying about losing time on Monday. Unless, it's too inconvenient for you."

"Nah, tomorrow is fine. What time did you have in mind?"

"Let me get back to you on that."

And with that Jim wrapped up the best conversation he'd had with anyone in a long time. He just sat back in his chair to drink it all in. Finally, all his aspirations, his long-awaited dreams were coming to fruition. Jim had finally landed the long sought-after job of a major league baseball announcer. That sound one heard was the monkey leaving the room after years of riding Jim's back.

Laura, Zach and Christine all asked what the cause of his jubilation was, like none of them had a clue already. With great pride, Jim announced to everyone that the Cardinals would be hiring him next spring. Each of the three offered their praises for landing the dream job, although Zach's sentiment wasn't as deep as that of Laura and Christine. It dawned on Jim that he had to consult with Zach in his office for a moment. He then excused himself from the ladies so he and Zach could have some time in private.

The two men sat down behind closed doors. Zach gently rubbed his white beard while Jim released a huge sigh. An awkward bit of silence ensued for a brief period before either spoke. How strange this was for Jim to let Zach know he was leaving the station to pursue his lifelong ambition. And how uncomfortable it was for Zach to be losing the shot in the arm his station needed as a result from the heroics two months earlier. Zach blinked first.

"You know," he began as he toyed with a pen on his desk, "I kind of anticipated this was going to happen. I mean, I know you've always had the talent, Jim, but you just needed the big break." Zach then exhaled a short laugh before continuing. "I'll let you in on a little secret, Jim. All those times you were promised the moon by that agent of yours in New York, and every time you were shot down by reality, I breathed a sigh of relief. I've always had selfish reasons even before that night you saved Langston's hide from Gillies Creek. But I couldn't hold on to you forever."

"Look, Zach, I know it's kind of weird for the both of us." Jim hesitated before going on. "I don't want to give you the proverbial two weeks' notice bit. In fact, Zach, I'll stay on until you get a replacement for me. Or, at least for another month or so."

"I would appreciate that. The Flying Squirrels will miss you. Richmond will miss you. This station will miss you, and above all, I'll miss you. I wish you nothing but the best."

"Thanks, Zach." Jim smiled. "I'm sure there's a younger version of myself out there who would kill for the opportunity to come here and do the Squirrels games."

"The problem is he'll want to move on to bigger things, too, eventually. But I guess that's how it goes in this business."

The two then rose from their seats. At first Jim and Zach gave each other a hearty handshake. And then Zach extended his free left hand around Jim's shoulders in a sign of friendship.

The new Cardinals' voice asked Zach if he could keep a lid on the announcement of Jim's defection to the Cardinals until after he and Tony signed the contract in New York the next day. Even the giddy baseball man, still flying on cloud nine over the call from Tony, didn't want to divulge the story to Vince during his last sportscast that morning. As a person of honor, Zach promised not a word would go out until he was ready to allow it.

Jim quietly left Zach's office. He wanted to start making phone calls to family members and friends, especially Anne. Hell, he wanted to shout from the rooftops! But he noticed the time. Ten oh-two. He was due to be on the air again in less than ten minutes. Given the shortness of preparation for the day's final report, he thought it wise to do his sportscast and then head straight home to his apartment and make all the necessary calls from the comfort of his living room.

He turned to Laura. "Please don't say a word to Anne. I want to break the news to her myself."

"Not a peep." Laura winked with a smile.

Just as he was grateful to Zach for keeping a media lid on the announcement, so, too, was he glad that Laura would honor his request for secrecy from Anne until he felt ready.

Chapter Thirty-Three

The moment he was able to plop himself down on his living room sofa, Jim made calls left and right over his landing the Cardinals' play-by-play job. He first spoke with his sister, Diane, who would later tell their mother, and also with his brother, Dan, who worked up in Allentown as a civil engineer in the city. And then there were the calls to Marty Leary and Alan and Joyce Langston. Madison would have to wait until she arrived home from school. Everyone was delighted for Jim having landed the job of his boyhood dreams. And he in turn was grateful for their praise in wishing him well. Indeed, Jim was acting like the kid showing off his Christmas present to his friends. His own giddiness could not be contained.

However, he reserved the most important call for last. He called Anne at her office. Naturally, she was on a business call and he was told by her assistant to either wait or leave a message. Jim opted for the former. It was too important not to. Finally, Anne got on the horn. They chatted for a few minutes and exchanged idle talk until Jim was ready to give Anne the thrilling news.

"My agent, Tony Salerno, called me at the station this morning," Jim began. "The Cardinals want me to be their man next spring!"

Anne hesitated for a moment before issuing a response. "That's fantastic, Jim!" There was another dramatic pause. "So, I guess you'll be moving to St. Louis."

"Well, not right away, but I do want to get settled out there before the team starts training camp in Jupiter, Florida, in mid-to-late February." Now there was a delay with Jim. He detected that his love didn't share the same enthusiasm he had in landing the St. Louis position. "You don't sound too thrilled about it."

"Well, I knew this was a possibility. And if I appear ambivalent, you can understand why. I don't know if I can just go out there with you, Jim, without . . . you know . . ."

"C'mon, say it, without some sort of commitment." Jim sighed. "Look, let's just celebrate the new job tonight. What do you say we go back to that place where I first laid eyes on that gorgeous face over a month ago? I'll call and make reservations for the two of us to eat at the Tobacco Company."

"I don't know, Jim."

"Why, is there something important you have to do tonight? Now I won't take no for an answer. We're going to celebrate this together. Just you and me. Laura and Charlie can stay home. What do you say?"

Anne finally waved the white flag to Jim's persistent pleas. She agreed to meet with him around 5:30 at the restaurant. That was when he countered by telling her he would prefer to pick her up at her apartment around the same time and then they would ride together to the bistro. Again, Anne yielded to his wishes.

Jim laid the receiver back on its cradle. He stared across the room, thinking about the way Anne reacted. Jim couldn't blame her. He looked deep within himself. Anne deserved more, and he could not afford to lose the woman who seemed to bring back the joy he had been missing since his better days with Maureen. Anne stoked Jim's fires. She rekindled the feelings and emotions he once had toward women before Maureen gave love a bad name.

There was something he had to do. Jim had to express his deep feelings toward Anne, whom he equally loved on the same level with his daughter, Madison, and the job that awaited him four months down the road in St. Louis.

He glanced at his watch. Almost two. There were still a few hours before he would meet with Anne. That bought him enough time to do the right thing, the honorable thing. He grabbed his light jacket and scampered out of his apartment.

Chapter Thirty-Four

Jim and Anne were seated for dinner at the Tobacco Company. Anne, in keeping up with her disdain for meat except poultry on occasion, opted for the stuffed flounder. In a show of unity, Jim selected the same.

They had kept their conversation to a minimum. The only sounds there were emanated from disruptive chatter by diners from neighboring tables, the clanking of silverware and dishes being gathered by busboys, and table servants asking for orders. Although Jim wanted the *Richmond Times-Dispatch* to stop the presses for his personal lead story, he knew Anne didn't share his enthusiasm. She loved him dearly, but was there a solemn vow by Jim to put a seal on their bonding together?

After dinner Jim took Anne back to her apartment. He asked if he could use her bathroom. No harm there. Sure, why not. A full 15 minutes had elapsed since he had entered the bathroom and had not yet exited. Anne looked at the closed door and was becoming a bit concerned. Perhaps the dinner didn't sit well with her boyfriend. Curiosity got the better of her and so she went over to the bathroom door.

Anne knocked a few times and then asked Jim if he was okay. Jim pleasantly responded that he was fine, and then he ordered her to open the door to see for herself. When she opened the door, she was stunned by what she saw. Her eyes widened as big as saucers and her eyebrows peaked near the top of her head. There was Jim taking a bubble bath of all things, in *her* bathtub! He appeared to be very calm and relaxed, and was enjoying himself as the warm waters soothed him no end. He then extended an invitation for her to join him.

"You've got to be kidding," Anne laughed in response.

"No, I'm dead serious!"

"What has gotten into you? I think that new position is going to your head."

"I wanted to relax, and I didn't feel like waiting until I got home. Now, how about coming in?"

Anne looked at Jim as if he were crazy. Perhaps the giddiness of the announcement that morning affected his brain. She had strong reservations about accepting the seductive inducement, but then, he made a valid argument.

"Oh, c'mon, Anne! I did see you once before without your clothes on. And I promise not to look for any birthmarks. The water's nice and warm!"

Anne gawked in bewilderment. While she maintained an open smile, her forehead furrowed with perplexity. Anne appeared to be thinking about the invite for a few seconds before deciding to do Jim's bidding.

As she was disrobing, she noticed Jim's left arm was hanging over the side of the tub with his left fist clenched. She saw that he wasn't wearing his watch. Ah, but there was a surprise Jim was cleverly hiding until the right moment arrived. Meanwhile, Anne remained quiet as she continued to play along with his game.

When she had gotten completely naked, she carefully placed her feet in the foamy water. She then slowly immersed into the bubbles until she made herself comfortable in a sitting position. As hesitant as she was at first to join him, Anne took great pleasure in allowing the bubbly water to soothe her tired body. A sensuous smile creased her lips as she extended her legs and perched her left foot on Jim's right shoulder and then her right foot on Jim's left. She then playfully splashed a little water in the direction of Jim's face. Some of the soapy bubbles got into Jim's right eye, but he quickly got rid of it, so as not to cause any irritation. He chuckled softly as Anne laughed in return. That was the clincher. Jim was very pleased that she took the bait and seemed quite happy to be with him in the tub. But then came the real purpose for getting Anne to join him in the first place.

"You know," Jim began, "you ought to do something about the ring in your tub."

Anne's smile quickly evaporated. In fact she became indignant toward Jim's statement as she defended her housecleaning practices.

"Where do you come off by that remark? I'll have you know I keep my place spotless, especially in the bathroom!"

Anne was so ticked off she threatened to jump out of the tub right then. That was when Jim gently refrained her from doing so by coming up with a rejoinder.

"No, no, no. You've got me all wrong. I didn't mean the ring *around* your tub. I meant the ring *in* your tub."

And with that, Jim lifted his left arm, which he had purposely left outside the tub to keep dry. He then motioned his clenched left fist toward Anne. And with a twinkle in his eye, he opened it for Anne to see. What appeared in his open palm was a radiant 1½ carat diamond encrusted in an exquisite 24-karat gold setting, surrounded by diamond chips in a circle. The overhead lights gave the ring an alluring luster.

Anne was mesmerized by the ring's beauty. She sat in the tub with a disbelieving look on her face. *Wow!* Unlike her unfortunate near miss with Steve years earlier, Anne knew that Jim's offering was sincere. He took her left arm, reached out and grabbed a nearby towel to dry off her left hand, then gently placed the sparkling ring on Anne's left ring finger. What came next were Jim's heartfelt thoughts.

"You didn't think I was going to St. Louis by myself, did you? I want you, Anne. I need for you to be with me. I want to be your crying shoulder and for you to be my soul mate for the rest of my life. I can't promise everything, but I will promise my devotion toward you. You are everything I have ever wanted in a woman. What do you say, Anne? Will you marry me?"

Anne's eyes began to fill with tears, which began to flow down her soft cheeks as she grasped for the proper thing to say. As she was still searching for words in her delirium, she sprang from the tub to change positions. She couldn't have cared less if some of the water splashed over the tub and onto the tiled floor. She lay down next to Jim and rested her head between the left side of his face and his adjoining shoulder. Still fighting off her tears, Anne responded.

"Yes," she cried. "I want you to be my husband and I want to be your wife! Oh, God! I didn't think this day would ever come to me again! I love you, Diamond Jim Monahan! Did you hear me? I love you! You've made me feel so special!"

And with that Jim and Anne engaged in a long, lus-cious kiss that neither wanted to emerge from. When they finally did, Jim made another announcement.

"I know I told you I'm due to see my agent in New York early tomorrow afternoon. What I didn't tell you is that I had already purchased two round-trip plane tickets. I want you to be with me when I sign the contract. After all, my future is now going to be yours as well. Besides, didn't you say your family still resides in Brewster?"

"Yes," Anne responded as the last of the tears surfaced, "they do. It's about an hour or so by train from the city."

"Well, what better way to make our announcement to them than in person? You can do the bathroom detail when we get back Sunday night. I'll even help you."

"That would be great! And I'd love for you to meet my family. I'll even give you the grand tour of the town, how's that?"

"Awesome! And hey, if we ever run into that Steve char-acter up there, why don't you flash the ring in his face and stick your tongue out at him!"

Anne broke out in wild laughter and promised she would. The newly engaged couple then spent a few extra minutes in each other's arms in the frothy water until it came time to leave, lest their skin wrinkle like prunes.

After they dried each other off and got dressed, Jim told Anne the flight was scheduled on Jet Blue at 10:15 the next morning, with an arrival in New York at around 11:30. It was best to get a good night's rest and to allow ample time to get to Richmond Airport early enough to go through the pre-flight security screening. Anne at first agreed, as Jim told her he would arrive at 7:30 to pick her up.

Before he was about to leave, she took him by the hand. She didn't want him to depart so quickly, not af-ter what had just happened. She reasoned with Jim that they could take a quick nap in the airport before boarding and even snooze on the plane. *A sensible selling point.* Jim smiled and took off the sports blazer he had worn. He then followed Anne's lead into her bedroom for further celebra-tion and sensual stimulation. Jim certainly didn't want to disappoint his new fiancée!

Chapter Thirty-Five

They had spent a few extra hours celebrating their be-trothal the night before in Anne's bedroom, before Jim had to call a halt to their raunchy escapade due to the lateness of the hour. During a small break, Anne had called her parents to tell them she was planning to come up for a brief weekend visit.

"And I have a little surprise for you!" As she said it, she had looked over at Jim with a wide affectionate smile. Anne's mother had guessed she had become engaged. "Um, maybe! That's one of several possibilities!" She didn't want to elaborate and spoil the fun.

The next day Jim and Anne took the flight to New York and arrived at JFK Airport. Because of their short visit, neither one carried much in terms of excessive luggage. Less time in the baggage claim area. *Yes!*

The sun smacked New York with just a smattering of a few white clouds here and there. *Gorgeous early autumn day.* Jim and Anne gathered their belongings to the curbside of the terminal as a sea of yellow cabs awaited them. The first of the taxis rolled up to the couple. The cabbie looked up at Jim and, with a trace of a foreign accent, asked him where he would like to go. *Manhattan, 1165 Sixth Avenue.* After writing a few things down on a clipboard, the cabbie popped the trunk and then exited the taxi to assist with the placement of luggage. *Accomplished. On to the big city.*

As the cabbie punched in numbers on his meter, Jim looked at Anne with a smile. "Well, here we go!"

Anne grinned in return as the taxi sped off toward Mid-town. *Uh oh. Better call Tony.* Out came the Samsung. Jim phoned his agent to alert him when he and Anne were due to arrive.

The taxi zigzagged through modest traffic along the Long Island Expressway. Jim peered out the window for a closer look. He had been to New York several times before, but he was still in awe of Manhattan's majestic skyline and towering office buildings. Anne admired the cityscape as well, although having grown up in the metropolitan area, the city was more commonplace to her. Still, there was the mystique about New York City that held a special place in her heart.

Forty-five minutes passed. Jim and Anne finally arrived in front of the sandstone-colored office building off West 45th Street. Since it was a Saturday, there was no high traffic in the lobby to speak of. The couple approached the attendant behind the console. He was a short, slightly pudgy man with a receding hairline and a pencil-thin mustache. A gold plate was over his left breast bore the name: *Bobby.* Dressed in regalia befitting a Fifth Avenue doorman, Bobby asked if he could be of any service.

"Yes, my name is Jim Monahan. This is my fiancée, Anne Finley. I'm here to see Tony Salerno with the KMC Group. I believe he's on the 23rd floor."

"Could each of you please show some identification and print and write your names on the sign-in log?" Bobby asked in his mousy voice. Just doing his job. Security matters.

As Jim was signing, he asked Bobby if it was all right to leave their luggage next to him. The attendant gave a polite, but subtle nod.

The swift elevator ride took just a few seconds and Jim and Anne arrived at the floor of Tony's firm. The moment the elevator doors opened, there to greet the couple was none other than Salerno.

"Hey! There's my tiger!" Tony was even more gregarious in person than he was over the phone with his mile-wide smile. With black swept-back hair, he had a much thicker mustache than that of Bobby the lobby attendant, Tony approached Jim with a huge bear hug to match his imposing 6'5", 240-lb. frame. Jim reciprocated, although to a much softer scale. In fact, he was concerned if he was going to catch his breath after such a strong embrace.

When he finally released his death grip on Jim, Tony eyed Anne.

"And who's this knockout?"

"Tony, this is my fiancée, Anne Finley," Jim responded with great pride. "Anne, this is my agent, Tony Salerno."

"Fiancée?" Tony was stunned. And then he continued in his accent, associating him with his Staten Island upbringing. "Whoa, Jim! This is a big surprise! I must say, you sure know how to pick a winner! A pleasure to meet you, Anne!"

Tony took Anne's right hand in both of his meaty palms and then planted a soft peck on her right cheek.

Anne blushed. "Thanks, Tony. It's great to meet you, too," she beamed.

Tony then gazed at Anne while slapping his right hand hard over Jim's left shoulder. "Let me tell you something, Anne. This is your guy's lucky day." Tony then quickly turned to Jim. "Am I right, Jimbo?"

Jim simply agreed, perhaps out of nervous fear that Tony might squash him down with that huge paw of his. Tony asked when he had proposed to Anne. Jim casually explained the night before.

"Just last night, huh?" Tony was impressed. "I'm surprised you two still had enough strength left in you to come up from Richmond!"

Tony laughed as Jim and Anne smiled nervously at his illicitly implied remark. He then advised the couple to follow him to his office.

Jim had been to Tony's office a few years before when the Orioles were seriously considering hiring him, but this was the first time for Anne. It was a modest 12'x16' room with a view of West 45th Street below. Various pictures of Tony's clientele graced his walls, most of whom belonged to the broadcasting industry. Jim even recognized two prominent TV network people, one a man, the other a woman, with personalized autographs below their faces.

Anne was more intrigued by an 8"x11" gold framed photo on Tony's desk. Tony noticed Anne smiling at the picture. It was time for the host to elaborate.

"That's me with my family. That's my wife, Linda. Can you imagine we're almost married thirty years? Honestly! But I'll tell you. I wouldn't trade all the tea in China for her. Linda is still my main squeeze and passion, even after all these years! She's something special."

"Aw," Anne responded sweetly. "I take it these are your daughters."

"Yep. That's Brianna. She's 25. And the other is Danielle. She's a freshman at NYU. Hey, that reminds me. You two may not be the only ones with wedding plans. I think it's getting very serious between Brianna and her beau, Christian. I'll keep you guys posted."

"That would be great, Tony," Jim responded.

"Okay, enough of the light talk, guys. Let's talk turkey, or should I say, Cardinal!"

And with that Tony whipped out the contract forwarded by the Cardinals for Jim to review. It called not only for the main play-by-play position for all of the Cardinals' spring training, regular season, and potential post-season games, but also a dozen or so games as the chief play-by-play man on television whenever the team's main TV play caller, Rich Halley, would be called for a network Saturday afternoon assignment.

Another feature was one similar to Jim's present situation back in Richmond. Jim would fill in for weekday sports features and reports on the main radio station that carried the team's games in St. Louis, but only if they didn't interfere with the Cardinals' schedule away from home. The contract called for an annual salary of $300,000 over five years, the bulk of which would be absorbed by KHFR, the station that carried the Cardinals' games. It also called for a number of on air endorsements and personal visits Jim was obligated to do. And there was also a $50,000 advance bonus to help cover moving expenses. Of the salary, Tony's firm would take 10% commission.

Jim just stared at the contract for several seconds to absorb it all. It wasn't the money that had attracted him, although for his sake as well as Anne's, it did carry weight. But what mesmerized Jim was the position he had coveted since his days at Villanova—major league baseball announcer. He had to pinch himself to make certain this wasn't one of his dreams. Maybe he wanted to frame it.

Anne noticed hesitation on Jim's part to sign the agreement. She gave him a slight nudge to snap him out of his trance. Slightly embarrassed, he gave her and Tony a sheepish grin as he reached for the pen, offered by Tony to clinch the deal. The agent was more than happy to oblige as Jim placed his signature on a few pages. *Mission accomplished.* Jim handed the document back to Tony.

"Perseverance finally paid off," Tony smiled. "By the way, the contract commences February the 1st of next year. You'll be obligated to make appearances for the team at various functions and media sessions before you head down to Florida to join the club for spring training. Go get 'em, Jimbo!"

And with that Jim stood up from his seat and gave Tony a hearty handshake. Anne graciously thanked Tony for making Jim's lifelong ambition come true, to which he replied that it was nothing, when in actuality it was a win-win proposition. Jim got the dream job and Tony's firm made some bucks off of it.

"Hey, are you guys hungry?"

"Are you kidding?" Jim responded. "We're starved!"

"We haven't eaten anything since early this morning," Anne chipped in.

"Great! I know of a place not far from here. The food is excellent and the prices are very reasonable for Manhattan. Besides, it'll be my treat. What d'ya say?"

"We were supposed to head up to Brewster to see Anne's family, but I don't think they'd mind if we're delayed an hour. What do you think, Anne?"

"Sure! I'm all for it."

Tony then took the contract and made a copy of it. He handed Jim the copy while locking the original in his top desk drawer.

"I'll send Sam Waldman an email on my Blackberry that we sealed the deal, Jim. I'll also let him know I'll overnight the contract to him on Monday."

Jim, Anne and Tony then proceeded to leave the agent's Midtown office for the bistro Tony had mentioned. Jim still had to splash himself to believe this was all true. He couldn't wait to get behind the mic at Busch Stadium come April.

Chapter Thirty-Six

Jim and Anne enjoyed a delicious late lunch with Tony, and were now riding the Metro North train to Brewster. Anne had called her family on her cell phone and said her train was due at 4:13. Jim was reviewing the contents and finer points of the contract he had just signed hours before, but he periodically noticed Anne admiring the passing scenery of the foliage turning to bright gold, orange and crimson as they fast approached the stop.

When she wasn't looking at the trees and roads, Anne appreciated the gem on her left ring finger. "Our wedding day is going to be spectacular!"

Jim softly smiled. But then Anne's pleasant demeanor suddenly changed.

"What about turning the ring around to hide the gemstone inside my palm from my family? This way I could flash the rock at the same time we make the engagement announcement."

"Very clever, Honey," Jim pointed at Anne. "Now, you see, I am marrying you for your brains besides for your beauty!"

Anne giggled at Jim's quip.

The conductor announced the arrival at their destination over the PA system. The newly engaged couple quickly gathered their luggage and other personal effects as they prepared to head for the exit doors and made a quick departure the moment the doors opened. Once on the platform, Anne told Jim to follow her. Several months removed from her last visit to her hometown didn't fog her memory about where to turn in order to join civilization in the Putnam County village. Anne guided Jim up the staircase at the front end of the platform and then down another to get to street level. And there she advised him to wait at the bottom step while she surveyed the adjacent parking lot. Supposedly her brother was to be waiting there for them to take them to Anne's parents' home. Well, that was the plan.

Jim spent the time glancing around the tranquil and delightful setting of the town square of Brewster. Bucolic and serene scenery speckled with quaint mom-and-pop shops housed in well-kept brick and wooden structures. It was beautiful enough for him to want to sit down at a nearby bench and drink it all in. Before he could be fully absorbed by the charm of the town, however, he heard his name being called by Anne. Time to move. He turned in her direction and noticed she was being escorted by a distinguished gentleman about their age, sporting a full head of dark hair with a matching goatee. The man wore a snazzy mocha-colored leather bomber jacket, with a nondescript sweatshirt underneath, along with jeans and athletic shoes. Time for Anne to bridge the gap of mystery.

"Jim," Anne began, "this is my brother, Tom. Tom, this is my boyfriend, Jim Monahan."

"Boyfreh . . ." Jim responded, puzzled about why Anne introduced Jim that way and not as her fiancé. He was actually stopped in mid-phrase when Anne quickly held up her right index finger on top of her lips. Jim suddenly realized Anne wanted to spring the engagement in front of everybody at the same time, not just piecemeal.

"It's a pleasure to meet you, Tom."

"Likewise. But I really don't understand what you see in my sister, Jim."

Anne tagged Tom across his chest. "Will you just drive us to the house, please? Honestly!"

Jim was amused by Tom's good-natured ribbing, while Anne simply rolled her eyes at her brother's remark.

The trio boarded Tom's Nissan Pathfinder SUV. Jim discovered that Anne's brother was married and was a father of three. Tom also told him that he and his family lived in nearby Mahopac, and that he was a writer for the *New York Times,* mostly on investigative reporting.

"How's the decline of readership in newspapers affecting the *Times* and your job?"

"Well, it has hurt the industry as a whole. People think of the *Times* and think we couldn't be doing so bad because of the prestige the name carries. In essence, print journalism has taken a hit and we're just as vulnerable as everyone else. Say what you want about cell phones carrying the internet, laptops and those iPads and tablets, but when it comes to reading a newspaper, there's nothing like holding it in your hand to read it and not worrying about missing it if you lose it. So what's your line of work, Jim?"

"I handle play-by-play for the Richmond Flying Squirrels' Double A team."

Jim held his right index finger on his lips at Anne. It was his turn to keep a secret. Just as she wanted to wait to spring the surprise of her engagement to Jim, he wanted to inform her family of his new job as the Cardinals' play-by-play job all at once, too. *Touché!* Anne gave him a subtle smile acknowledging his own request for timing.

Tom made a left turn down a road and was slowing his vehicle.

"Well, here we are gang. And please. Don't ever say to Dad, *How are things in Brewster?* To his way of thinking, he resides in Southeast."

"I don't get it," Jim remarked.

"Oh, he always equates the core of Brewster with the immigrants living there," Anne countered. "He's one of those staunch flag wavers. I mean, we all have our love of country, but Dad . . . well . . ."

Tom pulled the Pathfinder onto the driveway adjacent to the house. The edifice was a beautiful A-frame house whose charming exterior would speak a wealth of stories if it could. An American flag, whose size could cover a picnic table, hung limp in the windless air atop a small pole on the front lawn. Tom mentioned that was the influence of his father, a former Marine. There to greet the trio were Tom's wife, Brea, their daughters, Caitlyn and Lara, and their son, Bryce. Introductions were in order as all three exited the SUV. Brea's welcoming of Jim was warm. The children on the other hand, given their age, were polite, but not as enthusiastic. *Typical.*

Meanwhile, Jim was admiring the pale yellow, wooden slat house. A sprawling elm tree stood in front to give the house comfortable shade in the summer. Luckily, there was hardly any damage to the tree from storms past, which could have caused problems for the structure.

"Anne, along with our brother Dennis and I were all raised in this house since childhood," Tom proudly told Jim. "Sixty years old, but well-maintained. That has a lot to do with Dennis' handyman influence. He's got this special knack."

Tom opened the front door and allowed the pair to enter first. Jim was captivated by the beautiful, yet understated décor of the interior. Of particular interest to him were a walnut bookcase, an elegant cherry wood china cabinet, and an embroidered settee, with an intricate sewn floral pattern, that appeared to be there more as show rather than a place to sit. It reminded the broadcaster so much of the quaint charm of the Langston house. A petite older woman in her mid-seventies walked in from what Jim presumed to be the kitchen.

Anne addressed the older woman with a, "Hi, Mom!" The two women embraced each other and exchanged soft kisses.

"Mom, this is my boyfriend, Jim Monahan."

"Pleased to meet you, Jim," Anne's mother replied as she gently shook Jim's hand. "I'm Doris."

As Jim replied in kind, a second person of similar age came down from upstairs. He had a shock of white hair on his head and a face that resembled a mountainous road map. Jim knew the man had to be the patriarch of the Finley household. He was slightly intimidated as he recalled the first time he had met Maureen's father years ago. Then a thought occurred to him. He realized he was older than he was when he first met Maureen's dad and could relate to Mr. Finley better. Besides, Jim was a father of a daughter, and there would come a day when Madison's beau would fear him. The anxiety factor abated. Still, he felt a lingering hint of trepidation.

Just the same, Anne's father examined Jim like he had just landed off a flying saucer. Anne walked up to her dad and gave him a hug. Placing a soft kiss on his face, she introduced her father to Jim.

"How do you do, Mr. Finley?" Jim said warmly as he reached out to shake the patriarch's hand.

"Boyfriend, huh?" The elder Finley was reticent to reciprocate. That was his nature, especially given the fact he was a veteran of the armed forces and was brought up to be suspicious of unknown parties. Mr. Finley didn't seem too keen on the idea on the relationship forged between his Anne and Jim. That was when Doris intervened.

"Oh, Pat, lighten up, for God's sakes. Jim seems to be a nice man."

Where was Anne's other brother, Dennis? Doris explained he might not come around until well past seven that evening. Anne was anxious to reveal the news to her family. Like a pot of boiling water about to gush over the sides, she could not contain herself. Dennis would have to be clued in later.

"Listen, everyone, I have something to tell you," Anne began.

"Uh, let me explain my secret first, since it does go hand in hand with the other," Jim interceded.

Anne yielded to Jim. He made a slight apology to Tom, because he didn't tell the whole story to him when he was driving them to the house. Jim explained that he was hired by the St. Louis Cardinals as their play-by-play radio announcer next spring, with some work on TV doing games on occasion. Pat, being a big time baseball fan and loyal Yankees diehard in particular, was impressed. Unexpectedly that gruff veneer Pat had put up earlier fell away. Jim was extremely pleased to see the reversal in Pat, accentuated by the patriarch's acceptance. Even Doris and Tom were amazed at learning the news. But now there was the really important announcement. Jim smiled at Anne as she stepped up.

"Jim and I are engaged!"

Anne proudly turned around the gold band on her left ring finger to show the dazzling rock for everyone to see. A roar of approval went up as everyone took turns kissing and congratulating her. Tom was the first person to walk up to Jim to extend his congratulations.

"Welcome to the family, Jim," Tom smiled as he and Jim shook hands.

Both Doris and Brea went up to Jim and each gave him a kiss and a hug. But now it was Pat's turn. *Hmm, this might not sit well.* He didn't show much emotion at first toward Jim. Instead he came out with what appeared to be a stern warning.

"Be careful, Son," Pat began. "You'd better be good to my Anne. I'm an ex-Marine, you know."

"Yes, sir," Jim replied. "I can assure you I will do everything to make sure Anne is accorded with every amount of love and companionship I can give her."

Then Pat did something out of left field. He walked up to Jim, shook his hand and gave the announcer a firm pat on his right shoulder, "Take care of her, Jim." Jim smiled back at Pat and gave Anne's father his solemn oath that he would.

"Hey," Doris chimed. "Pat and I have a bottle of Moet champagne with a 1991 vintage that we've been saving for a momentous occasion and I declare this as the one!"

As Doris went to retrieve the bottle, there was a discussion about when the marriage would take place and where. Pat brought up the fact that the Finley family was Catholic. Much to their delight, Jim told everyone he was brought up in the same faith. But there was a matter of Jim having been divorced. The idea Jim was once married and broke his union with his first wife did not sit well with Pat. Anne had to set the record straight with her suspicious father.

"Dad, I'll have you know Jim's first wife cheated on him and had a baby with the man she had an affair with," Anne began. "She was the guilty party. I don't think you can condemn Jim for that, can you?"

"You should cut him some slack, Dad," Tom piped in.

Even Doris came to Jim's aid. As reluctant as he might have been, Pat conceded and gave Jim his proper due. But then the elder Finley brought up a point of contention. He would like to see his daughter married in a church in front of a priest. How could that possibly happen with a divorced man, a fellow Catholic no less? Jim offered a possible solution.

"I have been preparing myself for that scenario ever since I thought about buying the engagement ring for Anne. I read that the Church has this thing called a Decree of Invalidity."

"You mean an annulment, don't you?" frowned Pat.

"No, not exactly. That would make the daughter my first wife, Maureen, and I had together illegitimate. This would require presenting a formal case before the Church with purpose to prove the shallowness behind our marriage. I'm hoping Maureen's act of infidelity may prove how insincere she was about our marriage to begin with."

Doris posed a question. "When are the two of you leaving back for Virginia?"

"We have a seven o'clock flight tomorrow night," Anne responded.

"Why don't the two of you come with Pat and me to church tomorrow and speak with Father Carlo afterward to get his reaction?"

"I think that would be great, Doris," Jim replied. "And seeing this Father Carlo brings me to another point. Since Anne and I will be moving to St. Louis eventually, we think it would be great to have the wedding done here before the move. My family comes from the Philadelphia area and it won't be a big deal for them to come up here."

A local wedding. What could be better? The family gave a big thumbs up of approval. Tom, Brea and Doris offered to help coordinate the ceremony and reception festivities. Both Anne and Jim mentioned that they didn't want anything too ostentatious. Although this was to be Anne's first trip down the aisle, she pointed out her age and didn't feel the need for anything too extravagant. As for Jim, this would be his second marriage and he didn't need all the pomp and circumstance accorded his first time. Tom offered a suggestion.

"What about the Arch Restaurant on 22?"

Tom's choice was met with universal approval. Doris commented how the food and atmosphere were very good there and Anne's recollection of the size of the place was just right, given the fact they expected fewer than one hundred guests to be there.

Although Jim and Anne hadn't set a date, they projected sometime in late January would be ideal for the ceremony, since they would have to be house-hunting in the St. Louis area before the start of spring training in late February.

"Well, Anne," Jim said to his fiancée, "I guess that's another place we'll have to hit after seeing the padre tomorrow."

"The only thing you guys will have to worry about then would be if we get socked with a snowstorm that day!" Tom added.

"Bite your tongue." Anne smiled at her brother.

With all the talk abuzz concerning Anne's engagement to Jim and the initial wedding plans themselves, Doris had completely lost track of time. Suddenly she went into a dither about the roast and other accoutrements connected with dinner. Anne quickly volunteered to assist her mother, with Brea ready to lend a helping hand, too. Brea decided to drag Tom into the kitchen to have him help with some of the more arduous tasks.

Jim felt like the odd man out and wanted to aid the others, but Pat stopped him in his tracks.

"C'mon, Jim, you need to stay with me. The Yankees have a playoff game on just about now. Besides, there are a lot of questions and topics I'd like to discuss."

This was the skull session Pat wanted to go over with Jim. Anne overheard what was going on, and she gestured to Jim without Pat seeing her to humor him. Jim shrugged his shoulders and agreed to keep the Finley patriarch company.

Chapter Thirty-Seven

Roast chicken, complemented by braised asparagus spears, wild rice, and carrots. The dinner won the hearts of everyone, with the exception of Pat. He would have preferred a thick, juicy sirloin porterhouse, but had to acquiesce because his red meat-disdaining daughter was present.

Brea had given permission to her daughters and son to watch television while the adults remained at the table. Naturally, the discussion centered on the wedding plans and reception. While the Arch Restaurant was on the A list to visit the next day before Jim and Anne skipped town to head back down to Richmond, Tom asked what kind of musical entertainment they had in mind. It was actually a rhetorical question. When Jim and Anne were stuck, Tom offered a solution.

"I've got a good friend who is a musician. His name is Matt Caswell. I believe he's a part of a band. Let me ask him if his group would be available and what they would charge."

"Having a live band would be great," remarked Anne.

"And I can have one of my photographers from the *Times* shoot the pictures. How many can say they had their wedding photos shot by a *New York Times* photographer?"

"Hey, don't forget my brother is very good with a video camera," Brea piped in. "He has all the latest stuff and has professional editing equipment."

"And as for flowers," Doris added, "my very good friend, Elaine Paxton, runs a nursery and floral shop in town. I can quiz her about possible floral arrangements."

Jim smiled and shook his head at the outpouring of everyone's suggestions and efforts to make his eventual golden moment with Anne a memorable one. He was eternally beholden to Anne's family for their offerings of ideas and support.

"Gosh," Jim pleasantly remarked, "Anne and I are overwhelmed with all of your help."

Pat was practically the forgotten man at the table, what with all the nuptial banter going on.

"I couldn't care less about all of this frivolous talk," Pat began. "As far as I'm concerned, I would just as well order take-out for the reception and have it here in the house. And then I'd play a few Frank Sinatra records for the musical entertainment. Yeah, that's how I'd like it."

Needless to say, his suggestions were laughed off by everyone. However, Pat was giving the visitor a stern look. Jim had spoken of his daughter, Madison, to everyone. Anne even told her family how she had forged a very good bond in her brief time with Madison. Anne had lived away from the Finley home for quite some time. But she was also three times the age of Jim's daughter. A full-fledged adult. How would Jim feel moving further away from Madison, just an adolescent? If his current distance and infrequent visits with her were bad enough now, imagine the distance he would have to make up between St. Louis and Philly. Pat broached the subject with his visitor.

"I was just a bit curious, Jim. How often do you see your daughter?"

"During the Squirrels' regular season, I can only go see her when Richmond is playing in either Harrisburg or Reading. You know, towns within an hour's drive from Philly. During the off-season, I make every effort to go see her at least once a month. A few times I've gone twice a month."

"That's got to be tough on you, and I imagine it's hard on her, too. But let me ask you. How do you think she's going to feel about you moving to St. Louis? I think they only play the Phillies once a year in Philadelphia, right?"

Jim was getting a little uncomfortable with Pat's grilling and was beginning to squirm. He began tapping his right index finger on the table as a sign of nerves. It reminded him too much of Michael Langston and his penchant for instigating. But unlike Michael's case, Pat had every right to ask these questions to the man who was going to marry his flesh and blood. Perhaps Pat wanted to test Jim on his level of devotion. After all, if Jim gave an answer that made him come off as a little uncaring toward Madison, how could he muster up any love for Anne? Jim had to come up with some answers, even though everyone aside from Pat would rather have him sidestep the issue. *Think fast.*

"We haven't really had a chance to discuss it yet, Pat," Jim began. "Oh, I told her nearly two months ago about the possibility of me going there. Needless to say, Madison wasn't too thrilled with the idea at first, but then she supported me. Personally, I wish Madison could come with us. Anne has met Madison and the two of them got along great."

"Madison, I take it, lives with your ex-wife, right?"

"Yeah."

"Tell me something, Jim. What was the reason you never got custody of your daughter after the divorce?"

"The judge ruled that I'm not home half the time while I'm having to cover the baseball team on the road. There wasn't anyone there to act as guardian while I was away in Erie or something."

"Is that why you want to marry Anne, to have a nanny caring for your Madison?"

Gulp!

"No. Anne and I had this very same discussion a few weeks ago. I'm going to give Anne all the love and care she deserves. But just as you love and have concern for your daughter—otherwise you wouldn't be asking me these harsh questions—I also have those feelings toward my daughter. But to be frank, I haven't mapped out that plan yet, if I do it at all."

Tom saw where this was going. He didn't want the magnificent news of Anne's announced engagement to be disrupted by their father. He asked Doris if the coffee was ready, perhaps an intro to change the subject. When she said it was, Tom volunteered to get it for everyone. Brea and Anne told Doris to sit while they retrieved the two apple pies and whipped cream for dessert.

"Gosh, two pies?" Jim queried.

"It was the end result stemming from the last of the basket of apples we selected from the orchards a month ago," Doris replied.

While everyone was dashing about getting various plates and cups, sugar and milk to go along with the coffee and dessert, Jim wanted to take a moment to speak to Pat in private.

"You know, underneath that ex-Marine exterior lies the heart of a devoted husband and family man. You may not want to express it, Pat, but I can tell by your eyes."

"Oh, do you now?"

"Yes. And do you want to know something? I can picture myself in ten or fifteen years from now grilling the young man who wants to marry Madison. What are you going to do for a job to help support Madison, Son? How much do you really love her?"

"I got news for you, Jim. Doris' father was the same way with me fifty years ago."

Pat broke out in laughter over the thought. Jim joined him. And that was a good sign. Perhaps the old veteran wasn't so tough after all, as a softer side was emerging.

Chapter Thirty-Eight

At Doris and Pat's urging, Jim and Anne spoke briefly with Father Carlo at St. Lawrence O'Toole Church after Mass the next day. Time to come clean without the privacy of a confessional box. Jim had mentioned briefly to Father Carlo about his previous marriage and how it could be declared invalid. The priest, who had yet to celebrate his thirty-seventh birthday but was already in line to be elevated to the title of Monsignor by the Diocese's Archbishop, didn't have the time to talk at length or discuss the matter in detail. He did, however, ask Jim if the baseball man could email him all the criteria associated with it. Jim wrote down Father Carlo's email address.

"I promise I'll have something sent to you tomorrow," Jim mentioned.

"I'm not altogether pleased to hear of your previous failure down the aisle, Jim," Father Carlo replied, "but I promise I will view the topic with complete openness."

There was another piece of unfinished business left before they were to head back down to Virginia that evening. Early that afternoon, Doris and Brea took them to meet with the people who ran the Arch Restaurant. Anne had been to the restaurant a few times in her past, but it had been some time since her last visit. This was Jim's first.

Brea drove up the long secluded driveway that accented the quaint building. Jim loved the country home exterior and the rich, cherry wood arched door. The baseball man was particularly drawn to the elegant stone column chimney at the front of the establishment, which said all were welcome.

Once they stepped inside, he was captivated by the exquisite décor—so much so that he was oblivious to the hostess trying to communicate with him. Anne asked if the manager was available to speak with them regarding the usage of the bistro for her upcoming wedding reception. As the hostess walked away, Jim continued to marvel at the place. He liked the candelabra lights adorning the rich walnut walls. Doris couldn't help but notice his affection toward the restaurant.

"I see the place meets with your approval," Doris smiled.

"Hey, what's not to like? The place looks superb!"

A woman almost the age of Anne emerged from the back. She was smartly dressed and walked toward Jim and the others with an air of sophistication. The woman's beauty was only matched by that of Anne.

"Hello," she warmly greeted everyone. "I'm Jill McIntosh, the General Manager. Colleen was telling me you're interested in booking a date to hold your wedding reception."

"That's right." Anne smiled in return.

"Why don't the four of you please come with me to the back room?"

Jill led them to a private room that held about 80-odd guests. The intimate appeal was just right for Jim, because he was expecting only a mere handful of guests on his side, while Anne's extended family wasn't exactly large either. Still, neither Jim nor Anne were willing to commit until they saw what Jill had to offer. The blonde asked them to have a seat while she went to another area to obtain a book with charges.

Jim watched as Jill continued her way toward the back office. He then turned back to Anne and looked at her hair. Anne's expression wasn't favorable. She looked like she knew what he was thinking and decided to squelch his thoughts.

"Don't even think about me dying my hair blonde!"

Jim burst out laughing. Doris and Brea also joined in the amusement, although Anne maintained a serious air about her statement.

In a short time Jill returned with a heavy bound book. She reviewed a myriad of options with Jim and Anne, as Doris and Brea observed as interested parties. After the crunching of numbers, it wasn't long before the newly engaged couple decided upon one of two possible dates in late January, which would still leave them with ample time to house hunt before Jim was to report to the Cardinals' camp in late February. As a sign of good faith, Jim even allowed Jill to charge $1,500 to his credit card toward the eventual payment of the reception.

The selection was complete. Among the only things that stood in the way were the date, what food to serve, and finalizing the payment. Jim and Anne were relieved the first hurdle was cleared, while Jill was happy to book the wedding dinner.

With the restaurant mission accomplished, Brea drove Jim, Anne and Doris back to the house. It wouldn't be long before the couple would say their goodbyes to the Finley clan and prepared to head back to Richmond. Things were coming together for Jim. But there was still one element left, which Pat had touched upon the night before. It was irritating Jim in the back of his mind.

Chapter Thirty-Nine

The jetliner took off from JFK Airport without a hitch. Jim and Anne rested comfortably in their seats as the plane headed toward Richmond, with a brief layover at Baltimore-Washington International.

Despite having a window seat, Anne preferred reading the magazine she had picked up at Kennedy as darkness prevailed over the early evening sky. Jim, meanwhile, reclined in his seat, trying to catch some zees. However, the thought that niggled at him as they had left the Arch Restaurant that afternoon had returned to torment him again. The alarm clock, in the form of Madison's future, kept ringing inside Jim's head, so much so that he couldn't keep his lids entirely shut.

Anne couldn't help but notice her fiancé staring into space. "Hey," she began softly, "what are you thinking about?"

Jim didn't want to bring up what was on his mind so readily. He needed an excuse. "Oh, it was great to meet your family and all. And their help and hospitality were great. But I would also like to introduce you to my family. How about we drive up next Saturday? My folks will put us up just as your family did. What do you say?"

"That'd be great!"

"I've already told them about you. And now I've got better news for them." He saw that his answer wasn't totally acceptable to Anne. *Perhaps her own intuition is kicking in,* he thought. Jim wanted to hold it back. But she had a look that said she wanted to flush out the entire truth from him.

"I know you told me your family doesn't live that far from where Madison lives. You're not planning on swinging by that house with that bitch of an ex-wife of yours there, are you?"

"Well," Jim confessed, "I do want to see Madison. Perhaps if you can stay for a short time with my family while I visit her, that would be best. Maureen's not any fonder of seeing you than you are of seeing her."

"Are you going to tell Madison of our engagement?"

"Absolutely. It wouldn't be right if I didn't. But, uh . . . there is something else I'd like to discuss with her." Jim hesitated for a few seconds before continuing. "I'd like to ask her if she would be willing to move with us to St. Louis."

Jim knew Anne wasn't surprised that the subject would come up again. They had discussed it a few weeks ago when leaving the Langston house, and, of course, Pat brought up the same topic the night before.

"You know," Anne began, "I remembered when you first approached me on the idea before I met Madison." Anne sighed. "I fondly recall how the two of us clicked, especially after that nearly disastrous mishap in the bowling alley parking lot. I'll let you in on a secret, dear. I really don't look at myself as a caretaker for Madison. Quite the contrary, I'm beginning to believe I could serve as an alternate mother and help give her the guidance she seems to crave." Then Anne smiled as she stared up at the cabin's ceiling, reminiscing over the bond they had forged, and then looked at Jim with great warmth. "Okay," Anne beamed, "let's go for it!"

"Do you want to know something?" Jim asked rhetorically. "The more I look at you and talk with you, the more I know I'm making the right decision taking you down the aisle with me."

Anne giggled as she and Jim embraced in a passionate kiss.

One of the flight attendants strolled by and noticed the couple smooching. The plane was about to descend at Richmond Airport, and there was the issue of making sure the passengers were securely fastened to their seats. She nervously smirked at the thought of interrupting them, but there was the matter of her job obligation, plus safety regulations. Clearing her throat certainly got their attention.

Jim and Anne abruptly ceased their lustful exchange. Both looked awkward as they turned their attention to the attendant, sheepishly belting themselves in. The attendant smiled and continued to walk down the aisle to check on other passengers.

They peered at each other a moment before breaking into spontaneous laughter, thinking about how they were caught in the act of *necking*. They might be middle-aged, but they were acting like a couple of teenage high school sweethearts. And there was nothing wrong with that.

Chapter Forty

It was back to the old grind again for most people the following Monday morning, but this was no ordinary start of the week for Jim. The new voice of the Cardinals met with Zach Moser when he first got in, asking if he could make his defection announcement on Vince Wallace's morning talk/news program. *Green light. Go for it.* Zach gave Vince the okay to do a lead story involving Jim, but not to reveal the story until the news director asked Jim about it first, over the air. The announcement was no surprise for Vince. The moment Tony gave word to Jim on Friday that he had gotten the St. Louis gig, news around the station had spread like wildfire. But despite all the talk, not a word was mentioned by any of the station's on-air personalities that weekend. And the only Richmond listeners who knew of Jim's hiring were Anne and a sprinkle of others.

The on-air announcement had to have the dramatic build-up, though. Hey, ratings sells spots! And Vince played along with the gag to perfection. A couple of times he cryptically informed his listening audience of some important news involving one of the staff announcers, but he wouldn't reveal much in order to tease the listeners into staying on to find out.

Finally the time came for Jim to come on with his first sports report. As was his custom, Vince asked a lead-in question to Jim before the baseball man opened up with his report, trying to soften the hard edges. But Vince didn't want Jim's opinion on how the Top 25 faired on Saturday in college football, or the spectacular ending to the baseball playoff game between the Phillies and Reds, or even how the Redskins lost to Detroit. This was a question which would hit Jim hard.

"So, Jim, I've been telling the audience since I first came on that there was an important bit of news that had to be leaked out, and I understand it involves you, is that right?"

"Uh, yeah."

"Well, all of Richmond would like to hear, my friend. Tell the audience what the deal is."

"Actually, it's two things; one thing I'm sure you weren't even aware of, Vince."

Vince raised his eyebrows, but didn't say a word. But now the news/talk show host was as curious as the listeners.

"First of all, with great regret, I am leaving the station and my job as the announcer for the Flying Squirrels. I'll be moving to St. Louis next spring to take on my new role as the play-by-play man for the Cardinals."

"Whoa!" Vince gave the audience his best impression of being surprised, although he, like the rest of the staff, knew of Jim's imminent departure. "Did you hear that, folks? Diamond Jim Monahan is moving up to the big time! Hey, maybe it won't be too long before you'll be on ESPN!"

"Let me work on the Cardinals' job first."

"You mentioned there was a second bit of news, Jim. What can possibly top that?"

"Well, Vince, I'm not going to St. Louis alone. I'll be getting married over the winter."

This announcement floored Vince like a torpedo sinking a battleship. The newsman wasn't prepared to handle this one. At first there was silence as Vince looked at Jim with astonishment. But, ever the showman he was, Vince had to recoup and get back his swagger.

"Did I hear you correctly, Jim? You're getting hitched?"

"That's right."

"Oh, my God! Well, Jim, I'd just like you to know you've broken the hearts of a lot of ladies listening in. So, who's the lucky gal?"

"Her name is Anne Finley. Annie, babe, if you're listening right now, I love you!"

There was still the matter at hand with Jim having to do his sports report, but it didn't appear he, Vince, or anyone else at the station, cared if Jim had to give his report or not. The focus seemed to have shifted to Jim's personal life, and that was okay.

Jim still had to give his report several times again. And by the time the eight o'clock hour rolled around, news of his upcoming changes would seem old hat. However, for the time being, Jim once again was making the news, instead of reporting it! And even Vince was going to milk it for all it was worth.

Chapter Forty-One

Talk about news traveling fast, the station had gotten a phone call from the TV station where Amy Johnson worked. The news of Jim's defection to the big league St. Louis team and his announced engagement sprouted wings, and Amy's news department caught wind of it. The blonde reporter was wakened out of her sleep by her bosses after being on the air the night before reporting on a building collapse in the city. They could've selected another reporter, but the hierarchy knew Amy had developed a rapport with Jim since the Alan Langston rescue story two months earlier. To hell with rest. Amy was sent out on a mission.

Zach Moser had been contacted by the TV station, who said that they wanted to conduct an interview with Jim on the announcement. The station manager gave them the green light to come over, as long as it didn't interfere with Jim's schedule of air time. *Why not? More free publicity for the station.*

As Amy and her crew sped their way to the radio station, Jim prepared for yet another sports report. *Eight thirty-two.* The novelty of his double news flash had worn off considerably, although Vince introduced Jim each time with some comment regarding the big changes coming the baseball man's way. Vince was happy for Jim as much as he was working at rousing the ratings gods.

Laura Mazursky walked into the open area where Jim was revising his script. The heck with reporting to Zach first. She immediately strutted toward him with open arms and a broad smile. Caught off-guard, Jim couldn't help but stand to receive her greeting.

"Jim! Congratulations!"

Laura and Jim hugged each other as she kissed him on the cheek. Jim had to release his gentle grip on Laura so he could get back to work.

"You know," Laura continued, "Anne never called me about the news. I'm a little upset at her for that."

"Please don't be angry at her, Laura," Jim responded. "I only proposed to her Friday night. And then I took her with me Saturday morning up to New York to sign the contract for the Cardinals' job with Tony Salerno. I knew she had family up in Brewster, which isn't that far from Manhattan, so we visited her family that afternoon to break the news to them. We didn't return to Richmond until about eight last night, and boy, we were exhausted."

"Okay, I'll make an allowance. I still need to speak with her. So, when's the big day?"

"Probably late January, just before we move to St. Louis."

Just then, Laura's phone began to ring. She answered it and was told by the receptionist that Amy and her entourage had arrived to do the story on Jim. Even the baseball man didn't expect them to come that soon. He told Laura to relay a message to them that he would be available once his 8:40 report was over with.

Zach overheard the discussion. While he enjoyed the added publicity with the camera crew at his place, he didn't want them to linger too long. Zach motioned to Lisa Hillenbrand to tell Vince the news/talk host would have to double as the sports reporter on this one occasion. As he saw Lisa take off, marching orders in hand, Zach then gave instructions to Laura.

"Tell Maggie to let the TV crew in."

Zach's directive stunned Jim. *Skip a report?* Nonetheless, he put aside the report he was prepared to go with and saved it for his 9:10 slot. Seconds later, Amy and her crew infiltrated the station. Amy spotted Jim and immediately gave him a similar greeting to Laura's earlier. Jim joked that he couldn't remember the last time so many women came up to him with such enthusiasm.

"Are you ready, Jim?" Amy asked with a broad grin.

"Let's go for it!"

Shortly thereafter, the glare of the TV lights came on as Amy delved into her hastily prepared questions for Jim. He answered all of Amy's queries. The TV reporter then quickly interviewed Zach and, for a brief moment, grabbed Vince's attention during breaks. When she wrapped up her taping, Amy approached Jim once again.

"Is it possible I can ask your fiancée if the crew and I can interview her at her job?"

"Hold on, Amy. Let me ask her for permission."

He dialed her work number, knowing she had a penchant to get in a few minutes early. Four rings, then she answered.

"Hey, Love," Jim began. "Did you sleep well last night?"

"I didn't feel like getting up, but I did."

"I made the announcement of the new job and our engagement at 6:10 this morning on the air. Did you hear it?"

"Yes," Anne replied with a grin, "and that was so sweet of you. I love you, too."

Jim then switched gears and told Anne he had just been interviewed by Amy Johnson and that the TV reporter wanted to get her reaction. She told him her company probably wouldn't allow the cameras to be permitted on the premises, especially since she had yet to speak to her superiors to inform them she would need to leave the Richmond office in due time. How about a phone interview instead? Back to Amy.

"Anne's company isn't too keen on the idea of your crew being there, but if you want to ask her questions, I'll hand the phone over to you so you can speak to her."

It wasn't the whole loaf she was looking for, but Amy accepted Jim's offer. She took the phone from him and pleasantly spoke with Anne. All the while, Jim was enjoying every second basking in the spotlight. Just then he remembered a phone call he had to make from his apartment later. It would be to Maureen and it would concern seeking her permission to see Madison that upcoming Saturday. None of the negative vibes running Jim's mind about his impending conversation with his ex were ones he wanted to share with Amy, for fear of spoiling the moment.

Chapter Forty-Two

Jim was relaxing that early afternoon in his apartment. He had received many calls on his answering machine. One of them came from Marty Leary, who couldn't believe Jim was turning in his fraternity sweater of the Divorced Men's Society of Richmond. Jim did call Marty back, and even went so far as to invite him, as well as Ed Holtermann, informally to the wedding. What was more shocking was that Marty accepted. It appeared bygones would be bygones and that everyone had a right to change his or her own mind on views now and then.

Jim then dashed off an email to Father Carlo, as he had promised he would. Jim had dirty laundry he had to put out, and he pinned down Maureen as the perpetrator. It pained the baseball man to write the letter and to recall some awful memories of a life that once was, but he knew a written missive was the only method he could possibly use to pave the way to accelerating the process and gaining the acceptance to get the church wedding Pat Finley and others wanted them to have.

And then came the moment he really dreaded. Jim had to place the call to Maureen. To him, talking to his ex was the equivalent of a heroin junkie sticking himself with needles, if only to get a fix of nirvana later. Maureen was the needle. Spending quality time with Madison was the intoxicating bliss at the end.

Jim finally got up with the nerve and dialed Maureen's number. When she answered at the other end, he felt uneasy. Her voice alone sent a chill down his spine. But this was no time to equivocate. He pressed forward.

"Hello, Maureen. It's Jim."

"What the hell do you want? I suppose you'd like to see Madison."

"That's right. In fact, I'd like to see her this Saturday, if you don't mind."

"You'd better not bring that hooker with you!"

Oh, if Jim could have reached his hand through the line, he would have shoved Maureen's face into a wall! He wanted to throw the phone across the room, but not before telling Maureen to go fuck herself. However, he knew he had to keep a level head. Pressing his legs down to suppress his pent-up rage, Jim calmly held his tongue and with great composure restated his request, while assuring Maureen that Anne would not be present.

"If you were referring to probably the sweetest and the most well-mannered woman on the planet, no, Anne will not be there. Now, can I see Madison on Saturday, please?"

With an economy of words that weren't laced with any more venom, Maureen conceded to his wishes. Knowing he had achieved his main goal, he hung up to avoid any more conflict with his ex.

He sat on his easy chair and stared into space. Maureen's caustic remark burned in his gut like acid. So much so that he just wanted to take things and break them to release his suppressed anger. After all, it was bad enough that Maureen treated Jim without any respect. It was another thing entirely for his ex, with such an unflattering reputation herself, to refer to Anne the way she had. He clenched his fists and closed his eyes in order to make the anguish and fury go away.

However, his anger turned into sadness. A couple of tears streamed down his face. Perhaps he felt he had failed to defend Anne's honor against Maureen. Perhaps his own manhood was threatened. Then his thoughts turned to Madison. If there was any more important reason to save Madison from the Bell household, it was Maureen's inflammatory comment about Anne. Not only had he seen Madison as a square peg in a round hole in the Bell household, but he needed to change Madison's outlook on life, which could affect her for years to come. He didn't want to see Maureen's abusive and obnoxious traits rub off on his daughter. He needed to see her grow to full maturity with Anne's sweet and loving disposition.

The thought of taking Madison away from Maureen became more of a crusade, and Jim prepared himself for the battles ahead.

Chapter Forty-Three

Without an ounce of hesitation, Anne agreed to go with Jim to meet his family that Saturday and break the big news to his side. The weather wasn't suited for going anywhere, with heavy rain up and down the northeast corridor, but that didn't dampen their spirits.

Unlike Anne's hometown of Brewster, Wayne, PA, still hadn't thoroughly embraced the fall, but a few trees here and there had leaves of a bright gold, crimson, and orange. It would be a another week or so before autumn would make its mark on the Philadelphia suburb, and then two more after that before the branches would become bare.

Jim drove up to the driveway leading to the ranch-style house on Penn Road. It had been a few months since he'd visited his mother and sister, but his family understood he totally had to devote his entire free time to seeing Madison in nearby Bryn Mawr. Baseball snagged the rest.

A luscious lawn graced the front of the simple brick home. Near the front door were a pumpkin and two gourds, a sure sign of the season.

Hearing the car arrive, Jim's sister, Diane, emerged from the house. She was average looking with glasses. Diane had boyfriends in her past but she never married. She was resigned to living the rest of her life as an old maid, but that was fine with her. Marriage was never a priority with her. Maybe she ought to get together with Michael Langston. A perfect *singles* couple.

"Hey, little brother!"

Diane embraced Jim briefly as each gave the other a soft peck. Jim heard Anne clearing her throat behind him. Hey, that was the cue for introductions.

"Oh, Diane, this is my girlfriend, Anne Finley."

The two women pleasantly shook hands.

Meanwhile, Jim surveyed the house and grounds. The majestic maple trees shielded the home on either side. Diane looked at Jim as if he hadn't been there before. She commented that the place hadn't changed since he was there last. Jim just smiled. It felt good to return to his roots once more, like seeing an old friend.

"How's Mom doing?" Jim asked.

"Why don't you go in and see for yourself? Oh, Dan and Alice are here, too." She referred to their older brother and his wife.

With Anne in his shadow, Jim entered the house. Sitting in the living room watching some mindless television program was his mother, Mary. Well into her eighties, Mary was a frail woman who could get along by herself when Diane was at work, but she needed her daughter's assistance on weeknights and weekends. However, the question remained about how much longer that part time attention would be enough. Diane was at least ten years away from retiring from her state office job, and she was hoping she wouldn't have to rely on a home care attendant. But Diane was preparing for just such an emergency, should Mary falter. *Back-up plan. Good thinking.*

Mary was still mesmerized by the mind-numbing show. Jim stood alongside her and tried to get her attention, but she was still transfixed to the tube. He didn't want to resort to it, but he was forced to shut the TV off with the remote in order to make his presence known. Startled by the sudden loss of picture, Mary turned around and then noticed Jim. She looked up at him and was immediately startled. Mary held her right hand to her chest and smiled.

"Jim! Oh, I'm sorry I didn't see you come in."

Jim raised his hand to signal his mother not to get up. He then bowed to kiss her on the left side of her face and introduced Anne. Just then his older brother, Dan, holding a lager in his left hand, entered the living room along with Alice. Jim and Dan gave each other a bear hug. After he exchanged kisses with Alice, he showcased Anne.

"Where are Eric and Alexandra?" Jim asked, referring to Dan and Alice's adult children.

"Eric's out with his girlfriend," Dan commented. "What's this now, Alice, number seven for this year?"

Everyone laughed at Dan's comical response. But Alice playfully slapped him to set the record straight.

"No, it's not!"

"Sure seems that way. Oh, uh, Alexandra went with some old college friends of hers up to New York City."

"That's where we were last Saturday," Jim countered. And then with a little dramatic pause, he revealed why he and Anne were in the Big Apple. "I had to sign that contract with my agent. You're looking at the new play-by-play man for the St. Louis Cardinals."

Everyone cheered and clapped over Jim's new job, joining a special elite circle of announcers who report activities at Major League Baseball games. He absorbed all the plaudits and congrats from his family. Then he made the second big announcement, that of his marrying Anne. Dan and Alice were equally as enthusiastic in hearing that bit of news, too. They stepped forward and welcomed Anne personally with a lot of affection.

Diane and Mary were a different matter altogether. They had seen Jim shot down like a duck in the sky after what Maureen had done to him. Even though he was more than capable of making his own rational decisions, given the fact that he was approaching 50, Diane and Mary were a little protective of him and didn't want to see him get hurt again. *A lot of ambivalence here in their reaction.*

Jim couldn't help but notice their restraint. He had to convince them Anne was not Maureen number two! He took his right arm and stretched it across the top of Anne's back. Cupping his right hand on top of Anne's right arm and drawing her closer to him, Jim addressed the skeptical ladies.

"I know what you two are thinking," Jim began his speech. "Here's this crazy guy thinking the second time around is going to work. Well, let me assure you, Anne here is a completely different person from Maureen. She's much sweeter, more outgoing when you get to know her well, and I think, ten times prettier than Maureen."

"Well," Mary began, "as long as Anne makes you happy, Son, that's what matters most."

"Me, too," Diane responded. And then she turned toward Anne. "Please, Anne, this is no disrespect toward you.

It's just that my mother and I saw what Maureen did to Jim. I'm sure you can understand."

"Hey, don't worry about it," Anne assured the both of them. "I had the privilege of meeting Maureen a couple of weeks ago. I wasn't too fond of her either."

It appeared the barrier had been broken. Diane embraced Anne and welcomed her into the Monahan fold. Respecting Mary's physical problems, Anne bowed down toward Jim's mother to receive the elder Monahan's blessing, which pleased Jim very much.

Dan asked if he was going to see Madison now that he was so close. Silly question. Jim told his older brother he was . . . alone. He then explained to everyone that Anne wasn't welcome at the Bell house and asked if they would mind entertaining her while he visited Madison. Besides, it was only twenty minutes away. No one minded in the least. In fact, it was a great way for everyone to familiarize themselves with Anne and get to know her personally, and she them.

Jim kissed her and told her and the rest he didn't plan to be too long with Madison. It would be just enough time to make it a quality visit.

Anne looked at Jim and asked, "Are you going to ask Madison about what we discussed last weekend and how she would feel about it?"

Ever the curious eavesdropper, Diane cocked her head as a sign of inquisitiveness over what Anne was referring to. She approached her younger brother.

"What's Anne talking about?"

"Uh, I'll explain later," Jim answered.

And with that, Jim walked out the door. As he approached his car, he attempted to formulate the proper way to approach Madison on the subject. Then he said to himself, *Screw it!* and decided to wing it. With the rain having abated somewhat, he slowly pulled out of the driveway.

Chapter Forty-Four

Maureen was her sweet, lovable self when Jim arrived, which was the equivalent of being involved in a train wreck and calling it a pleasure trip. Pleased that he didn't have Anne in the front seat with him this time, the dour Mrs. Bell gave him a stern warning to make sure he brought Madison back to the house by six that evening. He did everything but press his hands together and bow. Jim assured her he would uphold his end of the deal as Madison exited the house and headed promptly toward the passenger side up front with her father.

Jim warmly greeted his daughter as she stepped inside the car. *Fast food? Absolutely!* Slowly pulling out of the driveway, he was relieved to put Maureen in his rearview mirror and watch her grow small and distant.

It wasn't long before he and Madison came across a Wendy's restaurant and decided to eat there. Once they got settled at the table with their food, it was time for him to open up the dialogue he needed to exchange with his daughter. He took a big gulp of his soft drink and sighed.

"I didn't bring Anne with me so that your mother wouldn't rant and rave like she did a few weeks ago, but that doesn't mean I didn't bring Anne with me to the area."

Madison's eyes brightened when Jim told her the news.

"Do you mean Anne's here?"

"Yeah, she's with Grandma Monahan and Aunt Diane. Uncle Dan and Aunt Alice are over there, too."

"Could I see Anne and everybody else?"

Jim checked his watch. *Two twenty-five.* He did a quick calculation in his head. He figured it was only fifteen minutes to his mother's home in Wayne. If they finished their meal within the next ten minutes, it would leave a good two and a half hours to visit his side of the family. That was plenty of quality time to spend with them. And even though the time spent with his family would infringe on his own personal time alone with her, he figured it was worth the sacrifice, judging by Madison's reaction to hearing that Anne was up there, too. Jim agreed to take her there on the sole condition that she was not to say a word about it to her acerbic mother. Madison consented to her father's compromise.

After taking another bite of his chicken sandwich, he thought it was the right time for him to disclose his latest bit of news.

"The St. Louis Cardinals hired me to broadcast their games beginning in the spring."

Madison knew two months before that the prospect of Jim being hired by the Redbirds was a strong possibility.

"I guess I'll be seeing less of you," Madison replied with mixed feelings in her tone, "especially during the summer."

"Uh . . . yeah," Jim sighed remorsefully.

Then Jim dropped the bombshell that he was marrying Anne. Whoa! Jim had to go into spin control.

"Look, I . . . uh . . . I'm sorry if that upsets you, Maddy. I mean, I didn't . . ."

"It's okay, Dad," Madison interrupted. But her saddened face told a different story. "I feel a little happy inside for you. Really. I'm glad to see you're rebounding from being divorced from Mom. But it'll also mean I'll hardly see you and Anne."

Jim noticed Madison's crestfallen appearance. The time was right for him to make his third revelation. This, however, was going to be in the form of a question. "Honey," Jim began, "you and I have had some strong and candid conversations in recent months. But besides words I've also noticed your body signals and facial expressions when it comes to staying with your mother, Harley and Reed. I can see you want to break away."

"Oh, Dad. It's not that, really."

"Then what is it? Madison, I have been fooled in the past, but not this time. Now I can tell."

"What makes you so sure?"

"Women have intuition, but men have gut feelings." Jim paused briefly before continuing. "Hey, remember when we ate at Pat's in Philly back in August? You brought up the fact that no judge would side with me if I had petitioned to have you come live with me on account of my being away for so long doing road games with no one else home. Well, you're fast approaching 16, which is certainly old enough to fend for yourself until someone was to arrive until, say, five or six. That's where Anne comes in. What I'm trying to say to you, Madison, is that both Anne and I would love to have you come live with us. We're getting married in late January and then we'll move out there shortly after. Now, I don't want to make you feel uncomfortable. This has got to be your decision and, trust me; there is no right or wrong answer here. If you need to spend time thinking about this, I'll understand. This is something you have to think over clearly. It can't be a rash decision. And just like the other things I spoke to you about, I don't want you mentioning this to Mom. Okay?"

Madison nodded in agreement. But despite Jim's suggestion of wanting her to mull it over, she appeared to have made up her mind.

"Dad, I want to live with you and Anne."

Upon hearing her answer, Jim sprang from his seat and Madison rose from her chair as the father and daughter firmly embraced each other. A tear could be seen streaming down from the corner of Jim's left eye. He kissed Madison on top of her head as he began to loosen his grip on her. With great joy written across his face, he told Madison to finish her lunch so they could go over to Wayne. Madison smiled and assured him she would speed it up.

Chapter Forty-Five

Jim's family was delighted to have seen Madison. They just lived a few miles away from Bryn Mawr, but for Mary, Diane and Dan, they might as well be as far away as Jim, for all the visiting time Maureen afforded them. And while she was happy to see her paternal grandmother, aunts and uncle, Madison was especially pleased to see Anne again, and Anne felt the same.

"Dad told me that you two are getting married," Madison began. "I think that's pretty cool! Did he get you a ring?"

"Yep," Anne smiled. "Take a look!"

Madison was spellbound by the dazzling gem in the same way Anne had been in her bathtub the week before. She made a remark to her father that he had good taste. Jim smiled and politely bowed to Madison in accepting her plaudits.

"Listen up, everybody. Anne and I would love to have Madison come live with us. And Maddy has gladly accepted the offer!" Jim announced to his family.

Jim's siblings pulled him off to the side. Diane and Dan were concerned about the legal grounds to pursue the matter.

"You better get a better lawyer than the one you hired when you were divorcing Maureen," Dan cautioned.

"I promise I will, Dan. But I also want to make known the fact that the circumstances will tilt more favorably to my side this time. There'll be an adult home when I'm away with the team, plus Madison is more mature and is desperately looking to get away from Bryn Mawr."

However, Diane was adamant that Jim choose the right lawyer wisely. Cocking her head slightly, Diane remembered a good friend of hers who had gone through a terrible divorce and was successful in getting everything she deserved.

"Let me call Valerie and get the name of the attorney she used."

Upon overhearing the conversation, Anne agreed with Diane that they needed to use someone who had a good track record. Jim might have seemed a little uncomfortable being forced into a decision, but without a compass to point him in the right direction, Diane's solution appeared more sensible.

"Please, Diane. Let me know as soon as possible."

Jim looked at his watch. Gee, almost five. He reminded everyone the witching hour was coming up. Trying to inject some dry humor, Diane made a sarcastic remark to make certain Jim emphasized the *witch* portion of the word in an obvious reference to Maureen's caustic demeanor.

Jim took exception. "As much as I agree with you, I still have Madison present, and Maureen is still Maddy's mother. Just please tone down the negativity."

All at once, Diane conveniently remembered seeing on TV earlier that a program on wedding preparation was coming on one of the Discovery channels. Dan interrupted, stating there was a big college football game he wanted to see, but Diane reminded her older brother this was *her* house and that she paid the cable bill. Goodbye Ohio State vs. Penn State. Hello *Bridezillas*.

Jim told Madison he had to take her back to Maureen. While the adolescent was not pleased to be saying so long to her dad's side of the family, she was more saddened to be bidding Anne adieu. That was when Anne reeled Madison in to give her comforting thoughts.

"Hey, it's not the end," Anne said. "In fact, your father and I will do all we can to make sure we take you with us to St. Louis."

Whatever frown Madison wore moments earlier at once vanished, replaced by a bright smile with the soothing news that Jim and Anne wanted so much for Madison to be a part of their lives on a full-time basis. Jim knew this is what she craved.

With farewell exchanges having been completed, Jim took Madison with him to return to Bryn Mawr. Madison assured her father she was sworn to secrecy about her visit to his family and Anne, and of what Jim and Anne's plans were for her.

"Zip the lip!" Madison giggled.

Jim gently stroked the back of her head and smiled.

Chapter Forty-Six

As miserable as the weather was on their way up to Pennsylvania the day before, they were surprised by a complete 180-degree turnaround with abundant sunshine and temperatures hovering to near 70 for their return home. Before they left, Mary and Diane extended a Thanksgiving invitation to Jim and Anne, which the newly engaged couple accepted happily.

Jim was driving on the Beltway around Washington. Anne, who had been sleeping in the front passenger seat since they scooted past Havre de Grace, awoke abruptly. With a big yawn, she grumbled slightly and began to look around at the surrounding landscape. One tree looked like the other. She couldn't distinguish where she was. Looking over at Jim, she gently stroked his arm. He stole a quick glance at his lover and offered a smile. Anne reciprocated.

"Did you have a good snooze?"

Anne was still trying to extract the few remaining cobwebs from inside her head. "Yeah," she yawned in reply. "It did me good. By the way, where the hell are we?"

"We're on the DC Beltway, I believe in Prince Georges County. A weekend day on the Beltway is better than driving it on a weekday. Besides, I didn't feel like driving through the Capital District. I've seen the Capitol Building before."

Anne didn't say anything in return, which was an indication of her agreement with Jim's route selection. As she continued to be attracted to the green scenery around her before it, too, would change colors in due time, she said, "Your family was very nice. And your brother, Dan, is some comedian."

"Oh, he's a character all right."

"And it was great to see Madison, too. Tell me, how was she when you took her back to Maureen's house? I mean, she didn't say anything about what happened yesterday, did she?"

"Not a peep. Maddy acted as though nothing else had happened. And that's the way it should have been."

Anne extended her left hand to stroke Jim's right thigh gently. For a split second he glanced at his affectionate fiancée and gave her an appreciative grin, letting her know he liked it very much.

Jim continued to press for home. As he arrived at the Virginia border near Alexandria, he began to reflect on three major hurdles he thought he would never attain. He finally got his plum big league job, found a new soul mate, and possibly wrestled Madison away from Maureen. But there would be no imperiled Alan Langston to help him achieve notoriety to impress the Cardinals, nor an intrusive but concerned Laura Mazursky to latch Jim to the love of his life. What would it take for Jim to achieve the triple play? What would it take for him to get Madison? And for all he had accomplished in the last two months, there would still be many hearts broken if he couldn't reach for that last brass ring, the most important of which was having Madison be with Anne and himself.

Anne noticed his furrowed brow. She didn't have to ask. The hurdle to leap over to get Madison was the most difficult. She had to give Jim some comfort and ease his mind. "Hey," she began, "I know what's bothering you. I want you to know, Honey, that not only am I one hundred percent behind you in getting back your daughter, but I feel very confident we're going to win."

Jim was curious why Anne thought that way. "What makes you so sure everything's going to turn up roses?"

"Instincts." Anne looked at some more scenery before continuing. "You don't seem confident about a lot of things, Jim."

"What do you mean?"

"I mean I'll bet you didn't think that big baseball job was going to come through, and it did."

"Well, you haven't known Tony as long as I have. I've been promised the golden lode by him many times in the past, and all I got was the dirt of the earth. Let's just say I was skeptical."

"Okay, and what about when Laura first told you about me? You didn't seem so sure it would work."

"How do you know? You weren't even there!"

"Oh, we girls do talk to each other," Anne smiled.

"Oooh, just wait until I see Laura tomorrow!"

"Hey, be nice!"

Jim smiled to assure Anne he was only kidding about doing anything diabolical.

"In a few months, we'll be Mr. and Mrs. Monahan. That worked out!"

"Yes, it did."

"So, why not the idea about getting Madison? Look, Jim, if you keep up with this negative thinking of yours, you'll never get her. No lawyer will want to represent you, unless you feel like throwing money away. And as for the judge, if you come off as indecisive, then for sure he won't rule in your favor. You've got to show a strong conviction. You've got to have a backbone. I'm not trying to nag you about this, Sweetie, but I'm just telling you what's for your own good. It won't bode well for you if you don't."

Jim knew Anne was right. It was time to show some nerve and push forward. Anne noticed his countenance improve, and she hoped her little morale boosting pep talk had changed his outlook.

Chapter Forty-Seven

Jim was relaxing in his apartment late Monday afternoon. He had opened his email and found very good news. Much to his surprise, both from the quickness of its decision and the outcome itself, he received a notice from Father Carlo. His church approved the matter of moving forward with the wedding ceremony to be placed, based on the stipulations agreed upon. Jim was very pleased and wrote back to the priest to thank him for the great bit of news and to say he and Anne would arrive at a date very soon.

The baseball man called his fiancée to let her know of Father Carlo's decision.

"Great news, Love," Jim opened. "I just got an email from Father Carlo giving us the green light for the wedding at St. Lawrence O'Toole!"

"That's terrific!" Anne exclaimed.

Now she could tell her family, especially her traditionalist father, that the sacred ceremony would take place within the walls of her hometown church. Jim wanted to call the Arch Restaurant and inform Jill McIntosh of which date they would select.

"Hey, it's Monday, Jim. They're closed on Mondays. I'm looking at their business card stating so. In fact, they won't be open until Wednesday."

"Damn," Jim sighed, "you're right."

"You could still call the marriage license bureau in Brewster. Just gather all the necessary information we'll need to obtain the license."

"Good point." End of call.

He was about to phone Brewster and find out the number to call the bureau when he received an incoming message from Diane. She had the name of the attorney recommended to her for him to consider hiring in the matter of taking custody of Madison from Maureen. He quickly gathered a pen and a piece of paper and wrote down the name of the lawyer. *Thanks Diane!*

"It's only four thirty," Diane remarked. "There's still a chance you might reach the attorney before the day is through."

"Great! I'll call him the second I get off the phone."

That was a cue for Diane to hang up so he could make the call. "Until next time, sis." Chat over.

Jim stared at the name and number of the lawyer for a while. David Epstein. It wasn't the attorney he had used when he and Maureen went through their divorce years before, so right off the bat it was a sign of improvement. Besides, Jim was in a much better position than he was during that fateful time in his life when he and Maureen parted ways. Still, with some trepidation and a degree of skepticism, he studied the name one more time before picking up his phone.

He dialed the cute number Epstein had: 610-555-4LAW.

After a nominal wait, he heard an automated greeting. *Ugh! One of those. Okay, just play along.* He punched in a number from the menu selection and waited hopefully to be transferred to Epstein. Instead, a woman came on the phone. Unfazed by the delay, Jim identified who he was briefly and that he was referred to Epstein. The woman began taking down some information from the baseball man. *Oh, great,* Jim thought. *The guy isn't even in!* But, lo and behold, the woman asked him to hold for a moment while she connected him to Epstein. *She must be some sort of gatekeeper to weed out any joker trying to get through to her boss.*

A couple of minutes had passed before Jim was finally able to hook up with Epstein. It was a cordial exchange which lasted but two minutes. In the end Epstein invited Jim to his office for a free consultation to discuss the matter further. As much as he dreaded traveling to the Northeast for the third week in a row, he knew this was important enough to sacrifice his body and make the special effort. He agreed with the attorney to meet Epstein on Friday at three o'clock in the afternoon. For that to happen, he would have to take time off work, which required a little chat with

Zach Moser the next day. Legal business. Zach would understand.

After hanging up the phone, Jim glanced at his watch and realized he had promised Anne he'd call Brewster to learn the requirements of obtaining a marriage license up there. Which meant he had to make another call . . . *immediately!*

Chapter Forty-Eight

With Zach's blessing, Jim was able to take off the following Friday, allowing him to take another trip to the Keystone State. Actually, Jim had left Richmond the previous afternoon. Mary and Diane were more than happy to put up lodging for him that Thursday evening so he could feel well rested before seeing David Epstein.

Anne would have loved to come up with him, especially since she had a stake in the Madison custody matter, too, but her job was too demanding for her to get away. Anne did encourage him about meeting with the attorney, and felt confident he would represent the two of them well.

The skies were a mixed bag as a threat of rain imposed itself upon the area. Jim drove his battle-worn Civic for the 20-minute drive to Epstein's Norristown office. The leaves were turning more and more, and with November only a week and a half away, it wouldn't be long before the trees would become totally bare.

Jim parked his car in the rear lot of the two-story red brick building that housed the firm of Garrett, Epstein and Kohner. A slender woman in her late twenties, sitting behind a desk, received him upon entry. The receptionist was keying in information on her computer, but she was fully aware of Jim's presence.

"May I help you, Sir?" The woman asked the question without even looking at him. He thought it was rather peculiar for her not to glance at him at least, but perhaps it was her way of multi-tasking.

"Yes, my name is Jim Monahan. I have a three o'clock appointment with Mr. Epstein."

The receptionist finally broke away from her data entry and offered a seat to Jim while she called Epstein's office. Much to Jim's surprise, the woman flashed a hint of a smile at him as a way of welcoming him to the office. *Well, she actually does have a pulse,* he thought.

After confirming with Epstein that Jim had arrived, the receptionist returned to her typing duties. It was like nothing had happened as the young woman cocooned herself. Jim then took her advice and sat down on one of the plush chairs in the waiting area. Once settled, he looked around the light-colored walls with the firm's name in raised lettering above the woman's head. A few potted ferns and a couple of paintings graced the sides of the room so as not to give the place a completely sterile look with its eggshell walls.

He noticed an array of various periodicals arranged in neat rows. Jim was almost afraid to touch them, given the attention the receptionist no doubt accorded them. He decided to pick up one of magazines that began one of the rows, a two-week old edition of *Time.* Jim began to leaf through it when he heard his name being called. Stunned by the surprise announcement, Jim looked up in the direction of the voice. There in a doorway stood a thin man in his mid thirties. He wore a conservative gray pinstriped suit with a cranberry necktie over a traditional white cotton dress shirt. The man also had a pair of horn-rimmed glasses and dark, close-cropped hair.

"Hello, I'm David Epstein." The man smiled as he extended his hand for a shake.

"Nice to meet you, Mr. Epstein," Jim reciprocated, giving the lawyer a firm grip.

"Won't you come this way, please?"

With Epstein leading the way, the two walked up a set of carpeted steps and veered to the left at the top. There, Epstein walked into his office and asked Jim to have a seat. As the lawyer opened a manila folder and began to scan a few pages of notes, Jim glanced at the room. Behind Epstein's high-back leather executive chair was a collection of books containing past cases, which Epstein no doubt used for reference. Standing between Jim and the lawyer was an oversized walnut desk. A few knickknacks graced its surface, although the one thing that stood out the most was a picture of Epstein, a woman near his age, a young boy and a baby. Jim presumed the others were Epstein's wife and children. His mind wandered around the room some more as Epstein continued to review a few more pages. Jim spotted a couple of pictures of a schooner and a square-mast rigger. *A boating enthusiast. Maybe I should introduce Epstein to Marty Leary's plastic surgeon client, Dr. Seymour Klein. Perhaps the two of them could go fishing together on Klein's boat.* Jim smiled at the hilarious thought.

Suddenly Epstein said the word *so.* It snapped Jim out of his line of thinking as the baseball man then gave his undivided attention to Epstein.

"I reviewed the notes of our conversation on Monday," Epstein began, "but perhaps you'd like to fill me in on other details."

As painful as it was for him, Jim recounted the time Maureen came up to the area and visited her family a few years ago and that fateful night she ran into Harley Bell. And then along came their child. But the damage had been done already as Jim and Maureen were headed for an ir-revocable severance. Jim told David how he lost in the cus-tody case because of his job as a minor league baseball announcer and the requirements the title demanded with relentless road trips. He paused for a moment. Instead of dwelling on negativity, Jim switched gears to reflect on all the marvelous things that had happened to him lately.

"Well, thanks to some notoriety from saving this guy's life a couple of months ago, my agent said the Cardinals were interested in having me try out for their soon-to-be vacant head play-by-play job."

"The Cardinals? As in St. Louis?"

"Yep. One and the same. I met my agent up in New York two weeks ago to sign the contract with the Birds."

"Congratulations, Mr. Monahan. But you've still got road games to cover."

"Well, yes, but I just exchange a bus ride for a plane flight. It's still the same time difference."

"What I'm trying to say is that your daughter is still alone. Sure she'll be 16 in a half-year, but she's still a mi-nor. There is no adult supervision or guidance."

"I've got some more news for you. I'm getting married in late January. And my wife-to-be has a typical nine-to-five job. She and Madison have hit it off pretty well. Anne, that's her name, will take good care of Maddy whether I'm in Chicago or LA."

"That still might not convince a judge to overturn a decision in spite of what love and care your fiancée might provide for your daughter."

Up until then Jim had been calm in his dialogue with Epstein, except recalling Maureen's tryst. But now he was growing desperate, in need of a legal miracle. "You don't understand, Mr. Epstein. My daughter can't stand being in that house anymore. Maureen practically ignores her. Where the hell is the love there? She needs me, and I need her. And I'm confident Anne will give Maddy all the love and affection as if she were her own child. Maddy will run away if I turn my back on her now! I swear she will! And to what, who the hell knows? Please, Mr. Epstein! I need your help!"

David sat back in his chair. He pursed his lips while resting his extended fingers against them to absorb the situation thoroughly. David told Jim he would have to engage the services of a psychiatrist to analyze Madison. Jim raised his eyebrows at the thought, but David gave him lucid reasoning. If the psychiatrist can get to Madison and find out the cause of her angst of remaining in the Bell household, it might help justify Jim's plea to get his daughter out of there. And this brought the consultation to another major point.

Up until then, Jim had identified Maureen only by her first name. He told David only that Madison lived with Maureen and her husband in Bryn Mawr, which is part of Montgomery County, hence the need to fight this in the county seat of Norristown. But David wanted to learn more. The lawyer began to write down on a separate piece of paper the new last name of Maureen and the identity of her husband.

"She's married to Harley Bell."

David released the grip on his Cross pen. The attorney convulsed briefly, like a deep-seated fear arrested his body. He stared directly at Jim and for several seconds did not say a word. David needed to confirm the name.

"Did you say Harley Bell?"

"Yes, that's right. Do you know him?"

David sighed and reclined back in his chair. He removed his glasses and started to rub his eyes. That was when David revealed both he and Harley served as members of the board for the Montgomery County Business Development Council.

"I also know what Bell does for a living and the money he makes," David continued. "They can hire a very good lawyer for their side."

Jim was getting pissed off. It served notice as a red flag that David would rather wash his hands of the whole deal. Jim decided to deliver a punch to the gut. "Listen! Are you afraid of damaging your relationship with Bell as a fellow board member, or is it that you're not confident in beating their hired suit?"

Now David's pride was under attack. He glared at Jim at first with the baseball man thinking David wasn't up to the challenge. David told Jim, "Let's go," as he picked up Jim's gauntlet. David then mentioned he would require a $2,000 retainer, plus expenses for documentation and court appearances. Jim promised the attorney he would mail a check next week to cover the retainer. Offering Jim his business card, he stood up and shook hands before his new client departed. Jim was relieved the hurdles were finally cleared. Game on.

Once outside the building, Jim trotted to his car. *Got to make a call.* He hastily phoned Anne at work. After all, she had told him to call her once he was finished with Epstein. Seconds later he got through to Anne and explained their exchange.

"Well," Jim began, "Epstein was a little hesitant at first to represent us because of a conflict of interest and Harley's money, but he finally decided to push forward."

Anne was relieved Epstein was going to take the case. But she then asked Jim a direct question.

"Are you confident in hiring Epstein after he balked at first?"

Jim hesitated for a moment. A degree of lingering doubt spun inside his brain, but those thoughts were soon zapped away. He issued a statement of conviction that accepting Epstein would be a wise choice after all. He then told Anne he loved her and would see her tomorrow evening after he returned to Richmond.

Chat with Anne done. Ignition turned over. It was on back to his mother's house in Wayne to discuss the matter with Diane and Mary. The wheels to get Madison back were in motion. But was Jim truly convinced about selecting Epstein, or was he just kidding himself?

Chapter Forty-Nine

A little more than a month had passed since Jim met with David Epstein. Everything was coming together like a jigsaw puzzle. The date for the wedding had been set for Saturday, January 29th with the ceremony to be conducted at the St. Lawrence O'Toole Church in Brewster at two, and the reception at the Arch Restaurant at five. Jim and Anne would tie up the marriage license issue in person when they were to travel up to Brewster around Christmas to see her family. Tom Finley's friend, Matt Caswell, agreed to perform, along with his band, at the reception. Laura Mazursky agreed to be Anne's matron of honor, while Dan consented to being his younger brother's best man. The invitations had been sent, along with a note of Anne's bridal registry. And Doris and Brea picked the Sunday immediately after Christmas to hold a very modest bridal shower for Anne, given her brief visit with the clan that weekend.

There was still the matter of where Madison would wind up. Jim and Anne were praying the situation would be long resolved by the time they exchanged their vows.

They drove up to Pennsylvania a day earlier before their Thanksgiving Day dinner with his family. The early arrival gave Jim the opportunity for Anne to meet briefly with David Epstein. It was nearly one o'clock that Wednesday afternoon, and David wanted to get a jump on the holiday weekend, too. But knowing there were some minor loose ends to be tied up, and that Anne was curious to meet with him, David agreed to stick around for them.

Much to their delight, Jim and Anne were informed by David that the papers to proceed had been filed with the Montgomery Courthouse and that a tentative date to appear had been scheduled for Wednesday, January 12th. Before long, Maureen would be served notice, thus forcing her to hire her own legal beagle. Jim gladly signed a few more pages. Enjoy the holiday!

"I'll be in touch, should there be any late developments," David remarked.

"Thanks again, David," Jim said with a smile.

Buoyed by David's encouraging signs, Jim and Anne wanted to have a modest celebration. They were starved after the long drive up from Richmond. There was a diner across the street. Its glistening silver façade was well-maintained as was the surrounding shrubbery, and judging by the vast number of cars in its lot, the couple's impression was that the eatery had a good reputation for its food, cleanliness and service. Since they were not due to be at his family's house until after three, the decision to eat at the bistro was a no-brainer.

The hostess immediately greeted Jim and Anne and swiftly sat them in a booth halfway into the establishment. Once they were settled in with their menus, the hostess told them their waiter would be coming soon.

The interior was even better looking than the manicured exterior. And the glistening throwback soft drink logos gave the place a look of nostalgia, harkening back to the days when juke boxes ruled the scene. Clearly they had made the right choice of eatery.

As Jim was perusing his menu, he asked Anne her impression of David.

"I think you made the right choice," Anne replied. "I really like David. What's more, I'm pleased the procedure is moving along in a timely manner."

At that point a young man of dark complexion came over and poured water into each of their open glasses. After thanking the young man, Anne switched gears in the conversation. "I'm glad Madison is going to be there tomorrow."

"Well, I usually get Madison for Thanksgiving," Jim explained. "It's been that way every year since Maureen and I split. I always come up to see my folks on Turkey Day, so my family and I get Maddy for the day, while Maureen keeps Maddy for Christmas."

"You don't get to see Madison for Christmas?"

"Hey, there are a heck of a lot of days I don't see her. Besides, it's all part of my guy/gal theory concerning the holidays."

Anne sported a quizzical grin and cocked her head as she asked, "Guy/gal holiday theory? Oh, this ought to be good."

"Well, it's like this. Y'see, on Thanksgiving Day, men like to get together and watch pro football, so their wives, girlfriends, or in my case, exes, don't mind allowing the kids to be with Dad's family. I personally think it's all a plot by mothers so that fathers can't watch sports. On the other hand, women love the charm and beauty of Christmas and they want to be around their children with *their* families. What it really amounts to is a trade-off. I mean, just look at us. You're with me and my folks tomorrow and I'll be with you and your family for Christmas. See? It's the guy/gal theory."

Anne just laughed and shook her head at Jim's unfounded explanation as she took it all in her stride.

Their lunch decisions were made. Time for the waiter to arrive and take their requests.

Chapter Fifty

Jim picked up Madison from Maureen on Thanksgiving Day without incident. Apparently Maureen had not yet received notice she would be summoned to appear in court over the custody of Madison. It would have been ugly if she had already known. The only person under that roof who knew what was about to happen was Madison, and she was going to keep that under her hat until the time permitted itself. Madison wanted out of there anyway. As she had explained to her father, she looked at herself as a prisoner waiting to be paroled.

Another thing Maureen wasn't privy to was that Anne was with Jim and that she would be reunited with Madison for the second time in little over a month. Again, better to keep Maureen in the dark. Anne assisted Mary, Diane and Dan's wife, Alice, in the kitchen preparing the stuffing for the turkey as well as sweet potatoes, asparagus, carrots, and string beans to complement the bird. Occasionally, Jim and Dan also aided the ladies to ensure the meal would go well. Madison passed some time talking with her cousin Alexandra, while Eric looked somewhat disinterested in the Packers-Lions game on the tube and listened through headphones to his iPod. Green Day ruled over Green Bay.

When it came time for dinner, everyone sat in certain seats, with Jim being flanked by Madison to his left and Anne to his right. The sumptuous meal was spread out across the long linen-draped dining room table. Beverages of all types were laid out, from wine and beer, to apple cider and soft drinks. Before anyone had a chance to start to fill their plates, Diane offered a prayer of grace. Everyone clasped their hands and bowed their heads in respect.

Not long after everyone selected their choices, Dan rose from his seat. Holding his glass of white Zinfandel to the ceiling, he proposed a toast. He waited for everyone to pay attention.

"Folks, I'd like to wish Jim and Anne good luck with their new lives together."

Diane looked at her brother curiously. "Aren't you supposed to save that speech for January?"

"Yeah, but there's nothing wrong with saying it now, too."

Everyone raised their glasses and clanged them with whatever person's glass they were near. But just when they were through with their sip, Dan made another remark.

"I also want to wish Jim and Anne success with the courts in getting Madison away from that Wicked Witch of the Western Philly suburbs."

An even bigger roar of approval pervaded throughout the room. Maureen was not a welcomed name, and no one dared mention it for fear of getting a shiv in the back. Glasses were raised once more. Jim nodded to his daughter, giving her every bit of assurance he could that it was indeed going to happen.

When dinner was finished, everyone chipped in with clearing the table. Food and beverages were put away as Diane and Mary prepared a care package for Dan and his family to take home with them. Since Jim and Anne were staying overnight again, and Madison had to be returned later that evening to the Bells, no separate items were stashed away for them.

Over an hour later, Diane, Anne and Alice graced the table with two huge pies, one pecan and the other pumpkin. There was a generous helping of freshly prepared, real whipped cream and vanilla ice cream to slather on the desserts. Coffee and other beverages were also served for all to choose from.

However, Jim, Dan and Eric would have none of that. Their bellies were full and the tryptophan from the turkey spurred on drowsiness. Instead, the three men decided to brave the crisp 45 degree temperature in the backyard sitting on metal chairs, with glasses of aged scotch and custom-made cigars in hand. Smoking was not permitted in Mary's house, so the trio had to resort to smoking the stogies in the dark autumn chill. Six o'clock. Nightfall had already enveloped the land. The patio light was the sole source of illumination preventing the men from tripping over themselves.

The three of them were chewing the fat over a vast array of subjects, from Eric's female carousel to Jim's new position and the outlook for the team. Then Dan brought up the subject of the court hearing.

"So, how confident do you feel about this guy Epstein representing you and Anne?"

"I'm, uh, I'm good," Jim replied hesitantly.

"You don't sound so sure of yourself."

"There was this matter of Epstein and Harley Bell being members of the same County Board, but Epstein gave me his assurance there wouldn't be any conflict."

"I hope not, for your sake."

"Well, I look at this way. Politicians are all of the same cloth more or less, yet they bang themselves over each other's heads to get the positions or win approval on bills."

"That's true. I just don't want you winding up like you did the first time with that nutcase you had for an attorney."

"The circumstances are all different this time."

Diane popped her head out from the screen door. She saw her brothers and nephew sipping and puffing away. Not pleased, she frowned and just shook her head in disbelief, feeling the need to reprimand. "At least you should be inside with us, Jim. You've got your fiancée in here with us, and I'm sure you don't want her to get the idea this'll be your way of relaxing all the time after you get married. Besides, your daughter is inside, too. Before you know it, you'll have to take her back to Brunhilde."

Jim sucked in his lips in a point of embarrassment. *Yeah, Diane is right.* He downed the last of the scotch and put out what was left of the cigar. Excusing himself from the conversation, he trudged back inside.

Dan pointed at him as he remarked to his bearded son, "Now, you see that, Eric?" Dan asked rhetorically. "This is what you have to look forward to should you ever finally settle down with a woman."

"Gee," Eric chuckled, "maybe I should keep searching. What do you think?"

"Hell, yeah! My god, you've got your whole life still ahead of you! And believe me. Mom and I are in no rush to be grandparents anyway."

Meanwhile, Jim had to trade in his conversation of politics and the latest gadgets on the market for hearing subjects he'd rather avoid. But he promised his sister he would remain with the women inside. Jim was only hoping Dan and Eric would become numbed from the cold, forcing them inside, too.

Chapter Fifty-One

The following Tuesday was exhausting for Jim. Not only did he have to perform his usual broadcasts, but he also did some promos and even had to appear at one of the station's local sponsors, a local tire dealer, to sign autographs. With everything, he didn't get back to his apartment that afternoon until well past three.

When he arrived, he noticed the answering machine was blinking with three new messages. He played the first two. One was from Marty Leary, while a second was a solicitor. The third call, however, was the most interesting. It was from Maureen, and her expletive-laced message came over like a bullhorn. Apparently she received the summons to appear in court over Madison's custody. Jim just sat in his easy chair and listened with amusement to Maureen's diatribe. He creased a small smile and thought how wonderful it was to get under her skin. He played it several times and, as he heard each play, his level of laughter rose. But at the end of her message, Maureen demanded Jim call her immediately. He was going to seek out David Epstein for his legal advice on how to approach Maureen, but then figured his attorney might not even be in. Besides, Epstein would probably encourage Jim to call Maureen to establish some dialogue, but Jim knew it would probably amount to a shouting match.

He even thought about calling Anne to get her take on the subject. Perhaps he could play Maureen's tape for Anne's enjoyment. But then he rationalized it was best just to call his ex and approach her head-on. *Get the darn thing over with. Nothing is going to change Maureen.* Eyes closed, he took a deep breath. Jim had to muster every ounce of strength before he reached out to his ex. With his nerves fortified, he started dialing Maureen's home number. Four rings. She came on the line.

"Hello, Maureen. I got your . . . uh . . . message."

"What the hell are you trying to do, you goddamn bastard?"

"Trying to save Madison, what do you think I'm doing?"

"You've got some fucking nerve to think you're going to take Madison away from me! Well, I've got some news for you! You're not going to win! You tried before and it didn't work!"

"The circumstances have changed since then. First of all, in case Madison never told you, I'm getting married."

"Oh, and you think marrying that hussy is going to change everything?"

Just as he did a month earlier when Maureen lauded Anne in a similar light, Jim held his tongue. He closed his eyes and counted to three in his head. Then he clenched a fist and made an impression with it on a sofa armrest. This was Jim's way of getting around the unnecessary, nasty epithets being dished out by Maureen, and to release tension. He just wanted to pretend he didn't hear that callous reference.

"Anne will be there for Madison when she comes home from work when I have to go on road trips with the team, which by the way will not be the Richmond Flying Squirrels, but the St. Louis Cardinals. You see, I have gone and moved up the ladder despite your beliefs that I wouldn't amount to anything."

"Big freaking deal! I suppose that changes everything! Well, did it ever occur to you that our daughter is going to be a latch key kid until this Anne person comes home?"

"Oh, I must commend you for referring to Anne by her first name and not one of your more colorful terms. But to answer your question, I don't think Maddy will have a problem. You may be in the house by the time Maddy arrives home from school, but your presence is as significant as a speck of dust! Anne will give Maddy the love and attention our girl needs in the limited time they're together, more than you ever will!"

"Who the hell put you in charge of judging other people?"

"I don't have to judge. Maddy told me herself. You ignore her, Maureen. You may not want to admit it, but you do. And it's gotten to the point where she's threatening to run away. Why? It's because you appear to her to have evolved into a self-centered aristocrat whose dalliance with a moneyman has elevated her status in society. You're now more in love with the mirror and the opulence around you than with Maddy!"

"I'll see you in court, Mister!"

"Don't forget, it's Wednesday, January . . ." Jim heard the abrupt click on the other end, meaning Maureen hung up her phone. ". . . The 12th." His voice trailed off at the last part.

Jim looked at the receiver oddly. But his bewilderment was actually toward Maureen and how she had failed to recognize her own shortcomings, thus bringing the issue of Madison to light. He was going to call Anne and tell her what had transpired, but then decided it wasn't worth mentioning. Instead, the new Cards' sportscaster placed the receiver back on its cradle as he rose from his chair and walked over to the window overlooking the street from four stories above.

The skies were overcast as a system of potentially heavy rain was about to creep upon the Richmond area. Jim looked down at the traffic below and spotted the trees all barren as a result of the late autumn chill. The wind was blowing away candy wrappers and sheets from a newspaper as November took a curtain call. Jim hoped the dreary, bleak picture outside was not a portent in his bid to win Madison.

Chapter Fifty-Two

On the immediate Saturday, Anne had been fitted for her wedding gown. Also present were Laura and her mom, Carolyn. The admin tried on her matron of honor gown. Each complimented the other on the way the dresses looked so perfect, as if they were molded to their figures. With Doris Finley nearly 400 miles away, Anne emailed pictures of her gown to her mother with her iPhone, to which she responded back with instant approval. Julienne, the bridal shop owner, was quite pleased with the swift decisions.

Jim had already informed Zach Moser his last day as sportscaster at the station would be Friday, January the 21st. Jim wanted to leave at that point in order to cover his personal business, which included the last-minute wedding preparations. But he did clear a few days off from Zach prior to his departure. Two of those dates were the Thursday and Friday right before Christmas. Anne replicated the same schedule as she had already given the notice to Kleister's Richmond office and informed the corporate headquarters of her arrival to the firm's St. Louis location on Monday, February the 7th.

Thursday the 23rd was a blur for Jim and Anne. They booked an early morning flight to New York, and Doris was gracious enough to pick them up from JFK. But there was no rest for the weary after the two-hour flight, which included a layover at Washington's Reagan National Airport. The engaged couple asked Doris to take them to the marriage license office in Brewster first so that they could put that matter to bed.

A light coating of fresh-fallen snow blanketed the front lawn of Anne's parents' home. Garlands and holiday lights festooned the gutters and frame of the house. An unlit plastic smiling snowman stood in the middle of the front garden. A huge evergreen wreath, speckled with pine cones and complete with a humongous red bow adorned the front door. And yet, with all the yuletide decorations all over the place, Old Glory was still atop the flagpole holding court.

Pat opened the front door and greeted the party. Anne raced out of the car to give her father a huge hug and kiss. Jim, on the other hand, was a little more unrushed, although he approached Pat with an open hand and a warm smile. Pat gave Jim a firm grip, as the elder Finley was beginning to embrace the idea Jim was about to become his son-in-law.

When they had gotten inside, Jim marveled at the large Christmas tree standing in one corner of the living room. It was beautifully decorated with intricate ornaments of different shapes and sizes, from angels to elves, and from secular to religious. Dazzling lights twinkled at varying times, while a thin roll of tinsel added a little glitter. A magnificently lit star crowned the apex. Although the tree wasn't real, Doris had gone to great pains to spray a pine-scented fragrance to give the faux fir tree some authenticity. Three stockings bearing the names of Tom and Brea's children hung on the mantle of the idle fireplace, waiting for Santa to stuff them with goodies.

Later that evening Jim decided to watch a film on one of the cable channels. Doris and Pat opted to retire, since they were preparing for the get-together with everyone invited over on Christmas Eve for the holiday dinner. Tom, Brea and their children were due to be over at Brea's family's house in West Haverstraw on Christmas Day itself, thus necessitating the Finley family version of festivities a day early.

Anne joined her fiancé on the sofa and cuddled up to him. Although Anne's parents didn't have an active fireplace any longer, the house was still fairly warm to insulate everyone from the early winter chill. But Anne used Jim's inner body warmth and generous left arm to caress and shield her from any sign of the cold. She didn't much care for the action movie Jim favored, but decided to go along with it. There would be plenty of opportunities to watch a chick flick some other time. Anne just loved being in his company.

While Jim was watching Bruce Willis shoot up the bad guys, Anne rested her head against his shoulder. She felt so relaxed with her man, she almost nodded off. But she had to stay alert. She needed to bring up a subject related to the reception, which was only a little more than five weeks away.

"I spoke with Tom earlier," Anne began. "He wanted me to see when you want to meet Matt Caswell."

"Matt Caswell?"

"You know, Tom's friend who's going to play at the reception. He just wants us to hear him and his band and maybe exchange some ideas, like what song are we going to play as our first one."

"I guess you're referring to the one we'll dance to by ourselves?"

"Uh, that's the general idea."

"What about Peter Frampton's *Baby I Love Your Way?*"

"I know the song. That's a sweet one."

"Or maybe The Beatles' *Something.*"

"That's a good one, too. Maybe Matt and his group can play them back-to-back."

"Not a bad idea. We can call him tomorrow and perhaps go over that with him." Jim decided to spice up their tender moment together by moving his right hand underneath Anne's sweater

Anne stopped him from going any farther. "Hey! This is my parents' house. You have to show them a little respect."

"Well, we're two middle-aged adults, not a couple of teenagers. I mean, it's bad enough we're sleeping in separate rooms."

"That'll change after the wedding. Then my parents will allow us to sleep together when we're here."

"You mean your *father* will allow it. Oh, well. Good things come to those who wait." Jim resigned himself to just cuddling with Anne on the couch, which suited the human resource analyst just fine, considering all they had accomplished in one day.

Chapter Fifty-Three

Christmas Eve dinner went off very well at the Finley home. Everyone was there, including Anne's other brother Dennis, who brought along his girlfriend, Jessica. There was the exchange of presents, with Tom having to explain to Bryce and Lara that old St. Nick paid an early visit to their grandparents' house because of the jolly fellow's hectic travel schedule. Caitlyn, on the other hand, was old enough to know the truth about the legendary yuletide hero of folklore, but Brea gestured for her not to say anything to her younger siblings.

Christmas Day was almost anti-climactic, if that could be an apt description of the venerated holiday. Oh, sure, there was the morning Mass that Pat, Doris, Anne and Jim attended together. And they even chatted briefly with Father Carlo to review details on the preparations for the big event, now only a month away. Of course there was dinner that evening, but it was downgraded to leftover turkey and other items remaining from the night before.

The day after was a stunner for Anne. After attending Sunday Mass that morning, Doris asked Anne if she would mind the two of them going out for a short drive to go over some new floral arrangements Elaine Paxton the florist might come up with. But on her return to the house, there was an eerie silence about it. Anne recognized Tom's Pathfinder in the driveway and Dennis's Buick out front. She had figured they might have gotten together with Jim and Pat to watch NFL football on TV.

Anne opened the front door. As she did a thunderous yell of *Surprise!* resonated throughout the living room. At first she sported a look of shock as she spread her outstretched fingers across her face. Her mouth was initially open in awe at the reception, but that soon morphed into a wide grin. There to greet the bride-to-be were Brea, Jessica, Diane and her mother Mary, Dan's wife Alice, their daughter Alexandra, and a couple of Anne's female cousins and aunts. Probably the most shocking attendee of the group was Laura Mazursky, who, like Anne and Jim, made the trip up from Richmond to be there for the shower.

Plenty of exchanges of conversation among the women filled the air, and an ample helping of some catered food and beverages on a side table. Of course, the event was capped off by the smattering of gifts bestowed upon Anne.

While the women were having a grand time in the living room, Jim, Pat and Dennis were in the finished basement, watching the Jets playing the Dolphins from Miami. Tom would have liked to have been there with the guys, but while Brea was celebrating with the other girls upstairs, someone had to stay home and watch their young children. Despite the presence of area rugs upstairs, the men could distinctly hear the scuffling of high heels on the wooden floor above, as well as occasional excited squeals of laughter and joy.

The basement was beautifully done with smooth walls and a tiled floor, courtesy of a home improvement contractor Pat hired years earlier. He'd thought about putting a wooden floor down similar to what he had on the upper floors of the house, but Dennis and Tom talked him out of it because the below ground area could be subject to a potential flood disaster, which would ruin the boards.

Although the work was mostly done by the contractor, there was evidence of Dennis's own handy work here and there. Things such as the washer and dryer and heating and air conditioning units for the house were nicely hidden from view by doors and dry walls to cover any eyesore. A big flat-screen television graced the center of the basement with an accompanying entertainment center.

While the guys moaned how a Jets receiver dropped a sure touchdown pass, Dennis, whose specialty was cabinetry, wanted to know more about his future brother-in-law. With Tom and Brea's children present at the Christmas Eve dinner table, it was difficult for Dennis to communicate with Jim at any length. And with Jessica with the other women, Dennis wasn't being tugged by his significant other.

Dennis was a cross between his conservative father and very progressive brother. He was completely clean shaven and sported a shock of dark hair, similar to Tom's. A cigarette every now and then was usually his bent, but not to the point he was thoroughly addicted to the cancer sticks. His moments when taking a drag were quite private. Dennis also sported a modest tattoo on his left bicep. A heart with the name Gisele written across it. That was the name of Dennis' first wife, who was tragically killed in a car accident years earlier. When she first started dating him, Jessica was a little uncomfortable seeing that mark, but then understood why he never got rid of it. Although Jessica had gotten used to seeing it, Dennis had thought about getting rid of the tattoo altogether if they were to take their relationship to the next level.

Pat was beginning to doze off a little from drinking one too many beers. That gave Dennis and Jim a chance to get more acquainted without the patriarch butting in.

"Boy, those girls are really whooping it up upstairs," Dennis began.

"Yeah," Jim responded. "I'm surprised your dad didn't get up."

"Who, him? Nah, once Dad has a couple in him he's out like a light."

"Gee, we may have to keep him away from the open bar we're having at the reception."

The two men shared a lighthearted laugh. Then Dennis asked Jim for a progress report on the pending court case. Jim didn't say much in return, except that he was confident he and Anne stood a good chance of winning. The sportscaster then went on a different track while trying to keep the subject of the Madison matter in focus.

"I'll tell you something, Dennis. I do love your sister very much. But there was a situation about three months ago that cemented the deal. I took Anne with me one weekend to Pennsylvania so she and I could go out for a spell with Madison. There was a mishap in the parking lot of a bowling alley. Madison foolishly stepped into the path of an oncoming vehicle. She was okay, thank God, but there was something in the way Anne took charge to comfort Madison and attend to her needs. Maybe it's because of maternal instincts many women possess, even if it's not their child,

216

but Anne demonstrated her devotion and dedication to ensuring Madison's safety and well-being so well that I can unequivocally trust her with my daughter's life."

"Wow! That's a powerful statement. I know Anne's always rued the day she learned she couldn't have a child of her own. Now here she is with the possibility of becoming a mom of sorts."

"And she'll be a damn good one!"

Just then Pat awoke from his nap dazed, not realizing where he was at first. He inspected the room and recognized it was his basement. Then he spotted Jim and Dennis, both of whom greeted him with a sarcastic *good morning,* although the clock read well past two in the afternoon. The ex-Marine didn't utter a word, but only gave them a nasty sneer. Pat then glanced at the TV and began to watch the rest of the game. He saw a wide receiver on the Jets deliberately knocked down by one of the members of the Dolphins' secondary before the ball was thrown in his vicinity. Pat's blood started to boil. His eyes bulged, only to be matched by the veins in his neck. That was when the Finley patriarch leapt from his chair with his arms waving.

"Aw, c'mon! That's freakin' pass interference!"

Dennis softly smiled at Jim and quietly told the sportscaster his father was back.

Chapter Fifty-Four

Nearly two weeks after Jim and Anne popped the cork off the champagne to ring in the New Year, the day of reckoning had arrived. Wednesday, January the 12th. The day when the couple would bring their case to Family Court before a judge in their attempt to wrestle Madison away from Maureen and Harley Bell.

The trip to Pennsylvania the day before was brutal. A nasty winter storm wreaked havoc on the highways. Accidents and abandoned vehicles were in mass numbers as they pockmarked hockey rink excuses for roads and snow banks cleverly cloaking guard rails and dips. What would've been a five-hour trip under normal conditions turned out to be a ten-hour odyssey. But heeding the warnings of many meteorologists, Jim and Anne left Richmond early that Tuesday morning in order to arrive at his sister and mom's house by seven o'clock, in time for a good dinner.

Then there was their day in court. The storm that swept through the Mid-Atlantic region had moved well up to northern New England and Canada. The result of the precipitation produced a six-inch snow covering around the courthouse. As treacherous as it was to drive though, the leftover snow gave the Norristown community a picture postcard look. Tufts of snow frosted barren tree limbs like icing on cupcakes. And despite the bright sunshine, the temperature was not due to get above the freezing point that day.

Jim and Anne gingerly walked up the icy steps of the building, trying not to create a new dance routine on the slippery surface, despite the presence of sprinkled calcium carbonate pellets. Much to their surprise, they spotted David Epstein waiting for them at the top near the building's entrance. The attorney was delighted his clients made it that day. Jim's testimony was critical.

David wore a navy blue winter coat over his sharp charcoal gray pinstriped suit with a white shirt and conservative red tie underneath. He eschewed wearing a hat, but wore a woolen band around his head to keep his ears warm, and a Kashmir scarf wrapped around his throat. David removed his right glove to shake Jim's hand. Anne, meanwhile, was still quite cold and wasn't brave enough to expose hers. Instead, David gave Anne a pat on her left arm. He told them to go inside and meet them in the adjacent waiting room while he waited for the psychiatrist he had hired to interview Madison a couple of days earlier to arrive.

Just after Jim and Anne entered the building, David heard his name being called. He turned around. *Harley Bell*. The Philadelphia financier was dressed in similar attire to that of the attorney. And Harley approached David with some purpose as the former dashed up the slick steps.

"Hey, David," Harley yelled with a smile. "How are you?"

"I'm okay, Harley." David didn't offer the same greeting. His client was actually going up against Harley's wife. The attorney's skeptical expression suggested that Harley's grin was spurious at best.

"Listen," Harley began, "we all know why you're here. Personally you need to suck up some cash from Monahan's bank account. I don't mind that at all, David. No, on the contrary, I'm glad you're making a buck or two. We're on the same committee to promote the county's business and I'm all for it."

"But."

Harley grinned at David. The attorney stiffened as though expecting what was about to come next.

"I can't see Maureen upset. She's unbearable. As far as I'm concerned, I couldn't care less where Madison ends up. She's not my daughter. But I'm married to her mother. You know her lawyer, Miles Canfield, don't you?"

"I'm quite familiar with him, yes."

"Well, then you know he hates to lose. Maureen hates to lose. Why don't you do everyone a favor, David? Just go belly up like a cockroach on this one."

"You want me to do something totally unethical?"

Harley shrugged his shoulders. "Just a suggestion. But, uh, I just want you to remember one thing, David. I got you on that committee, and I can easily get you off of it, and all the little perks that go with it. Think it over, buddy."

Harley gave David a couple of quick taps on his left shoulder and proceeded inside the courthouse. David stared down at the steps in front of him, looking for answers. Once Harley was out of sight, David began to mutter to himself.

"I appreciate my position on the county business committee, but I owe my best effort to Jim's case." David looked at the courthouse with contempt. "Shove the seat and all the niceties up your ass, Harley. I'm going to fight for what's right for my client!" And with that David remained outside the building as he continued to wait for the psychiatrist to arrive.

Meanwhile, Jim and Anne arrived in the waiting area outside the courtroom. Much to the dismay of the sportscaster, he easily spotted Maureen across the room, sitting next to a nattily attired man about her age. He was her attorney, Miles Canfield, a good friend of Harley's. Canfield appeared as slick as his swept back hair, very confident in himself, with an ego to match. And then Harley entered the room for good measure. Sickening.

Jim couldn't bear to watch the threesome any longer, even though Anne was in the same line of sight. Repulsed by their presence, he instead decided to focus on a paint chip on the far right wall to avoid looking at them. He loosened the knot in his necktie and opened the top button of the dress shirt he wore under his navy blue suit. *Relax, Jim.*

David suddenly appeared in the room with a gentleman who looked to be in his mid-to-late sixties. The gentleman's bookish veneer was accentuated by the thick glasses he wore and his receding hairline. Like the other men, the gentleman wore a suit, beige in color. David brought the man over to Jim and Anne for introductions.

"I want you two to meet Dr. Leo Sternberg," David said to Jim and Anne. "I want you to know I have used Dr. Sternberg on many cases before. He comes with impeccable credentials, is a Penn State alum and a graduate of the University of Pennsylvania School of Medicine."

As the three were about to exchange handshakes, a female court officer appeared in the room. In a voice that would rival anyone, she made the announcement of all parties in the Monahan vs. Bell case to follow her into the courtroom next door. David turned to Anne and asked her to sit in the gallery. Although she would have a stake in the matter, this was still Jim against Maureen. Even Harley would have to take a backseat in the proceedings.

In the courtroom, the officer ushered all parties in to take certain seats. Maureen and Miles were ordered to assume seats behind the table to the judge's right, while Jim and David were instructed to the seats behind the opposite table. All interested members who were curious, Anne, Dr. Sternberg and Harley among them, were directed to the back gallery seats.

As he fidgeted in his seat waiting for what was to come next, Jim noticed the judge presiding over the case had already taken his seat behind the bench. Mid-to-late fifties in appearance, a few extra pounds accorded him, judging by how his face filled out, and an ebbed hairline, not nearly as pronounced as that of Dr. Sternberg, but thinned out near the front just the same.

Jim scanned the room and noticed its austerity and silence. This was, after all, a courtroom and not some sports bar. His perusal stopped when he came across Maureen and Miles. The matronly court officer then made an announcement.

"Case number 74683," she began. "Monahan versus Bell. All parties are present. Both attorneys are present. The honorable Harris McDonnell presiding."

With that out of the way, Judge McDonnell began to recite the circumstances necessitating the court appearance. His delivery was as vanilla as the atmosphere, but he made each point of contention very clear. McDonnell then asked both counselors to give their opening statements, to which David went first, followed by Miles. The adjudicator gave David the first crack. The attorney wasted no time in calling Jim to the stand.

Swallowing the last ounce of nerves jabbing him, the sportscaster rose from his seat and proceeded to the stand.

When Jim stood in position, he was sworn in by the same court officer, raising his right hand while placing his left on the Bible. The officer offered a prepared statement, and Jim identified himself for the court's records.

"Have a seat," she commanded.

David slowly walked toward the baseball man to begin a barrage of questions. "Mr. Monahan, explain to the court your occupation."

"Currently I am a sportscaster on a local radio station in Richmond, Virginia."

"You say currently. Is there something you wish to divulge as far as employment, or should I say, future employment goes?"

"Yes, in about a month from now I'm moving to the St. Louis, Missouri area to become the play-by-play radio voice of the Cardinals' baseball team."

"Now, for the non-sports followers present, this means you will be calling the action on the field of all the Cardinals' games this coming year, whether at home or away, is that correct?"

"Yes."

"When the Cardinals play games away from St. Louis, you will be with the team, regardless of what city that is?"

"That's right."

"When you and Mrs. Bell divorced each other three years ago, you were broadcasting minor league games down in Richmond?"

"That was when the Braves were still in Richmond. They've since moved down to Gwyneth, Georgia. I almost moved with them, but then came along the promise that Richmond would get another minor league team, which became the Flying Squirrels, so out of loyalty to a lot of people down at the station, plus other broadcasting commitments down there, I remained in Richmond."

"There was a concern by the courts of your being away with the baseball team for road games, and that no one would properly look after your daughter Madison at the time."

"Yes, she was just twelve at the time and during our divorce proceedings the judge said he had an issue with that. I didn't have a leg to stand on."

"How will things be so different this time, given the fact you'll be away for various amounts of time this summer?"

"By having Anne as my new wife, Madison will always have the proper care and adult supervision an adolescent needs when I'm not there. Also, Madison will be turning sixteen in three months. There are a lot of young people who go off to college and live in campus dorms before their eighteenth birthday. Madison has matured into a very capable young woman to handle herself until Anne comes home from work. And don't forget, except for those road games, I'll still be home by the time Madison arrives home from high school."

David appeared satisfied with the lucid explanation of the direction and plans Jim had devised for an eventual reacquainting himself with Madison. He adjusted his horn rim glasses and thanked Jim for his time. But just as soon as David returned to his seat, Miles rose from his. It was time for the counterpunch by the opposing counsel.

Miles approached Jim with a smile as ingenuous as they come. He was the shark waiting for the prey, as if knowing his victim was possibly vulnerable. Glancing briefly at some index cards he held in his left hand containing a few notes he had made when Jim was questioned by David, Miles took over.

"You seem to have it all planned out, Mr. Monahan. You'd be home for your daughter until it's time when your new wife comes home at about five, giving you enough time to get to the ballpark to do your games. And even on those days when you're in Chicago or Cincinnati, or wherever the Cardinals play, there is only a little down time when Madison will be by herself until Anne arrives, say about two hours from then."

"That's right."

"Ah, but there's something you overlooked. You see, I make it a point to investigate everything. I'll bet you didn't know your fiancée has to travel to her company's corporate headquarters in Orlando, Florida twice a year, did you?"

The news of Anne's company travels fell on both Jim and David like a ton of bricks. Jim sat stunned as he glared at Anne for answers. David also looked in her direction. He begged Judge McDonnell to interrupt Miles' questioning for a brief moment. McDonnell gave him just one minute.

223

David stood up to meet Anne at the railing separating the courtroom. She whispered the reason for the trips. David nodded in assent as he then rotated and addressed McDonnell.

"Your Honor," David began, "I want to assure the court that Miss Finley hasn't gone on any business trips to Orlando or anywhere else for that matter in three years, and she doesn't foresee this happening in the near future either. In a cost-cutting move, her company eliminated the need for such unnecessary trips."

Miles had to counter David's claim.

"Miss Finley doesn't foresee this happening? Well, I suppose she can tell us who will win the elections in November, or perhaps give us the winning lottery numbers? The fact that Miss Finley did go on such trips in the past lends some credence that the possibility still may exist, Your Honor. And that turns me back to you, Mr. Monahan. What kind of provisionary plans do you have should such a possibility arise? Neither one of you will have any relatives close by. And, please, I loved your analogy about kids going off to college just over a year or so older than Madison, but she is still technically a minor."

"I can assure you, Mr. Canfield, when Anne and I, and hopefully Madison, arrive in St. Louis, we will acquaint ourselves with trustworthy neighbors and we'll develop contingency plans to tend to Madison should such a time occur."

"In other words, a wing and a prayer," Miles smiled smugly. "You may step down, Sir."

Jim stood up from the jury box seat and began to walk back toward his chair next to David. As he did, he looked at Miles with anger and reserved a greater dispassion for the attorney's client.

David stood up and called Dr. Leo Sternberg to the stand. The psychiatrist began walking from the gallery and was sworn in. After he went over Dr. Sternberg's qualifications, David asked the doctor some direct questions.

"Dr. Sternberg, you had a chance to evaluate Madison Monahan yourself. What were your conclusions?"

"I found her to be a very troubled child. She has developed an aloof relationship with her own mother, Mrs. Bell, or should I say Mrs. Bell has ignored Madison."

"In what way?"

"Well, Madison told me that ever since Mrs. Bell and Mr. Monahan divorced each other, her mother has paid Madison only lip service. The child needs and requires attention and care. I mean, the fact that Madison is well taken care of in that she is properly fed and maintains a great degree of proper hygiene, has a wonderful array of clothes to wear, and a beautiful roof over her head, doesn't necessarily equate her to be a happy adolescent. Madison has told me she would rather run away than stay any longer in the Bell household, and that disturbs me. That does not bode well if there is a wall between the mother and the daughter. And this could fester into problems as Madison matures into an adult. This lack of an alliance could develop into low self-esteem and may alienate her from the rest of society to near-dysfunctional proportions. Madison needs that love now, and from what I found in my session with her, she isn't getting that."

David was through. As he retreated to his seat, Miles got up and slowly walked over to the doctor.

"You used the term *alienate,* Doctor, but it sounds as though my client is currently doing the same to her daughter, correct?"

"From what I found in my session with Madison, yes, I am drawing a similar conclusion."

"My client is a highly respected person in the community in which she lives, almost as prominent as that of her current husband. Mrs. Bell serves on many committees and boards, a couple of which are directly tied in with the high school Madison is currently attending. If there were no love for Madison, why bother serving on boards that oversee Madison's educational needs?"

"While it is certainly wonderful that Mrs. Bell has all these altruistic motives in helping the community at large, especially at the high school, she ought to be focusing her attention on one individual, and that's Madison. It's like you needing a car to drive around, but ignoring the engine light when it goes on. Let's face it, we live in a fast-paced society, but sometimes you have to slow down and devote your attention to specific needs."

"Now let me ask you something, Dr. Sternberg. Who would you say is more important for a female teenager to gravitate to? Her mother, who went through similar feminine problems years earlier, or her father, who may have had masculinity issues as a teenager, but certainly can't equate with what his daughter may be going through."

"Personally I do not see the relevance in this situation . . ."

"Answer the question, please," Miles interrupted.

Dr. Sternberg sighed and agreed that a mother is better suited to be associated with the daughter than a father. With that said, the psychiatrist was asked by Judge McDonnell to step down.

Miles examined some papers on his desk. After rifling through some sheets, he then approached McDonnell and asked if he could call Maureen to the stand in order to defend herself. The gruff adjudicator allowed the request. Jim gave David a puzzling look, but his attorney didn't say a word. In fact, David gestured his right index finger at Jim as a way of telling him to keep quiet so that he could concentrate on what Maureen had to say when it came time for him to cross-examine her.

"Mrs. Bell," Miles began, "I'd like you to please tell the court why there seems to be some misunderstanding between you and your daughter Madison, and why she wants to, as Dr. Sternberg put it, run away."

"I just can't understand why," Maureen replied. "Madison has a wonderful home to live in. My husband certainly makes a very good income to fall back on. Madison goes to a private high school, and she gets the best in terms of care, clothing and love. I just don't understand her behavior."

"Well, apparently there is something that is disturbing her to make such a statement to Dr. Sternberg."

"I don't know. I do know when she comes home from school she'll spend a great deal of time on the computer, no doubt being influenced by things she sees on the internet. And then she gabs or texts with her friends on her phone. It's not like I don't try to get her attention. She just comes home and buries herself in all the things I just rattled off."

"No, there's something more to it. There has to have been something else that triggered Madison's reaction."

"I have a possible theory. I think ever since my ex-husband Jim shacked up with that floozy back there, his attitude has all of a sudden changed and now he's on this crusade, influencing Madison's thought processes."

Anne had sat quietly throughout the proceedings, except when she had to give an explanation to David on the company trips. But when she heard Maureen refer to her by a derogatory term there was only so much abuse she could take. She puckered her lips and narrowed her eyes like her pent-up anger was about to come to a head. Anne's face turned a beet red. As much as she wanted to suppress it, Anne had to fire the missile. This was a side Jim never had seen before. But inside he thought it might be best for Anne to let the world know she wasn't going to accept Maureen's insults any longer.

"Floozy?" Anne leapt from her seat in the back and began to shout at Maureen. "Who are you to call me a floozy? Listen, you fucking bitch, I'll tear your fucking lungs out!"

"That's typical of the type of woman Jim would pick," Maureen commented. "Flying off the handle."

Anne had to be restrained from going past the railing by two court officers. McDonnell banged his gavel several times to restore order in a hearing that was developing into a circus. He then came out with a loud decree.

"I want that woman removed from the courtroom, never to return! Escort her to the waiting room!"

Jim was now furious at the ploy by Maureen to get Anne's nerves unraveled, causing the latter's ejection. He had to come to the defense of his ousted fiancée.

"Oh, that's just great, Maureen! You are really a fucking piece of work, do you know that?"

McDonnell scowled at Jim. He had laid down the law by evicting Anne. It appeared Jim never got the message. That was when he ordered David to control the temper of his client. David angrily told Jim to sit and cool his heels before the sportscaster might become the next casualty. Jim serenely sat in his spot and did not say another word. But if you had gotten close enough you might have seen the steam still coming out of his ears. With order restored, Miles continued the line of questioning.

"So," Miles continued, "you believe Miss Finley is the reason we are going through this exercise?"

"I don't have any other explanation. Besides, from what I understand of this woman, she never married, nor did she have any children of her own. Maybe this is her way of having that child she could never have otherwise."

Miles then directed his next statement at Judge Mc-Donnell.

"What Mrs. Bell just said is true, Your Honor—at least the part about Miss Finley bearing children. I've obtained medical records to substantiate the claim that Miss Finley does not possess the ability to conceive. As for Mrs. Bell's other viewpoint, well, that is just theory, but an interesting one at that."

Miles stepped away to allow David a crack at Maureen.

"First of all, Mrs. Bell, what you just told Mr. Canfield and the court is just theory. It's just your opinion."

Maureen began to squirm just slightly in the jury box seat. Her brow furrowed. She wasn't taking too kindly to David's tone of voice. She still owed a reply to David's statement.

"Yes, that's true, but it's still a good enough reason for all that's going on."

"You claim that when your daughter comes home from school, she barely says a word to you as she immerses herself in cyberspace and chats with her friends. You make mention of the fact you try to reach out to Madison in order to win back her love, always being there for her, yet I have found you with your husband on the countless dinners and functions on the community business board. I know that for a fact because I've seen you there."

Miles' expression showed he wasn't appreciative of the direction David was taking this. He appeared infuriated as he rose from his seat to voice his rebuttal.

"Objection, Your Honor. Counsel is now doing an irrelevant character assassination on my client, for what purpose I don't know."

McDonnell responded that he would allow David's bold statement. The adjudicator gave Jim's counselor the nod to proceed, but reminded him that he would allow only so much slack. David acknowledged McDonnell's charity, cleared his throat, and forged ahead.

"The only point I wish to make of all this, Mrs. Bell, is that you seem to devote a lot of time and energy to things not directly connected to Madison. You may lay claim to stating that Madison retreats to her room upon arrival from school, but I'm just curious to know how much of an effort you make to reach out to her. Don't answer that. It was a rhetorical question."

Maureen gave David a dirty look as the latter returned to his seat behind his desk. McDonnell advised her that she could step down, but Maureen didn't move so readily. She still harbored ill will toward David as her eyes appeared to be shooting daggers at him. Maureen was so engrossed at glaring at David that McDonnell had to remind her a second time to go back to her spot next to Miles. But the judge's order went unheeded. Finally, McDonnell motioned to one of the court officers to physically escort Maureen back. This time she got the message and headed back to her seat.

Once Maureen was settled, McDonnell made an announcement that Madison was to appear before the court that afternoon at three. With a swift tap of his gavel, McDonnell ordered everyone to reconvene at that time. At the lead officer's command, everyone in the courtroom rose as the judge made his way to his chambers.

With McDonnell completely out of the room, everyone was left to his or her own devices. Jim excused himself from David as the sportscaster raced out of the courtroom and into the adjacent corridor. He turned to his right in the direction of the waiting area, hoping to find Anne there.

The scanning of the large room didn't take long. To his relief, he spotted Anne, but he was deeply troubled by what he saw. There she was with her head down. She had a few facial tissues crumpled on her lap, and her face appeared red as though she'd been crying. Jim was saddened to see his fiancée in such a morose state. He slowly walked up to her and sat down on the vacant spot to her right. With a subtle cupping of his hand around her left shoulder, Jim gently pulled her toward him.

"Hey," Jim began softly, "what's with all the crocodile tears?"

Anne was still sobbing. She dried her reddened eyes again as she tried to regain her composure. "I screwed things up," Anne quivered. "I let that witch get the better of me with her insult! I couldn't control myself! I'm sorry, Jim! I'm sorry for everything!"

"C'mon, if it'll make you feel any better I gave Maureen a piece of my mind as you left the room. The judge threatened to toss me out, too."

"But this isn't like me. You know that. That floozy remark really got to me!"

"Believe me, Anne, I was livid, too. Maureen should've just referred to you as my fiancée and left the name-calling and the gutter talk out. Maureen never had any sense of decency, and this only proves it."

"Yes, but I'm afraid we may have lost any chance of getting Madison because of what I did! I wouldn't be surprised if you decided to leave me right now after what happened!"

Jim wanted to lay the cards on the table with Anne on this aspect. He took his free right hand and tenderly turned Anne's head toward him.

"I want you to look at me." Once he had Anne's attention, he continued to say what he had to, from the heart. "No matter what happens later this afternoon with McDonnell's ruling, I want you to know it will not change my love for you. We are still going to get married in two weeks. You are my soul mate. You complete me."

Whatever frown Anne had expressed earlier disappeared. Instead, she sported a warm smile as she softly pressed the right side of her face up against Jim's left shoulder. Having calmed Anne down, Jim suggested the two of them head for lunch.

He mentioned the diner they had eaten at the day before Thanksgiving was only a few blocks away. It was as good a place as any as Jim wanted to erase Maureen's words from Anne's memory.

Chapter Fifty-Five

Two forty-five. Everyone gathered back in the waiting room—that is, everyone except for Madison. She was due to arrive soon to make her appearance and add her own reflections to this drama between her parents.

In one corner were Maureen and her attorney Miles Canfield, no doubt strategizing on how things should be played out when Madison took the stand. Harley, who had made his face known that morning, had to go back to his Philadelphia office.

In the other corner sat Jim and Anne with their hired gun, David Epstein. While no one took anything for granted, there was an air of confidence on David's part that Madison's testimony just might close the deal for them.

Nearly ten minutes had passed and it was almost time for both parties to return to Judge McDonnell's courtroom. But where was the star of the hour? It was almost to the point to put out an APB on the whereabouts of Madison, as both sides grew nervously curious why she hadn't shown up yet.

But, just when all hope appeared lost, Madison arrived. Maureen, who purposely sat by the main entrance of the waiting room, was the first to greet her daughter. The mother gave her a lot of doting attention, probably more so than she had given Madison all month up to that point. Miles hailed Madison's entrance, although one could question his sincerity. But Madison would have neither of them. Their manifestation of deceit was that apparent. Instead, Madison sought her father and Anne out. She found them. Madison sped across the room, as Jim welcomed her with open arms and a big smile. They barnacled each other. Anne sat patiently for her turn, and Madison didn't disappoint. A moment worthy of a photo to be sure, but David wanted to spend a minute or two with her.

"Hi, Madison. I'm David Epstein. Your father hired me in this case. Now, just to let you know, you're going to sit in the witness box in front of the judge. I'm going to ask you some questions and I'm quite sure Mr. Canfield—that's your Mom's lawyer—will be asking you questions of his own. The most important thing to remember, Madison, is to be truthful and forthright. It's okay to be a little nervous. I would, too, if I were in your position. But if you contradict yourself during the testimony, or say something that might clash with something you may have already said, the judge is going to pick up on that, and that might not look good for you. Just give it straight from the heart, okay?"

Madison assured the lawyer she would. David smiled and gave her two light pats on her left shoulder. At that moment, the female court officer, who had been escorting both parties in and out of the courtroom earlier, arrived to call everyone inside. First Maureen and Miles exited, and then Madison, Jim and David followed. When she turned around, Madison noticed Anne didn't move from her seat and became concerned. She glanced at her father, puzzled, but Jim simply drew a deep sigh. He knew why Anne wasn't following suit, but remained tightlipped. Demanding answers, Madison gazed back at her future stepmother.

"Aren't you coming, Anne?"

Embarrassed to give Madison the real reason why she couldn't show her face in the courtroom, the human resource manager had to think of some excuse and fast.

"Well, the case is between your parents, Madison. They prefer I sit in here. Good luck."

Anne smiled as she saw Madison and the others leave the waiting room. But the moment everyone was out of sight, she reverted to her melancholy disposition.

Judge McDonnell was already in his place behind the bench when everyone entered the courtroom. Jim, David, Maureen and Miles occupied the same chairs behind opposite desks while Madison was told to sit in the gallery with Dr. Sternberg and a few others to uphold a sense of impartiality toward the proceedings. The court officer told the judge that both parties and vested interests were present. McDonnell asked David to proceed. Without hesitation Jim's attorney called Madison to the stand.

Madison stood up from her gallery spot. After releasing a slight sigh, she began her stroll to the box. Madison kept her eye contact to the front of the room, never once glancing at either parent. Jim watched his daughter walk past him, showing a look of hope that she might do well. Maureen, on the other hand, offered a visage that said, *you'd better not blow this!* Once settled, the line of questioning began.

"Miss Monahan," David began, "you met with Dr. Sternberg, the man sitting in the back with the light-colored suit the other day, did you not?"

"Yeah, it was on Monday."

"How did your session with him go?"

"Um, it was okay. He just asked me a lot of questions like you're doing."

"Well," David said, "I assure you I won't do as much probing as he did. Now, you weren't here this morning for the earlier part of this hearing, but I had asked Dr. Sternberg what had transpired between the two of you. He made a very profound statement indicating you had told him you might consider running away from home, is that true?"

"I did tell him that."

"I don't understand it. It seems you have everything someone your age would want: nice clothes, a great school, a beautiful home, a generous income from your stepfather. Would you please tell the court why you still feel this way?"

"I feel my mother has alienated me. She doesn't care if I exist or not. She's too busy wrapped up with all her activities and my bratty three-year-old half-brother. And forget about my stepfather. To him I'm just an accessory that came with the rest of the baggage when he got involved with Mom."

"That's a pretty strong accusation."

"Well, it's the truth."

"Before Dr. Sternberg, had you spoken with anyone on the matter besides your father, like a guidance counselor or some very close friend?"

"They don't want to hear anything. The guidance counselor is never around and my friends have their own hang-ups. I know my father is concerned, but there is nothing he can do in his present state."

"Until he gets married to Miss Finley in the other room. That would change things dramatically. Tell me, Madison, how do you feel about Miss Finley and the prospects of her becoming your stepmother?"

"I think she's pretty neat. Anne helped nurse me when I got injured in the parking lot of that bowling alley in Ardmore. She seemed to be pretty concerned. I like Anne a lot."

David smiled at Madison as he began to pull away. The door was left open for Miles. He rose from his chair and walked up toward Madison, but not without studying the situation beforehand. Once he was set, Miles began his line of queries.

"You know, Madison, your mother is very concerned about you. I mean hearing all this talk about you taking flight. That disturbs her no end. And do you want to know what she told me and the court this morning? She said that you have a habit of heading straight to your room when you come home from school—practically locking yourself up in there. If this is true, I'd like to know why."

"Why don't you ask her? How many times, Mom, did I want your attention? You just ignored me!" Madison paused for a moment. She looked around the ceiling before continuing. There was a cry for help in her visage that didn't seemed to have been answered. "After a while of being ignored, you just say to yourself *whatever* and leave it at that."

"I'm sure there must be some little misunderstanding that a good talk could resolve."

"God, don't you get it? We should've had a talk about this a long time ago. Now it took this thing to finally bring everything to a head. Well, it's too late."

Miles didn't pursue the matter any farther. However, there was the issue of some trash concerning Anne.

"There's something you ought to know about what transpired this morning, Madison. When I was questioning your mother, Miss Finley, that's the woman your father is marrying to whom you referred to Mr. Epstein as *pretty neat,* flew off the handle and went into a tirade. Why do you think she's not in here? Miss Finley went into a rampage threatening your mother to the point that Judge McDonnell had to order her out of the courtroom for the duration of this hearing."

Madison looked at Miles in disbelief. How could such a mild, sweet and tenderhearted person like Anne react in such a manner? Madison then looked at Jim and David and wanted to know if all this were true. David had to quickly go in spin control mode and set the record straight.

"Objection, Your Honor. What Mr. Canfield neglected to tell Madison is what caused Miss Finley's outburst. I can paraphrase to Madison what her mother had said that provoked Miss Finley, or may I get the permission of the court stenographer?"

"Sustained," McDonnell replied. "Mr. Canfield, perhaps you'd better enlighten Miss Monahan with regard to the term Mrs. Bell used to refer to Miss Finley."

David then interrupted.

"If it may please the court, Your Honor, why don't we just have the stenographer read that portion that provoked Miss Finley?"

Things were falling out of Miles's grasp. He had to quickly turn the tables, or else risk losing the case altogether.

"That won't be necessary. But I would just like to add, why would anyone with any sense at all, given the venue, would react the way Miss Finley did, instead of showing some prudent restraint? Oh, and I trust Miss Finley's words were recorded by the stenographer, too. Think about that, Madison, should you ever cross Miss Finley in the future."

Miles was through with his questioning as Madison was then ordered by McDonnell to step down. As she was being escorted by a court officer to take a seat back in the gallery, Madison looked at her father. Miles's suggestive opinion left an indelible impression. Madison displayed an expression wondering if things would work out between her and Anne, or if Jim and Anne would always get along.

With Madison having taken her spot in the back, all eyes were then riveted on McDonnell. The adjudicator examined papers in front of him relative to the case, as it was time for him to render a decision. He pawed at his jaw as Jim and Maureen and their respective lawyers were sweating out the wait. McDonnell then cleared his throat to make his answer known.

"I have heard arguments from both sides. Both are compelling. But the most important testimony was that of young Madison Monahan. Whereas a young female's more natural connection should be that of her mother as opposed to her father, there must also be the bond that holds that relationship together. Judging from Miss Monahan's responses and, due in part to Dr. Sternberg's psychological examination of the teenager, Madison feels like an outcast in her own home. There are so many wayward teens who have taken flight from their homes in this country. The number is staggering. These teenagers leave their families for a myriad of reasons. And to where they go and how they wind up, only God knows. These kids come from all walks of life, regardless of social class, race, religion or ethnicity. I can see Madison becoming another statistic should she remain in her present state, and the consequences that may follow could be devastating to both her parents. For my own conscience, I cannot allow this to happen."

McDonnell glanced at both parents. The tension was tightening. "Now, Mr. Canfield brought up a very significant point concerning the behavior of Miss Finley this morning. Yes, Miss Finley did explode in the courtroom, so much so that I had to ban her from the rest of the proceedings. But I also see how Mrs. Bell's offensive provocation served as the impetus for Miss Finley's stormy reaction. I am willing to dismiss Miss Finley's outburst as an anomaly and her response to be natural, albeit strong, to Mrs. Bell's surly accusation."

The judge swallowed some air before continuing. "Young Madison appears to be a very sweet person who needs the love and attention she appears not to be getting at the moment. In just a little over two years from now, she will be able to live wherever she wants, with whomever she wants. At that point Madison will be able to make her own decisions. But for now, I must rule in favor of where I believe she will receive not only the proper care, but also be given the proper attention to her needs. Therefore, I am ruling in favor of Madison to be with her father, Mr. James Monahan, and Mr. Monahan's soon-to-be wife, Miss Anne Finley, to take effect on their wedding day, Saturday, January the 29th."

With a swift tap of his gavel, Judge McDonnell brought an end to the hearing. Jim and David gave each other a hearty handshake as they both exhibited broad smiles for winning the case. Madison stepped forward toward her father. Jim caught a glimpse of her approach through the corner of his left eye. He disengaged his hand from David's and quickly turned to his left to receive his daughter. Both Jim and Madison had a tear or two streaming down their faces as they embraced each other. He didn't say anything. He didn't have to. There was an etched expression of joy. Jim was happy he'd rescued his daughter from possibly leading a nomadic life. Madison was happy her father kept his word and that she'd be going to a home where lip service wasn't going to be the norm.

At the other table, Maureen zipped her eyes closed. She displayed a look of disgust, not so much over losing Madison's primary custody as to just losing anything at all to Jim. She widened the palm of her left hand and gently massaged her temple to relieve the anguish. Miles bent over to her and explained that they could appeal McDonnell's decision. But Maureen waved him off, in a sense telling him that there was no use in trying, since Madison had already made up her mind to bolt anyway.

In the meantime Jim, Madison and David left the courtroom. They gathered in the outside hallway where Jim thanked David one last time for all the work he did in making McDonnell's call happen. Then Dr. Sternberg offered his congratulatory handshake to Jim. More smiles and pleasantries were exchanged. David and Dr. Sternberg then departed. Jim then took Madison by the hand. They needed to extend the great news to a currently unwitting Anne.

Jim opened the door to the waiting room. He and Madison noticed Anne reading the present day's local newspaper. The human resource executive appeared more interested in passing the time to keep her mind occupied while waiting than in catching up on all the latest headlines. The father and daughter slowly walked toward her. Although neither Jim nor Madison said a word, Anne sensed they were near. She presently raised her head and looked at her fiancé and his daughter. Jim flashed a broad grin and gave Anne two thumbs up. Anne tossed the journal to the side and shot from her seat in elation. She quickly hugged Jim and Madison. The torment was over. The three of them were to be a cohesive family the moment Jim and Anne tied the knot in a little more than two weeks. Then Jim suddenly released his steely grip on the two.

"Let's celebrate tonight with my family," Jim said to Anne. He then looked at Madison. "I wish you could come along, Maddy, but I know it's a school night. See if your mother is still around so she can take you home."

"Jim," Anne interceded, "do you think it's a good idea for Madison to go with Maureen? I mean, your ex-wife just lost. She may be too bitter."

Jim took Anne's advice into consideration. He still told Madison to look for Maureen. If she had left or if she was too perturbed over losing the case, Jim would offer to drive Madison back to Bryn Mawr.

With the case finally settled, the only things left were the wedding itself and the eventual move to new digs in the St. Louis area. Another cloud was lifted from above Jim's head.

Chapter Fifty-Six

The wedding was a little over a week away. With weekend sportscaster Scott Larsen having been elevated to the weekday job as well as having been handed the Flying Squirrels' play-by-play position by Zach Moser temporarily, at least until a suitable full-time replacement could be found, it was time for Jim's emotional last sportscast at the Richmond station. It was a report not so much filled with scores from games the night before as it was reminiscing over so many memorable moments throughout his tenure there.

Vince Wallace and Jim exchanged banter with each other right up until the time Jim said his last goodbye to the listeners. When the station went into commercial, Jim and Vince gave each other a strong hug as the news director/on-air personality wished Jim nothing but the best in his next role as the new Cardinals' voice.

Jim arrived back at his desk basically to empty it out. He handled knickknacks of all shapes and sizes, some of which caused him to smile gently at the esoteric significance each piece held. As he quietly packed them into a small duffel bag, Laura came up from behind to plant a soft kiss on the right side of his face. Jim smiled and told her he would be looking forward to seeing her and Charlie up in Brewster in eight days.

Zach milled about in the doorway leading to his office. He noticed Jim gathering his personal effects and called out to the sportscaster before he left the station for the final time. Jim dropped his array of trinkets and paraded to the station manager's office. Zach shut the door.

"Have a seat, Jim," the bearded Zach ordered.

Jim took his spot in front of Zach's oversized desk. Zach then reclined in his high-back executive leather chair as the two began their conversation, still trying to come out with the right words, despite having rehearsed it.

"Well, I never thought the day would arrive, Jim, but here we are, the last hour."

"Gosh, I just can't believe it myself. Of course, I'll be seeing you next week."

"Yeah, Barbara and I will be there."

"Great! I know I'm leaving the job in capable hands. I mean, Scott has the experience, and God knows there's someone out there dying for the chance at my job. I think they'll do all right."

"I've got confidence in Scott, too, Jim, but let's face it. There's only one Diamond Jim Monahan. Which leads me to this." Zach grabbed a box off to the side. He offered it to Jim. The sportscaster was perplexed about what was inside. With a grin visible even through his white beard, Zach told Jim to open it.

When he did, Jim noticed a brand new, Swiss-made Tag Heuer watch. He carefully pulled the timepiece out of the box to give it a better look. He was dazzled by its beauty and expert craftsmanship.

"It may not be the proverbial gold watch, Jim, but I hope you like it. It's the station's way of expressing our gratitude and appreciation for your loyal service."

Jim was still in awe of the watch. "I'm speechless. I just don't know what else to say but thanks."

"I'm just glad you like it. I would've waited until next week to give it to you, but I was afraid you might mistake it for our wedding gift."

Jim laughed at Zach's joke. It was now time for him to ride into the sunset. A new chapter was about to begin.

Chapter Fifty-Seven

Despite the winter chill of 30 degrees, the sun was shining brightly on the auspicious day of Jim and Anne's wedding at St. Lawrence O'Toole Church. Recent snow made the roads a little tough to negotiate, but everyone who was supposed to be there for the ceremony had safely arrived, including the Virginia contingent of Alan and Joyce Langston, Marty Leary and his girlfriend of the week, Ed Holtermann, Zach Moser and his wife Barbara, and Laura and Charlie Mazursky. Of course, there was a special reason for Laura to be there, since she was the matron of honor. Tony Salerno made the short trip up from the city with his wife Linda. Jim couldn't ignore the man who had finally fulfilled his dream to get behind a major league mic.

The rest of the attendees included members of both families, with Anne's side getting the better benefit. Of the limited number people from the Monahan clan, there was no one more special than Madison. She sat in the front row on the groom's side of the pews with Grandma Mary, Aunts Alice and Diane, and Cousins Eric and Alexandra. Madison was so proud of her father. She and Jim exchanged smiles. The sportscaster then threw a wink at Madison for good measure.

The church organist began to play Felix Mendelssohn's, *The Wedding March.* The procession was to be brief. The first to appear were Dan and Laura, arm in arm. She wore a beautiful royal blue full-length chiffon gown, while the best man wore a traditional tuxedo with a royal blue cummerbund and matching bow tie, the same exact outfit Jim had on. When he reached the altar, Dan took his position next to Jim, while Laura took her place directly opposite. Jim looked at Laura as the two exchanged grins. Jim realized if it hadn't been for her, this marvelous day wouldn't have happened.

The next person to come down the aisle was Tom Finley's precious five-year-old daughter, Lara. She was the flower girl and was having a grand time flicking rose petals as she waltzed toward her waiting father. Once Lara was steered into the pew by Tom, it was time for the primary entrant.

With her right arm weaved around Pat's left, Anne and her father proceeded to make the slow, deliberate march toward the altar. She wore a traditional white satin full-length wedding gown, embroidered with pearls, while Pat wore a more subdued tux than that of Jim and Dan, complete with a black and gray striped necktie that more closely resembled an ascot.

As Anne and Pat slowly approached, Jim stole a quick glance at Madison. He began to think the day may not be too far off when he would have to make a similar trek and give her away to her prospective husband.

Finally, Anne and Pat arrived. Despite his proclivity toward high testosterone levels as an ex-Marine, Pat gracefully pulled back the thin veil over Anne's face. In true tradition, Pat offered Anne's hand to Jim, which the sportscaster gladly accepted. Just as he was on that first day, way back on that Friday of Labor Day weekend, Jim was captivated by Anne's lustrous smile to go with her beautiful face. And her pretty eyes sent Jim a sincere signal that said, *I want to be with you for the rest of my life.*

They faced forward. Father Carlo was not presiding over the ceremony. In his absence was Deacon Paul Manzarelli, who was more than capable of handling the rite. The ceremony went swiftly and was capped off by the exchanging of vows and rings. And after Jim and Anne smooched for the traditional kiss, the entire throng gave the newly married couple a thunderous ovation. Jim and Anne gladly accepted the plaudits from the congregation.

Chapter Fifty-Eight

All the wedding party pictures were taken indoors due to the sub-freezing temperatures. With only four people and very few immediate family members, there weren't a whole lot of pictures taken; just enough to occupy the time leading up to dinner at The Arch Restaurant.

Cocktail hour went quickly as Matt Caswell and his band took their places in front of the private room Jim and Anne had secured with Jill McIntosh. Matt was an engaging gentleman who thoroughly seemed to enjoy his side occupation a heck of a lot better than his day job. He took great pride in his singing and guitar playing as he put his heart and soul into every note played. The Eric Clapton wannabe was nailing every riff with intense energy.

He had told the principle players in the wedding that he and the band would introduce each of them into the room and that they were to enter through the doors from the back on cue. The band leader motioned his group to play lively music as he began to call out the names, one at a time.

The first to be introduced was Mary Monahan, who walked in very carefully with assistance from both her wooden cane and her daughter Diane. Once she was settled, Matt called out Anne's parents, Pat and Doris Finley, to enter the room. The proud couple smiled and waved at the gathering as they were taking in the cheers. Next was Lara Finley. The affectionate flower girl seemed to be cherishing the moment, and even bowed to everyone like a stage actress acknowledging an appreciative audience for her performance. Alas, the young Sarah Bernhardt had her curtain call curtailed by Tom, who picked up young Lara and brought her to their table. And then there were Laura and Dan. Both smiled and waved at everyone as they took their places at the head table.

Matt then cued his drummer for a dramatic roll on the snare drum. The red beard band leader cleared his throat for the final introduction.

"Ladies and gentlemen, girls and boys," Matt began, "here's the moment you've all been waiting for! It's time for the couple of the hour! Let's give it up for the new Mr. and Mrs. Jim and Anne Monahan!"

The band broke out with a jazzed-up version of *The Wedding March* as Jim and Anne entered the room and received a standing ovation. The newly married couple smiled and waved to everyone in accepting the crowd's cheers and adulation.

Anne then placed her bridal bouquet by her place setting as she and Jim walked over to the middle of the dance floor. Once they had gotten to that spot, Jim and Anne held each other in a pose as if they were about to slow dance together. Anne smiled and nodded at Matt who bowed his head in reply.

Matt and his group began to play. The keyboard player started with the electric piano. Jim quickly picked up on the song from just the first four beats. It was *Color My World,* and Jim became incensed.

"Hey! What the hell's going on?" Jim asked rhetorically. "This isn't *Something!*" He looked at Anne. "What is this, Anne, your idea of a sick joke?"

Anne looked up at Jim and smiled. "No, it's not a joke. And I'll tell you something else it's not. It's not Maureen's song anymore. It's my so . . . ugh! . . . *our* song, and I want you to color my world with it."

Jim looked at Matt and his group continuing to play the instrumental beginning of the song. He began to shed a tear. Anne became a little concerned.

"Look, if you want me to, I'll tell Matt and his band to stop."

Jim actually began to smile. He gave a swift response to Anne's statement. "No! No! It's okay, Anne. You're right. This . . . this is *our* song."

Anne's psychological ploy worked to perfection. She successfully removed the stigma that *Color My World* had carried from Jim's mind. The painful stings the song had jabbed at Jim's heart since his bitter divorce from Maureen were successfully taken away, thanks to her. The beautiful Chicago ballad once again endeared Jim. The sportscaster still had a few tears, but they were now tears of joy. Anne saw this and immediately grabbed a linen napkin from a vacated place setting and began to dab Jim's cries with it.

"Gee," Anne began, "I always thought only the bride got emotional at the wedding."

Jim laughed and humbly apologized. For good measure, Anne asked him if he was okay, to which Jim replied with a soft, "Yes." Then, with a sweet expression that would melt anyone's heart, Anne tenderly looked at Jim and began to speak in third person. "Now, Mrs. Monahan would love the honor of her first dance with her new husband. Does Mr. Monahan accept?"

"Yes," Jim replied with a broad grin, "Mr. Monahan gladly accepts."

Almost on cue with Matt beginning to sing the lyrics, Jim and Anne started their wedding dance. Each enjoyed the other's company as they affectionately looked into each other's eyes. Anne had always dreamt about getting married someday, but the road to the altar was always bumpy. Jim satisfied her desires and dreams. He was good looking, affectionate and easy-going. As for the groom, his experience with Maureen had made him leery of women ever since. But Anne's sweet, wholesome demeanor changed all that. She was the epitome of what every decent guy from high school through adulthood envisioned the woman in his life would be.

All the guests admired the way Jim and Anne were dancing and the love they were exuding. But perhaps there was no greater devotee than Madison. She watched intently with great joy how her father and new stepmother held each other close.

At the moment he finished the last of the few lyrics to the song, Matt encouraged everyone to give the newly married couple applause. The gathering all stood in unison and gave Jim and Anne a roar of approval. The couple turned toward the crowd and happily acknowledged the plaudits. As the musician was playing the flute, the ending segment of the song made famous by Walter Parazaider of Chicago, Jim and Anne resumed their intimate slow dance.

Because *Color My World* was such a short song, Matt and his band allowed only the newly married couple dance to it. But they quickly segued into *Something,* the ballad George Harrison stood out for the most while a member of the Beatles. Matt then made an announcement for everyone in the audience to join Jim and Anne in slowly dancing to that tender melody. And as couples began to crowd the dance floor, no one stood out more than Jim and Anne, who were right in the center.

Chapter Fifty-Nine

The gala affair entered its fourth hour. Dinner had long been served as the cake and coffee were being administered. Jim and Anne took the opportunity to make their way around the tables to thank each guest personally for coming.

Marty Leary and Ed Holtermann told Jim they were sorry to see him leave the group, but Jim quickly replied that someone would soon regrettably take his spot in the male lonely hearts club. Zach and Barbara Moser wished the new couple well. The station manager then made a comment to Jim.

"I happen to notice, Jim, that the Cardinals will be playing the Nationals in DC in late July," Zach began. "How about it if you could take a short trip in between dates and come down to Richmond for lunch? Maybe you can come on the air and talk about your new job and the team."

"I'd love that, Zach." Jim smiled. "I just might take you up on the offer."

Jim and Anne made their way over to Joyce and Alan Langston. Joyce then admiringly gazed at the two of them.

"Oh, Jim, Anne," Joyce started, "it was a beautiful wedding and the reception here is top notch. And Anne, you are such a lovely, gorgeous bride."

"Aw, thank you," Anne gushed. "It was so good that you and Alan were able to make it up here."

Alan then turned to Jim.

"You know. If it weren't for you, Jim, I wouldn't be alive to see all this. I just want to say from the bottom of my heart, thank you. I sincerely mean that."

"Do you want to know something?" Jim asked rhetorically. "In a quirky kind of way I need to thank you, too. If you hadn't been there at Gillies Creek that evening, I wouldn't have rescued you and garnered all the headlines, leading me to my new job with the Cardinals. And then there's your son, Michael, who reminded me that being divorced really stinks." Jim then looked fondly at Anne and pulled her toward him. "This is way better!"

Jim and Anne then turned toward Tony and Linda Salerno.

"Hey, Jimbo," Tony glad-handed his St. Louis-bound client. "We gotta keep in touch. You know the Cards come to New York twice this coming season. They play the Mets in early May and the Yankees in late June. What d'ya say? Don't be a stranger. We gotta do lunch in Manhattan."

"It's a date." Jim pointed at Tony.

The couple then meandered over to the table hosting Anne's immediate family. While Tom and Brea were busy through most of the event policing their three rambunctious children, they did take a moment to wish Jim and Anne well, as did Dennis and his girlfriend, Jessica. Doris and Pat also prayed that their daughter and new son-in-law would have a happy and fulfilling life together. But then Pat took Anne aside for a brief moment.

"Nothing made me more proud today than escorting you down that aisle and taking that dance with you a little while ago," Pat began. "We may have had our disagreements from time to time, but there was no disputing today, angel. You made me one happy father."

"Oh, Daddy, thank you so much!"

Pat stood up from his seat. He and Anne then gave each other a tender embrace.

Time for Mr. and Mrs. Monahan to amble over to Jim's family. Mary, Diane, and Alice graciously welcomed Anne as part of the Monahan sorority. Anne then made a clever quip.

"I kind of like the ring to the name," Anne remarked. "Anne Monahan. It has a nice alliterative sound to it."

Eric smiled at the newly married couple, but it was almost forced because he couldn't meet any new young women to add to his collection of dates. Alexandra, meanwhile, flashed a broad grin and raised the bridal bouquet she had caught from Anne a while ago. Jim laughed and said perhaps his niece could be next.

And then there was Madison. Jim's daughter still marveled at the way he and Anne had danced at the beginning of the reception. Anne squatted down to meet the seated Madison so the two of them could see eye to eye for a more intimate encounter.

"How are you doing, Madison?"

"I'm doing great," Madison replied. "This place is really neat. Maybe someday it'll happen to me."

"Just don't get discouraged if it takes a while. I mean, look at me. I'm going to be 45 in June. Look how long it took me. And if doesn't happen, so what? It's not the end of the world."

Anne looked away for a brief moment before continuing on a different matter. "Madison, just because I married your father doesn't mean you have to call me *Mom.* You can still call me Anne if you'd like."

Madison gave Anne's statement a little thought. Then she answered profoundly, "Just because a woman gives birth doesn't necessarily make her a true mother. She has to show love and care. I can see that in you, Anne. But if I inadvertently call you *Mom,* it'll be out of well-deserved respect, not because it's a given right."

Now Anne was becoming teary-eyed. A couple of drops emerged from the corners of her eyes and began to stream down her beautiful face. She grabbed Madison and gave the adolescent a tender hug.

"That's the sweetest thing anyone has ever said to me," Anne quivered. "Thank you, Madison! Thank you so much!"

Jim's attention was elsewhere. But when he turned around, he spotted Anne and Madison giving each other a drawn-out hug. *Gee, what brought this on?* Quizzical, he inquired what was happening.

"You wouldn't understand, dear," Anne responded with a little bit of sarcasm. "It's a girl thing, right, Madison?"

"Yeah, Dad. So butt out!"

"Well," Jim answered with raised eyebrows, "I know now I'm going to be outvoted all the time."

Anne, Madison, and Jim all shared a hearty laugh, with the new Cardinals' broadcaster realizing his new wife and daughter were just teasing.

Jim and Anne then excused themselves as they retreated to their seats at the head table. There waiting for them were Dan and Laura, the best man and matron of honor.

"You know, Dan," Jim began, "Alice is okay where she's sitting with your children, Mom and Diane. I'm afraid though, Laura, that Charlie seems a bit out of place."

"Oh, don't worry about him," Laura responded. "At least he knows Zach and Barbara from office parties in the past. And my parents are there with him, too. Charlie's hanging in there, but once in a while I do check on him."

"Jim and I have been talking, Laura," Anne broke in. "There are a number of people who have influenced Jim's fate and career in this room from Alan Langston to Tony Salerno. But you were also influential. If it hadn't been for you, Jim and I would never have met. We both love you and appreciate you for making this day possible and changing our lives for the good."

"Well, I'm not exactly Dolly Levi, but I'm happy I got the two of you together. You were definitely made for each other."

"So what's next, little brother?" Dan asked Jim.

"Anne, Madison and I will be heading out to St. Louis tomorrow after our stay tonight at the Marriott in Danbury. We'll say our goodbyes to everyone. Anne and I won't have the chance for a honeymoon now, but we'll get that opportunity down the road to make up for it. It'll be some time before I see you again. After we look at and eventually close on a house, it'll be time for spring training in Florida for me. I won't see you again until, gosh, late July when the Cards play the Phillies at Citizen's Bank Park. But we'll have a phone and then there's email. So don't be a stranger."

Dan and Jim gave each other a hearty handshake. For good measure, in a display of strong fraternal bonding, Dan bear-pawed his brother's upper right arm.

Matt Caswell and his band finished playing the last song of the evening. Time to call it a night for their festive gig. The bandleader saluted the gathering a good evening as members of the group started to take apart plugged connections to amps and speakers. The crowd gave the musicians a round of appreciative applause for their excellent playing to which Matt quipped that their CDs could be purchased online. Which label, Columbia Records?

As the band members began to pack up their instruments, the guests gathered their personal belongings to march into the frosty air of the evening. All passed by Jim and Anne one last time to wish them success as well as bestowing upon them their gift cards in appreciation of a wonderful night of merriment. Jim and Anne were both gracious and grateful in thanking everyone for attending. And after everyone had left, save for the immediate family members, Jim and Anne affectionately looked at each other. They could not believe all that had happened to them. But here they were still absorbing the magnificent night. However, there wasn't going to be much time to dwell on the enchanted moment. *Next stop: St. Louis.*

Chapter Sixty

They left the Brewster area that Sunday afternoon after countless emotional farewells from both families. Now two words came into vogue: think west. Jim's Honda Civic was packed to the gills with clothing and other various items. Room inside the cramped vehicle was so scarce the sportscaster felt like a circus clown driving a Volkswagen crowded with other jovial face-painted performers. Besides getting a new house when they eventually made it to Missouri, Jim was determined to get a new set of wheels. Anne felt the same about hers after she sold her Hyundai Sonata days before heading up to Brewster for the wedding.

Between the long affair the day before and the arduous driving on the highway, Jim was taxed like nobody's business. He could only push the envelope so much, and that included a stint where Anne actually drove as well. Lack of energy forced the trio to weigh anchor at a motel outside of Youngstown, Ohio, for the evening.

After a well-rested night at the stopover, it was back to attacking the paved ribbon of highway once more. Jim had estimated it was going to take about ten hours to complete the journey, so he wanted his wife and daughter to get an early jump. A quick breakfast was all the three needed as they set out to the open road.

Nine o'clock local time. The threesome finally arrived at the Gateway to the West. For Jim it was his second trip to St. Louis, but this was Anne and Madison's maiden visit. Of course, the most notable welcoming beacon was the towering Gateway Arch.

People from rural areas usually become awestruck by big cities. But those from major metropolises and/or their suburbs are more intrigued by new mega towns. Such was the case with Anne, who grew up not too far from New York, and Madison from the Philadelphia area. Both were fascinated, but not overwhelmed by, the many office buildings of the downtown area—block after block of towering fortresses of commerce.

"I'm really interested in the cultural aspects St. Louis has to offer," Anne mentioned.

"I'd like to know where the great clubs are," Madison added.

Jim raised an eyebrow hearing that bit of news. "Oh, really?"

"Well," Madison continued, choosing her words carefully, "maybe when I'm a little older."

Jim stumbled across a small hotel just on the outskirts of town. The hostelry might not have been the Waldorf, but its homey appearance said all were welcome. The area was okay. All three agreed the inn was the perfect choice to call *home* on a temporary basis, at least.

As he, Anne and Madison began to head toward the clerk's office to check in, Jim began to prepare a mental note to himself of the many things on his agenda for the next day. He had to notify the Cardinals he and his family were in town and to contact the real estate agent the team recommended to begin house hunting. Then there was Anne, who had to let the St. Louis office of Kleister know that she, too, had arrived.

Plus there was the matter of getting Madison registered for high school to continue her sophomore year. Of course, the last item was based on where the Monahan family would call home, which circled back to getting in touch with the realtor. And there was also the matter of both Jim and Anne each looking into getting their own new vehicles.

Indeed, there was a lot on Jim's plate. But enough of that. After spending the last two days seeing nothing but paved blacktop and white lines, all he wanted to do was get into a room and crash. Jim and Anne were to stay together with Madison in the adjacent room next door, but not before the three performed the unenviable task of unpacking the Civic. Jim was just grateful they had finally arrived at their destination.

Chapter Sixty-One

Tuesday morning arrived, and the first thing Jim did was to call the Cardinals' front office. Sam Waldman was thrilled to hear the team's new radio voice was in town. How about the realtor the team used to relocate players, coaches and office personnel? The club's Broadcast VP switched Jim to an admin, who gave him the name and number of Gail Sensabaugh. Jim told Sam he would report to the front office a week from Monday. Anne had already committed to starting her Missouri chapter with Kleister much sooner. As for Madison, Jim and Anne wanted to get the adolescent registered in school as soon as possible, but that depended on where the Monahan family would be living.

The next day the trio met Gail, who had them look at one house that morning in the suburb of Clayton. It was okay, but they were in total agreement that it wasn't for them. Too plain vanilla. That afternoon she took them a little farther away from Downtown St. Louis to the charming suburb of Kirkwood, where she showed the family a quaint A-frame white house. *Gosh, all that is missing is the paperboy riding his bike and flinging the morning edition of the* Post-Dispatch, *the next door beagle howling his head off, and a few lawn mowers changing the landscape of properties to give the neighborhood an aesthetic Norman Rockwell appearance.* The effervescent middle-aged blonde told them the house went through recent foreclosure as the former owners were forced to cede the property back to the bank.

"The bank would love nothing more than to unload this home," Gail said. "You could get it for a song."

Jim noticed the outside porch and how it was horribly painted over, it seemed, countless times. It was an eyesore that required a makeover. He suggested to Anne he might want the wooden boards and matching rails restored to the original look. But that required a lot of sanding, scraping and finishing.

Gail took them inside where Jim gave the living room a long look. He liked the earthy tone walls, but Anne and Madison begged to differ.

"I was thinking perhaps a very pale shade of blue or green," Anne commented to Jim. "Or maybe even a light beige. You want to make the room vibrant and alive and well-lit."

"Anne's right, Dad," Madison remarked. "This is too ugly and dark."

"What's wrong with it? It actually looks homey."

Anne and Madison looked at each other and then looked at Jim with scrunched faces. They then released a sound of nauseating disapproval. Gail feared the difference of opinion might squelch the deal. She nervously smiled at them and persuaded them to continue the tour of the home.

They strode past the dining room and made their way into the kitchen. Anne looked at the old wooden cabinets.

"I'm thinking makeover, Hon," Anne said to Jim. "Some new cabinetry could help. And, oh, what about installing a small island for food prep? I'd like to try some new recipes on you guys. What do you say to that, Madison?"

"Awesome! Maybe I can help."

"And we'll be the A Team of culinary cuisine queens!" Anne and Madison gave each other a happy high five. Jim and Gail were amused by the sight. Onto the next area.

They peered out in the back to take a look at the yard. The space wasn't overwhelming, but it wasn't modest either. A pair of rickety wooden steps led to the grass, which appeared somewhat parched and brown from the winter.

"I'd like to install a brand new wooden deck," Jim remarked. "You know, for those rare summer nights I'll be home? And I definitely want to do something about that lawn."

"I'd like to resume gardening again," Anne added. "Gee, I haven't done that since I lived with my parents back in Brewster."

"What about a pool, Dad?" Madison inquired. "I'll bet it gets hot and steamy here during the summer, right Mrs. Sensabaugh?"

"Oh, yes it does," smiled Gail.

"How 'bout it, Dad?"

Jim was put on the spot. "Uh . . . definitely . . . maybe."

Gail resumed the tour as she led the Monahans to the bedrooms upstairs. Jim and Anne loved the spacious master bedroom for themselves and liked the fact that there were two other bedrooms. Madison took dibs on one of them for her own while the extra room could be kept for a family member or friend who might sleep over. There was also an ample bathroom on the second floor, which Jim and Anne thought could use some small renovations to spruce it up a bit.

The tour continued as Gail led them to the attic above. While it wasn't the prettiest part of the house, as far as attics go it was large enough to hold those items dear to the hearts of the family, but not enough to display them to all visitors. Jim remarked a few of the floor boards needed to be replaced. *Okay, moving on.*

And then there was the visit to the basement. The dark, musty place had a slight scent of mildew. That prompted Jim to take a careful look at the base of the cement walls. The sportscaster was looking for possible waterlines, a telltale sign the basement may have been subjected to floods in the past.

"Any reports of flooding in this area, Gail?" Jim asked.

"Well, maybe in some pockets of the town, but not here. In fact, I'd like to remind everyone that there's a slight incline running from the house, thus forcing rainwater away from it."

Jim was impressed. He thought part of the basement had the makings of a possible rec room. But before he was going to invest money into refurbishing it, he wanted some reassurance.

The tour was over and everyone gathered in the living room.

"The place is listed for $420,000," Gail began, "but, like I said before, the bank would love nothing more than to get the house off its hands. I'm sure I can work a much better deal for you. Oh, and you might find this interesting for your daughter, Jim. The schools around this area rank among the best in the state."

That was the clincher. Jim was sold. He looked at Anne and Madison, both of whom nodded in agreement. "I know it's a comedown from that mansion you lived in back in Bryn Mawr, Maddy. I hope you don't mind."

"To tell you the truth, Dad, sometimes I got lost in that place."

"By the way," Gail interrupted, "besides being a licensed realtor, I'm also a licensed insurance agent."

"Wow," Anne marveled. "One-stop shopping!"

"Let's see if we can crunch some numbers and paperwork, Gail."

And with that Jim and Anne conferred with Gail in the kitchen in the initial stage of negotiations toward closing on the home. As the adults began to hammer away at the seemingly endless paper trail, Madison explored the house once more. Yes, the charming house was beginning to grow on the adolescent, too.

Chapter Sixty-Two

Ten days had passed since Gail Sensabaugh inked Jim and Anne to their new home in Kirkwood. Madison had registered for high school to continue her sophomore year studies, which began the Monday of that past week. Jim and Anne each purchased new sets of wheels. Now that he had expanded his household threefold, he landed a brand new Chevrolet Tahoe SUV to accommodate any big excursions he and his family wished to embark upon. As for Anne, she opted to lease a new Ford Edge for her daily commute to and from her Downtown St. Louis job that started earlier in the week.

Oh, yes, the deal for their new home was approved the previous Tuesday. Jim and Anne wasted no time in coordinating with Marty Leary and Laura Mazursky respectively with the moving company to ship the couple's personal belongings from their former Richmond apartments to their suburban home. Maureen shipped Madison's personal effects in a box and had it shipped to Kirkwood via UPS. The majority of the contents for Madison were clothing. Maureen enclosed a *nice* little letter informing Jim to go get his own furniture for Madison's new room. She was getting her last dig at her ex-husband.

Early that Saturday morning, the moving van showed up with their things. Jim and Anne spent nearly five hours with the movers, orchestrating which things had to go to which rooms. Jim added his own muscle to the three-man moving team to expedite the transition, while Anne and Madison assisted in light matters wherever they could.

Two o'clock. The movers had cleared the truck of all materials. After Jim signed off on the paperwork and compensated the three men with a gracious tip, the movers took off to return east.

Most of the furniture was in place, but they still had the daunting task of going through endless boxes and deciding where dishes, small appliances, and other minor items were to be distributed throughout the home. Definitely not an overnight task. But the Monahan clan needed a rest from all the uncrating chaos, at least for a couple of hours.

Jim was beginning to think about his new career with the Cardinals, which was to commence in earnest in two days. Just the thought of meetings in the front office and countless appearances and interviews with the media and sponsors made Jim's head spin. Being a major league broadcaster did have a price, but for Jim it was well worth it. The only thing he was not looking forward to was the upcoming trip to Florida the following weekend to be with the Cardinals as they prepared for the upcoming season in their spring training facility. Although many broadcasters wouldn't mind escaping the winter chill for a little Floridian warmth, Jim had just gone through a whirling dervish of a schedule. In just a little over two weeks' time, he and Anne had to travel up to Brewster for their wedding while picking up Madison along the way. Then came the immediate trek toward the St. Louis area, selecting and eventually closing on the house, getting new vehicles, and each establishing their jobs and Madison's school curriculum. He looked guiltily at his daughter and new bride.

"Gee," Jim began, "here we are, having just moved into a new house and getting ourselves to act like family and now I just realized I have to go to Florida next weekend and leave you guys."

"Hey," Anne responded, "Madison and I will be just fine. Won't we, Madison?"

"Yep."

"You see. You're worrying about nothing." Then Anne added. "At least you're home for Valentine's Day on Monday!"

Anne affectionately hooked her left arm around Jim's right. The sportscaster got the hint. *Hmm. Okay, Madison. Just maybe you might like to leave your father and stepmother to each other? Brilliant idea!*

"Uh, if you don't mind, Dad, I'm going to take a walk around the area and explore the new neighborhood. It's not so cold out and it's sunny. Maybe it's best if I leave you two alone for a while."

"Uh, sure," Jim added. "Just don't wander off too far."

After assuring her father she would heed his advice, Madison grabbed her parka and woolen ski cap and went out to take a stroll. Jim reveled in the fact he had his daughter back with him and not under the influence of Maureen.

After Madison left the house, Anne said, "I like the way Madison thinks. She definitely inherited her brain genes from her father."

"Well," Jim replied, "I don't know about that. But I do know we should take her up on her offer. What d'ya say, Mrs. M? We got the bed all set up upstairs."

"Lead the way, Mr. M."

Jim lifted Anne off her feet. She giggled as her husband began to carry her up the staircase. Jim and Anne planned to christen their master bedroom in a seductive way.

Chapter Sixty-Three

A week after the move, Jim said his goodbyes to both Anne and Madison, but promised them he would get them down for the first weekend in March to attend a Cardinals' spring training game. And whereas Jim hated to leave his new bride and the revitalized bonding with his daughter, he didn't mind trading the 40 degree St. Louis chill for the 80 degree Jupiter, Florida, warmth.

On his first full day at Roger Dean Stadium, the facility the Cards share with the Miami Marlins, Jim met skipper Lou Anzalone along with members of the team's coaching staff and the players. All glad-handed the new broadcaster. This was his second home. And while in awe at the way slugging first baseman Trevor Salazar kept crushing pitch after pitch over the leftfield wall, he was equally fascinated, if not more so, by the newcomers to the team, all trying to make an impression upon Anzalone. All this happened as Jim kept pinching himself to make sure he wasn't locked in a deep subconscious dream from the depths of fantastic images seemingly surreal.

There was Domingo Rincon, the slick fielding shortstop St. Louis had acquired during the off-season from Seattle to provide some defense and solid contact hitting. Taylor Hendrix, a big glove man for right field and a clutch hitter with some pop in his bat, whom the team obtained through free agency. And then there was Dallas McSwain, a huge lefthander with an imposing fastball measuring in the mid-to-upper 90s, perhaps challenging the starting pitching staff as the number two man in the rotation. But the hurler's pitching coach, Damon Attleboro, told Jim to keep his eyes on a youngster named Ysidro Rojas, a young Venezuelan righty who threw the ball even harder than McSwain. Attleboro said Anzalone salivated at the prospect of Rojas becoming the set-up man for closer Blake Collins, perhaps taking over for Collins down the road. *All right. Session over.*

After he returned to his hotel, Jim learned that ESPN Radio tried to call him for his take on the Cardinals the upcoming season. Jim was flattered the prominent sports network valued his opinion that much, despite the fact it was his rookie season with the club. He eagerly called the network on his cell phone and spoke with an intern there. Jack Hartig was going to be paying him a call in a half hour.

The delay gave Jim a chance to retreat to his room and unwind a little. When he got there, he was happy to see the housemaids had already turned on the air conditioning to offset the Floridian heat and humidity. The sultry climate begged Jim to eschew his top shirt and shoes before deciding to do his homework and write a few things on a scratch-pad. Preparation is the credo for being good at what you do, so he wanted to be well-prepared when Hartig called to answer the ESPN man's questions.

After writing a few notes he thought were sufficient, Jim peered at his watch. It would be another ten minutes before the call came in. He decided to use the spare time and call Anne to see how things were back home. Three o'clock. Anne had to be in her new office.

"Hey! How are things at the ranch with you and Madison?"

"We're doing okay. I got all those thank you notes out with our pictures. And, oh, we're expecting snow overnight. Would you believe it?"

"Gee, I feel guilty telling you I've got the AC on down here."

"Oh, my heart bleeds for you!"

"Don't worry. I've already made arrangements for you and Maddy to come down here the weekend of the 5th and 6th. You'll get to wear that bikini yet!"

Anne burst out laughing at the thought. Just then, the call he was anticipating came through.

"Listen, Sweetie. I'm expecting a call from ESPN Radio's Jack Hartig. They want to do a Q and A with me about the team. I'll tell you what. I'll call home tonight so I can talk with the both of you. Love you, Anne."

Jim didn't hear Anne's sweet reply, as he was in a race to pick up the room phone.

On the other end was Jack's producer, Liam O'Brien, who told Jim to stand by for a few minutes before Jack would come on. And after hearing seemingly countless ads for cars, beer, financial services and auto insurance, Jim finally heard the voice of Jack Hartig through on the other end.

"With us now is the new lead radio voice of the St. Louis Cardinals, Diamond Jim Monahan. How's it going down there, Jim?"

There was a pause. Perhaps Jim unexpectedly had stage fright. Or perhaps he was hypnotized by the commercials.

"Hello, Jim, are you there?"

The bell in his head pealed.

"Yes! Yes! I'm here, Jack. I do apologize. I . . . uh . . . I have to get used to the title."

Jim then lovingly looked at the smiling, sweet pictures of Anne and Madison that he had placed on the dresser directly opposite him, keeping up with the old tradition he had when he went away while still married to Maureen. He saw Madison's picture and thought how great it was to have her full-time once again. And then he saw Anne's tender, loving face and wondered if only he had met the woman of his dreams twenty years earlier.

"I have to get used to a lot of wonderful and beautiful things happening to me lately."

About the Author

    I am a graduate of St. John's University and also a member of the Romance Writers of America organization. I have one self-published suspense novel and a WGA-registered screenplay to my credit. I am the father of three children and currently live in Brooklyn, NY.

WEBSITE: http://www.molloyauthor.com/
TWITTER: https://twitter.com/AuthorMJM
FACEBOOK: http://www.facebook.com/michael.j.molloy.3